# UNDEAD ANNIHILATION

## A ZOMBIE APOCALYPSE THRILLER

## MATTHEW DOGGETT

FIVE BROTHERS PUBLISHING

# CONTENTS

Special thanks to the *other* Matt Doggett for providing the awesome title. And for always reading my work. I truly appreciate it.

# GET YOUR FREE NOVELLA

Head over to **MatthewDoggettAuthor.com** to get your free novella, *The Rise of the Vampire Merek*. You'll meet Merek soon enough, and this novella is all about how he came to be such a . . . Well, you'll see. It's a fun read. Plus, it will land you on my awesome email list that only awesome people are on. See you there.

# PROLOGUE

"You're a dead man."

Charlie glanced up from his near-empty drink at this proclamation, mildly curious. Toward the front of the room a thin, leathery woman cackled and dance-walked away from the bar and the man behind it who had misgendered her with his threat. The shimmying woman formed a skeletal smile with half less teeth than ought to have been there. She threw up double middle fingers and left the bar backward, using her bony ass to open the door as she left. The momentary intake of night air did little to improve the odor in the establishment.

Charlie turned back to his drink, wondering why BDB was always saying people were a dead man. He'd never actually seen a dead man here. Except for that one time Shithead Steve drank himself to death. But that was a slow process and Charlie only saw him for a few minutes when he was actually dead. BDB didn't say it then, when it would have been appropriate.

He slumped, his forearms resting on the wooden bar that had been carved and mutilated by thousands of knives, forks, glass shards, and metal pieces over the years. Names and insults and forgotten jokes now served to soak up spilled beer and vomit. Charlie's left arm covered the "s is hel" in "This is hell," while his right rested on a punchline: "And that was the easy way!" He had searched for the setup on many a drunken night, but it was buried or erased by other names, shitty jokes, or random symbols that meant something to people long since dead. Sometimes he thought that there never really was any setup at all. Just a punchline that begged for a beginning. He knew the feeling.

Charlie leaned back, the rusty metal legs of the barstool creaking softly, and looked around the bar— his bar, as he thought of it often. The red neon lighting seemed dimmer than normal tonight. A couple of rough-looking characters played a game of pool way off to Charlie's left, under a green-glass light that hung from the ceiling on chains. The sole pool table in the joint was about as lopsided as that crappy tower in Rome, or Italy, or *wherever*. Such things didn't really matter, especially not now. Such things as Italy were beyond his realm of worries or concerns, if they were ever even there to begin with.

Charlie turned the other way, looking toward the front door, and saw a couple of geezers shivering at a dark table in the corner, their eyes darting around the near-deserted bar, a dozen beer bottles standing like sentinels before them. Charlie wondered where Buck was and reached for his phone to check the time. His friend was two hours late. He'd never known Buck to be more than an hour late. He glanced at the door again, willing his pal to show up. It was a dangerous world out there. Yes, it was.

The bartender, a guy named Big Dick Bill, hovered around his cash register, next to which, Charlie knew, he kept a locked and loaded shotgun. Big Dick Bill was a slab made out of pure shit. The hard kind of shit that junkies get when they're constipated. The shit that feels like a brick coming out, and is liable to crack a toilet if your sphincter is powerful enough. At least, that's how Big Dick Bill liked to describe himself.

Anyway, that slab of shit was named Big Dick Bill because— you guessed it— he had a bulge in his pants the size of a cat-scaring cucumber. Charlie didn't know if Bill's dick was really that big, or if he stuffed his pants. Neither would've surprised him, but he spent an unnatural amount of time wondering about it.

Bill wasn't a bad guy, but he'd fuck you up if you messed with him. Yes, he would. Charlie called him over and ordered another beer and a shot of the good whiskey— he knew the price. Cash only, of course. Charlie took his wallet out and slapped down two hundred-dollar bills, covering the words "shit heel" carved into the bar. Just then the front door opened, and in walked Buck.

Charlie let out a little sigh. Then he noticed a strange look on Buck's face as his friend took a seat next to him at the bar, but strange looks were the norm as of late. Bill came over and nodded to Buck, who ordered his usual in a distracted manner. As soon as Bill left to fix his drinks, Buck turned to Charlie and said, "Holy shit, dude. I think I'm dead."

Charlie was drunk. "Yeah, I feel you, brother," he said. "We all feel that way these days."

"No, you don't get it," Buck replied. "I was in the outskirts and... And I was fucking killed. I'm dead, man. I'm fucking dead." As Buck said this, he looked down at the bar and read the same words he'd read there a thousand times before. "Fuck You," the bar said up at him. And for the first time in his death, Buck felt really and truly fucked.

# CHAPTER ONE

# VAMPIRE MEETS DOUCHEBAG

B efore the world ended, before everything went to shit, before the apocalypse settled on the globe like a picnic blanket over an anthill, the city went on much as it had for generations. People went to work. Some stayed home. People fell in love. Some found hate. Some people died. Some were born. Capitalism and its inseparable partner commerce marched toward oblivion smug and disbelieving, much the same as every other man-made system for the division of resources did, all around the globe. But underneath it all, there waited chaos. You could see it everywhere, at all times, in all places— if you looked. In some parts of the world it was easily visible. In others it was hidden away under streetlights and buildings and uniformed officers of law and order. But it was always there.

The animals lived and died by its rules. The wind and the rain were all quantified but were no less powerful— no less chaotic— for it all. Mayhem waited, biding its time in the hearts of man and earth and sky. It didn't have much longer to wait, then. For the day started much like any other, but ended like none before.

Bertrand Guirrez found himself, on the day in question, the day when the world changed forever, piss drunk in an alley, taking a piss. It's called piss drunk for a reason, after all. He had stumbled out of the bar's front door unzipping his pants and heading for the alley that bordered the establishment. It was barely nine o'clock in the P.M., but Bertrand had had a particularly rough day. And it was about to get worse.

His morning had started off like any other: he woke up in his rent-controlled apartment around 10 a.m. and checked his phone. Like always, he had messages. Clients asking to come over. Clients asking him to come to them. A couple of girls mad at him for something he'd done. But one message stood out above all the rest. It was a message from his boss, which read: *Need to talk. HMU when u up.* It couldn't mean anything good. If Bertrand was doing his job right, he would only hear from his boss one day a month, and today was not that day.

His job was not a normal job, and his boss was far from your average boss. Bertrand sold drugs, but not his drugs. He sold Champ Pulaski's drugs. If that name conjures up images of an incredibly white former middle-weight boxer-turned-gangster, your image-conjuring mechanisms are working just fine. Congratulations.

Champ's real first name was Vasili, but no one called him that. It turns out that one of the side-effects of repeated head-trauma, mixed with a healthy dose of rampant alcoholism, is a tendency to fly off the handle at the most minor of inconveniences. Unfortunately for Bertand, Champ also had a tendency to imagine slights and insults that were never there in any way, shape, or form. He'd been weathering the ups and downs of Champ's punch-drunk brain for almost two years when everything went to shit. Bertrand found himself, after his meeting with Champ, out of a job and facing an impossible deadline: paying off his not inconsiderable debt within 48 hours, or else. Bertrand still had damn near 5 pounds of cocaine, but it wasn't enough to pay off the debt. He'd been getting high on his own supply for a long time, figuring he'd make it up on the next batch. But he never did. Now there would be hell to pay.

I know what you're thinking, but no, you're wrong. Bertrand did not find himself in the same bar in which Buck would announce his death just over a day later. That would be a little too on the nose. But it was a similar bar, no doubt. Similar in that it sold alcohol, had a pool table (four, in fact), and was also frequented by low-lifes and hard-cases alike. Bertrand didn't fall into either of these categories, though. With a name like his, the only thing he could possibly be was a douchebag.

\*\*\*

Which was exactly the word that flashed through Diirek's mind as he approached Bertrand in the alley bordering the shitty bar. Douchebags were Diirek's favorite prey. Over the years he'd honed his douchebag radar to the point where he could smell their Hatchet body spray from blocks away. In the darkest of nights, from sewer grates, the tops of buildings, through crowds of people, Diirek could sense the popping of a collar. The use of the word "bro" or "babe" several times in one sentence would put him on alert. He could hear the uninspired catcalls that seemed to fall out of douchebags' mouths the world over, their insipid words acting as a beacon. One or two of these things did not make a douchebag. The combination of them, however, sent Diirek into stalking mode almost involuntarily. It was then just a matter of following the bright flashing neon sign that hovered over them, in his mind.

This was exactly how he came across Bertrand. Like almost every other night, Diirek slipped out into the city as soon as the sun set, letting his old friend the night take him where it would. On this particular night, he wasn't even specifically looking for prey. He was engaging in his version of watching a nature documentary.

Most alleys in most cities contain an array of tiny life marching through time, oblivious to, but dependent on, the human world that built the alley and provided most of the food for this life to thrive on. Diirek, being what he is, had the ability to focus in on the rats, beetles, ants, spiders, cockroaches, and other various alley dwellers and feeders. Diirek felt a certain kinship with the small bugs and critters that moved around in the dark. He, too, operated out of view of the human world at large. For the most part, anyway. Some things were simply unavoidable.

Much like a modern camera, Diirek— and others like him— could zoom his vision in on the smallest of ants marching across the mouth of an alley while he himself perched on top of an adjacent building. He could also focus his hearing in such a way. But, unlike a camera, he could still make use of his peripheral vision to keep aware of what was going on around him. This was how he came to notice Bertrand.

Diirek was enjoying the sight of several hundred ants— 362 at last count— attacking some maggots that had spilled out of a busted trash bag next to a dumpster. The maggots were much bigger than the ants, but were carried off nonetheless, one by one, the ants struggling all the way. He was enjoying the show from a fire escape above the dumpster, making use of the deep shadows in the back of the alley. Then a douchebag came around the corner to take a piss. This was not really a surprise to Diirek. He had heard the footsteps, the heartbeat, the breathing, the muttered words, and even smelled the guy's fear-sweat and body spray before he came into view. As soon as he turned the corner, one of those bright neon signs popped up above his head. "Douchebag," it said. Purple, blinking, and inviting.

*What the hell,* Diirek thought before jumping down off the fire escape in a soundless and graceful maneuver. One could even say he almost *floated* down to the alley floor, if one ever saw it and lived to tell. He was behind Bertrand before the first drop of urine touched the alley floor. But, being the gentleman that he is, and not wanting to get any douchebag pee on him, Diirek waited for the gently swaying man to finish his stinky-sour business before getting on with drinking his blood and killing him. Diirek turned his head back toward the ants and maggots while he waited, smiling at the show.

When Bertrand finished up and turned around he found himself face to face with a handsome, ghostly white man of indeterminate age. The man wore all black, which made it seem like— in the dark of the alley— he was a pale head floating six feet off the ground. And the eyes in that face had something strange about them.

Bertrand let out a girlish "yip" sound before a steely and cold hand grabbed his shoulder and another grabbed the hair above his ear and yanked his head down, exposing the left side of his neck. He made half-formed whining sounds as the man's jaw seemed to unhinge like a snake's, and his lips pulled back over gleaming fangs.

There was a flash of light far off in the distance. The sky brightened like the sun had come up for a second, changed its mind, and gone back down.

Diirek moved his strange eyes around, questioningly. His teeth were so close to warm flesh and the satiating blood underneath, but there was something happening that he had never experienced before. Which made it a very significant event indeed.

He sent his hearing out tentatively and discovered the rushing roar of sound coming swiftly toward them. He shut his hearing down, afraid it would be damaged. When the sound finally arrived both he and Bertrand heard the same faint roar and felt a warm wind sweep over them and through the city.

The two stood, as still as dead men, in the dank alleyway. Bertrand's urine had seeped down around his expensive sneakers. Diirek's expensive shoes weren't presently touching the ground. Without a word the pale creature re-hinged his jaw and let go of the terrified but confused Bertrand.

Together, they walked (Diirek's feet now on the ground) to the mouth of the alley and turned to look in the direction they thought the flash had come from. And there it was, seen between two skyscrapers, off in the distance: an illuminated mushroom cloud. The blast below gave it an orange tint from the ground up, which faded as they watched. It faded out of Bertrand's human sight, but Diirek could still see it, with his enhanced vision.

Then another flash from behind them. This one a little further away in the other direction. Another mushroom cloud, blooming out of the horizon, reaching up to lay claim to the sky, seen between the tall buildings of the cityscape. Then another. And another. From all directions now. Explosions all around them, but all far-off, and dreamlike because of it.

The two turned and looked at each other, mouths slightly open, eyes glazed in disbelief. "Well," said Diirek in his not-quite-European accent, averting his gaze after a second. "I suppose... Um. Just forget about what happened in the alley. This seems more important, I suppose." He kicked at a piece of trash on the ground, embarrassed.

"Oh, yeah. Totally, bro," Bertrand said, equally abashed. "Yeah. Wow. Crazy." Neither said anything for a beat. "I guess I'll go now," Bertrand continued. "Probably should visit my Mom. You know, end of the world and all."

"Yeah. That is probably a good idea," Diirek said.

Bertrand started to go, then stopped, turned back. "What about you?" he said. "Any family to visit?"

"Me? Oh, no. They all died a long time ago. Hundreds of years."

"Oh. Oh wow. So you're, like, really a vam—"

"Please, don't say it. You humans say it as if it's a curse," Diirek interrupted.

"But, bro? You were really going to suck my blood?"

"Listen, let's just not talk about it, okay? This has never happened to me before. It's embarrassing enough as it is."

"No. Hey, bro, it's okay. Really, it's fine."

More silence. People had begun to come out into the street in droves, looking around in disbelief and confusion. So far the lights were still on in the city, and many people were making cell phone calls, so the towers were still up.

"Well, hey, bro," Bertrand said, still drunk but feeling more sober than ever. "Do you want to come meet my Mom? I mean, if you don't have any family to go to..."

"Oh, no. I couldn't. That would not be appropriate, really. Thank you, though. Thank you for the offer. Really. I must be going."

And with that, Diirek disappeared back into the alley. Bertrand looked after him for a long moment, seeing nothing but a dark alley next to a shitty bar.

As Diirek made his way through the city, back to his current home, he groaned in embarrassment, and began to regret not killing that douchebag after all.

# CHAPTER TWO

# CROTCH-DRUGS, PROSTITUTES, AND FIRST ENCOUNTERS

A cell phone buzzed and chirped and vibrated out an old song from an old band that was slowly becoming popular again with "the youths." A horrible realization for the not-yet-so-old owner of the cell phone. He had taken pride in choosing a ringtone that was seemingly obsolete in the wide and varied opinions of "the cool." He identified the song as one from his generation, but in reality it had been released close to fifteen years before his birth. In fact, were he ever lucid enough to the point of self-awareness, Detective Kurt Atticus Weller would have admitted a lifelong identification with the generation directly preceding his. An idiosyncrasy that had set him apart from his peers since the day he was able to be a part of a peer group.

As the buzzing and singing and vibrating cell phone continued doing its job by alerting its owner— in this case out of a deep and troubled sleep— the very fact that he hadn't changed the ringtone to something less cool yet put him in a bad mood. And it was about to get worse. Much worse. Weller rolled over on the blanket-less mattress to reach for the phone on the nightstand, its weak, pale light the only illumination in the room. He realized he was completely naked when his crotch met with something flat, hard, and— powdery?

"What the—" he mumbled as he forgot about the phone and clicked on the bedside lamp on the nightstand. He looked down to find that he had rolled onto a hand-mirror covered in a small mountain of cocaine, much of which now coated his genitals and upper thighs. The white powder stood out in stark contrast to his dark skin. He quickly dismissed the thoughts of infection or incidental overdose. But he lamented the waste of good drugs as he started to try and salvage the leftovers.

The smell of warring perfumes and stale sex filled his nostrils as he gained his bearings. His dulled synapses started sparking the sleep off, and pretty soon they were firing like good synapses should. The events of the last week flooded his mind and he stopped. His phone went silent.

"*Former* Detective Kurt Weller... shit," he said to himself.

"What's that, baby?" A woman's voice sounded from outside the small pool of lamplight, causing Weller to instinctively cover what he thought of as his cocaine-crotch with his hands. *Cocaine-Crotch.... Good name for a band,* he thought, and laughed despite himself.

"Oh nothing," he searched for a name, but none came. "Ma'am."

She chuckled and got up off the floor at the foot of the bed and walked over to the wall, where she flipped a light switch. The sight of her— a beautiful but tough-looking blond woman naked in this shitty motel room— brought even more back to Weller. As she pulled on her clothes, he watched her and thought about the circumstances that had forced him on unpaid leave five or six days ago— he had no idea the date, at the moment.

He had never been one for drugs or prostitutes, which was all the better because he had been a cop for most of his adult life, but the injustice that had been done to him— the sheer audacity of it— sent him over the edge. It was like he was making up for lost time, snorting and fucking and smoking. He was no longer a cop, so why should he act like one?

The unpaid leave was just a formality. He was sure that they would fire him when their "investigation" was all wrapped up. He was being railroaded. Bent over like it was his first time. He hated it, but the drugs and the women seemed to help quell his anger. In truth, for Weller, being a cop was as much a drug as the cocaine currently coating his cock and balls. The danger, the grit, the badassery... he loved it all and used it as a crutch. It meant he was a damn good detective, if a little unorthodox.

The bathroom door opened and another woman— this one dark-skinned and dread-locked— came out wrapped in a towel and wet from a shower. Weller couldn't remember her name either, so he just smiled at her as she, too, got dressed. He thought about stopping her, about what it would be like to put his cocaine-crotch to use, but before he could act on his impulse his phone started to ring again. The screen lit up with the name of the last person he ever expected a call from. Captain Railroader herself.

"What the fuck do you want?" he asked, proud of himself for being civil.

"Turn on the TV," she said in a tone that brokered no argument. Something bad was happening. Suddenly Weller's mind was racing, dreaming up and pouring through all the terrible possibilities that could make Captain Shellbourne call him for help after all that had happened.

As he fumbled for the remote he didn't have any inkling that one of those scenarios might actually be happening. In his heart of hearts he figured it was all a sick joke or a false alarm. But everything changed forever when he found the power button and turned on the TV.

"We're so screwed!" The TV man— a local reporter whose name Weller couldn't recall at the moment— was the very definition of "freaking out." He was on the rooftop of some downtown skyscraper, running from edge to edge with his cameraman chasing him and pleading with him to calm down. Mushroom clouds could be seen in the distance, some fading away while others grew anew out of incomprehensible violence and destruction.

"We're live, dammit," the cameraman was yelling now, his voice picked up on the anchor's mic.

"We're dead! It's only a matter of time until they start dropping here! I can't die without ever having really lived. I've never even had sex with an animal! Any animal! I'm such a coward." And with those words, the sound was cut off from Mr. Freak-Out's microphone and the cameraman gave up trying to console him. Instead, he focused on the bombs or missiles exploding all around, swinging and zooming in on every new cloud sprouting from the earth, miles away.

Weller was speechless. Immediately his mind went to his wife— ex-wife actually. Like every other time he thought of JayLynn lately, the accompanying feelings were complex. He felt fear of losing her, although he'd already done that. Months ago now. He felt love and a special kind of hate that wasn't really hate for her— a feeling that he suspected only ex-husbands and wives were capable of. His first instinct was to call her, but he decided against it. He knew her schedule. She was at home, downtown. Far away from any bombs dropping, so far, anyway. He'd call her later, he decided. When he didn't have two ladies of the night in the room with him.

He continued staring at the TV while ineffectual noises issued forth from his phone, held next to his cocaine-crotch, his hand resting on his powdery leg.

He was torn from his reverie by the sound of someone snorting. He looked to his right to find that both women whose names he couldn't remember had gathered up as much loose cocaine as they could find and were taking turns sucking it up their noses on the hand-mirror. He couldn't blame them but was surprised at their reaction time. It would have taken him a few more minutes to think of getting high in reaction to these strange events. The women looked wild-eyed at the television when they weren't focused on the lines of white powder. Weller looked at them, at the room, his phone, his crotch, and made a decision. "Fuck it," he said as he tested his nostrils in preparation. "Give me that straw."

***

"We need every single available officer. Your past mistakes are forgiven, for now. We'll revisit your status if and when we survive whatever the hell is happening right now." Captain Shellbourne sounded scared. Really scared, Weller realized in some faraway back part of his mind. The words "your past mistakes" jangled around in the front of his cocaine addled mind like a pinball doing Mach 3.

He had only called the captain back after the three of them— Weller and the two prostitutes— had done all the cocaine in the room, including some he had brushed out of his pubic hair and from the various folds of his scrotum. The women didn't seem to mind.

So now, as the anger welled up inside Weller and the coke added fuel to the fire, it suddenly dawned on him that he could take this opportunity— if the apocalypse wasn't an opportunity then what was?— and use it to make the captain pay for what she had done to him. The humiliation, the lies, the degradation. And above all, the brush with death.

He took a few moments to calm down. Picturing her helped. Her wiry and brittle hair, leathery skin, small and compact body pacing nervously around her office at Police Plaza. Her normally furrowed brow on her pinched face replaced with a girlish and gnome-like look of concern and helplessness. The image made him laugh a silent and short laugh. Logically, he was sure it was possible for her to look helpless and hurt, but seeing is believing and Weller had never seen the captain wearing any other look than a combination of anger and determination. Trying to picture her twenty years younger was an exercise in futility. Surely she had been born with that same face, complete with newly-formed wrinkles and crow's feet, her lips a thin, pale line slashed between her nose and chin. Once again he laughed, this time at the conjured image of an infant with the face of his hated captain. He'd seen some ugly babies in his time, but this was something else.

It had worked. In a feat that sometimes seemed herculean, he had managed to keep his temper under control. Instead of screaming into the phone, Weller took a deep breath and spoke calmly, his voice devoid of emotion. "Where do you want me, boss?"

A plan had screamed into existence in the last few seconds. A plan Weller hoped to God was just as good in the cold light of sobriety as he currently thought it was, high as a fucking cloud. A goddamn mushroom cloud. Plus, anything he could do to not think about the end of the world as he knew it was a good thing, for sure.

She told him to report to the precinct within the hour. He grunted in reply and hung up the phone. He could tell by the look on the women's faces that they were more than a little freaked and looking to him for answers. "Sorry ladies, I don't know any more than you do. Get to somewhere safe as soon as possible and hold onto your butts."

They stared at him with wide eyes. Then they looked at the pistol resting on the nightstand under the lamp. "Either of you have protection?" Weller asked. The blond woman held up a can of pepper spray, the other a box of condoms. Weller sighed. "Okay, where do you want to go? I'll take you." They smiled. He smiled back and then proceeded to get dressed.

As the three of them walked past the unmanned front desk of the motel, Weller used his finely tuned detective skills to learn his female companions' names. Okay, so listening isn't really a skill, but Weller was feeling good about himself despite the chaos they were surely walking into. The blond, he learned, was Cindy. The one with dreadlocks was Mindy. He didn't know if those were real names or not, but it didn't really matter either way. He would get them to their destination, some twelve city-blocks away, and then he'd probably never see them again. Most likely because they would all be dead in a matter of days. But even if they lived, it was a big city.

Weller stepped outside first, his hand on his Sig Sauer P229 9mm pistol in his shoulder holster under his left armpit. He glanced around and then signaled Cindy and Mindy to follow. There were people all around the streets. More than normal, and all with a kind of nervous energy. Most traffic was stopped, the drivers on their phones either in or standing beside their cars. Some drivers were still trying to get to their respective destinations, weaving around the parked cars, honking horns, panic-stricken. Almost everyone was looking at their phones, waiting for news, on the verge of terror. Waiting for the other shoe to drop. Or, to be quite literal, the other bomb.

The combination of nighttime darkness and the buildings in this part of the city did much to block the view of any mushroom clouds or falling bombs, but people glanced nervously at the sky anyway. The clouds were high and blocked any moonlight from reaching the city, but so far the power grid seemed undamaged. Lights were on all over the immense cityscape.

As they walked, people glanced at them, but no one paid them much attention. Weller was glad for it. Although Weller had always been ready to fight at the drop of a hat, he had never experienced anything like this. Every step he took brought him closer to sobriety, and every step was a new opportunity to see the city like he'd never seen it before. That was what really got to him.

Back in the motel room, watching the newscaster lose his shit, it was easy to discount the unfolding events as unreality. Even though he knew something bad was definitely happening, seeing it on TV was like watching a movie. But here, out in the city, it was hard to ignore the fact that the world as he knew it was changed forever.

They passed 24-hour bodegas that were closed, some for the first time in years, the shopkeepers sitting behind locked doors with shotguns. Those braver shopkeepers who kept their stores open were not shy about making sure anyone who passed by saw their weapons on display. They seemed to think the best deterrent to a robbery was a loaded gun. But a loaded gun does little good against an unruly crowd. Weller knew that from experience.

Those apartments above the stores that had balconies were almost all occupied. People of all ages and races were out looking at the sky and the city below, trying to get a feel for what was happening. They were deciding whether they should stay or go, and where to head if the latter was deemed necessary. The trio heard frustration when phone calls to loved ones were dropped or went unanswered. They heard relief when the calls were answered and good news was shared, devastation when the news was bad. Both women made similar phone calls on the way. Most went unanswered. Weller thought again of calling JayLynn, but much like he'd done when they were married, he put it off. One thing at a time. He didn't want his attention divided. Especially not now.

The quickest way to their destination was through an especially run-down and dangerous part of town. A two-block stretch of dark doorways, busted windows, and vague figures sauntering down the sidewalk. Going around meant a long detour, so Weller decided to go through.

Thus far the city's inhabitants had been nervous, scared, and tense. Not a great combination, but still manageable, in Weller's opinion. But if good news didn't come soon, all hell would break loose.

In this part of town, however, Weller wouldn't be surprised if those individuals who called this stretch home had no idea what was happening outside their little world. Which was good and bad at the same time. Good because such news would probably send many of them into a crazed state (more crazed, anyway) and bad because they might try to assault the trio for any number of reasons. Starting with the fact that it was dark out. Weller thought about removing his gun from his shoulder holster but decided against it. While it would probably deter certain characters lurking in various shadows, it would surely provoke others. Best to try and get through without provocation.

They came to the end of the first block having only witnessed an extremely skinny man taking a rather large shit in an alley and some choice words hurled at the ladies from what seemed like every conceivable crevasse. As they crossed the street to begin their second and last block of this particular stretch, the street lights flickered and went out. Foreboding crept up Weller's throat like a swallowed centipede. He squinted into the dark and saw several figures creeping towards him and his lovely company.

"Are you fucking kidding me?" Weller said. "The lights go out right now? Right this second? And creepy figures in the dark! Great! This is some horror movie bullshit. C'mon, ladies. Let's pick up the pace." Weller was genuinely pissed. As if the universe was giving him the finger with all this apocalyptic, creepy nonsense.

When they made it to the other side of the street, Cindy and Mindy both screamed. The twitching figures were dead ahead and moving in. There was some sort of guttural moaning accompanying these tattered people, and it was giving Weller the creeps. He pulled out his Sig Sauer and held it at his side. He didn't see any weapons in the hands of the figures coming toward them. *You can't shoot people for being creepy,* he reminded himself.

"Okay you assholes, stop what you're doing right now!" He yelled at the figures that were surrounding them. "I am a cop! Let us by or you'll face the long arm of Johnny Law!" He chuckled softly. He'd always wanted to say that. Both women stopped and looked at him. *What a corny bastard,* he thought of himself. But what else was new?

Both the ladies yipped again as the figures closed in on them. They weren't stopping, and the sound was getting louder. Weller squinted through the dark and caught a glimpse of one of the creepy figures. It was an old man whose clothes were in tatters. His eyes were cloudy and he had open sores all over his face. Now it was Weller's turn to yip. Some kind of crazy homeless drug addicts, the likes of which he had never seen before.

He sprang into action, kicking the old man in the balls. He stepped toward Cindy and Mindy, who were holding up their pepper spray and condoms, respectively. The figures were reaching out, trying to grab the women as they backed away— into more figures. Weller was turned around in the dark but thought that he knew which way to head, so he began to clear a path.

He elbowed a crazed lady in the face, punched a man, whacked a teenager, pummeled an octogenarian, and pistol-whipped a portly young woman. It struck him as strange that none of the people he hit made noises other than that continual growl. They just fell or stumbled back into the night, not one of them screaming in pain. *Creepy.* Then he heard thwacking and grunting noises from behind him. He looked back and was not-so-surprised to find that both Cindy and Mindy were kicking some ass. The ladies were crotch-kicking, eye-gouging, and elbowing the stragglers that Weller had missed.

He yelled for them to come on. Cindy and Mindy's destination was a block ahead, if Weller was right. They jogged, Weller bringing up the rear, sure that the strange silent figures were right behind him. The lights came back on just as they reached the brownstone in which the women lived. Weller looked around and threw his hands up at the lack of creepy figures around. Super weird.

"Are you okay?" Weller asked Mindy, who was bleeding from her arm.

"I'll survive. I think one of those crazy bastards bit me! I'll get it cleaned out here."

"I would suggest staying behind that big door until we get some order in this city. Can't have people going around biting other people. No way. Not on my watch," Weller said.

He saw them to their door and they said their goodbyes. Weller noted the address and told himself that he would come check on them when he had the chance. Then he left, heading for the precinct downtown, happy he didn't have to go through the creepy part of town again.

# Chapter Three

# A Bunch of Crazy Shit

F ormer-but-possibly-recently-appointed Detective Kurt Atticus
Weller... So, maybe just forget the "former-but-possibly-recent-
ly-appointed" thing. Like he had never been railroaded. Never been
set-up. Never been screwed over by people he called friends.

Well, maybe not friends. Acquaintances.

Okay, co-workers, for sure.

So, let's start over.

Detective Kurt Atticus Weller (who, as far as we're concerned, had
never lost that title) made his way through the stunned city to the
precinct with a distinctly bad taste in his mouth. He had seen many,
many strange and terrible things during his eighteen years as a police
officer, but nothing like the dead-eyed crowd of near-silent psychopaths
that had assaulted him and the two beautiful sex workers he had been
escorting.

Over the course of his career he had seen a milkman lit on fire and
shoved up a chimney, many years after milkman had been an obsolete
job. He had investigated a murder committed with a number of outsized

dildos. (For the record, the size of those dildos did not threaten his manhood in the least.)

One of the highlights of his time in Vice was a strange and meandering investigation that included a fictional kingpin that was blackmailing bored housewives into dealing narcotics and running a brothel. Really their actions had been voluntary. A scheme in order to catch their cheating husbands, live a little, and make some extra money. In the pursuit of those goals, the women committed far greater crimes than adultery. But, of course, they didn't see it that way.

He had dealt with junkies and crackheads, nutjobs and weirdos, dickheads and douchebags. But he had never, ever seen anything like what he had seen on this night.

He kept thinking about striking the various perps in the dark. About how they didn't make a sound as they went down. He didn't care how tough you were or how many drugs you were on, when you took an elbow to the head from Detective Kurt Weller, you made a sound. He was certain he had broken a jaw or two in his mad rush to escape their clutches. Probably even an arm and a leg. But none of them had uttered a single sound of alarm or pain. Plus there was the wide range of age, race, and sex. What were the chances that old white women and young black men, teenage girls and senior citizens, trans and non-gender-binary folks of indeterminate age, would all end up in the same place, to take the same drug, and have the exact same response?

There was no chance. None at all. Weller's finely honed instincts (although subtly numbed from his recent use of narcotics) told him that something was very wrong. And that the bombs falling outside of his city were just the beginning.

As he turned the corner and brought the precinct into view his heart jumped into his throat. There was a crowd in a half-circle around the station's front steps, held back by heavily armed, uniformed police officers and plastic barriers. *Not again*, he thought. But then he realized that the crowd was yelling as if in protest. *Oh good, just a crowd of regular citizens, fearing for their lives and seeking answers*. That he could deal with. He approached and elbowed his way through the crowd, recognizing one of the officers on crowd control at the bottom of the steps. Jones. Judy Jones. She saw him and sidestepped to let him through the gap in the barrier.

"Hey, Detective," she said with a small nod, sounding harried and looking exhausted. "They told us you'd be coming."

Weller grunted in reply. "What's the deal with these people?" he asked, gesturing with his head toward the unruly crowd.

"They want answers that no one has. Nothing on the radio or the TV but local stations. We know as much as they do."

Weller grunted again and started up the steps.

"Hey, asshole!" One voice rose above the rest. Somehow Weller knew it was directed at him. *Of course the grunts don't know anything, but this guy in plainclothes looks important enough to have some answers*. It wasn't hard to put himself in the guy's shoes, but that didn't mean he liked being called an asshole. He stopped and slowly turned around to search for the offending citizen.

"You can't ignore us forever! Soon there'll be more of us than you, and we'll get some answers by force, if it comes to that!" It was a young guy, mid-twenties, with some sort of stupid haircut and a punchable face. *How did I know he would look like that? Damn, I'm good*, Weller thought to himself as he walked back down a few steps, stopping to stay slightly elevated above the crowd.

"All right, listen up," Weller used his cop-voice, which never failed to make people pay attention. It was an art, really. All eyes were on him now. He paused for effect, sweeping his gaze around the small crowd, looking people in the eye as he went. He sensed more than saw that Stupid-Haircut was about to say something else.

"Shut the fuck up, Haircut," he snapped just as the guy opened his mouth. "You want answers, you'll have to shut. The fuck. Up."

Weller loved doing this. And he could see that the four uniformed guards were loving it, too. Some sort of byproduct of being a cop, and the inevitable odds that it created with society at large, especially in America.

"During the London Blitz, the people of that fair city had two choices," he resumed, donning the effect of a leading man, recalling all the great speeches he had ever seen in movies. He stood up straight, puffed out his chest, and held the audience captive.

"The first choice, the choice that you people seem to have made, was one of fear and hysteria. They could have cowered in their homes and waited to die. They could have gone running to Churchill, demanding answers and threatening violence. Do you know what they did, instead?" He paused for effect. The crowd stared, silent. "They volunteered to help put out fires, clean up bomb-sites, and assist in the war effort. They went to pubs to drink beer and have a good time. They spent quality time with their loved ones. Hell, they even referred to the bombings like rain or snow. Like something to be endured with grit and determination. The point is, they were undergoing terrible losses while the rest of the world watched in disbelief. The Germans expected them to lose their shit. So did everyone else. But they let their better angels shine through. And this is the British we're talking about here... Just saying... So my question to you, citizens, is what are you going to choose? Fear? Or courage?"

Not his best work, but he beamed anyway, waiting for the crowd to disperse or to ask for information about how they could help to protect the city. Surely there were efforts underway already.

"Ahh, fuck you!" a woman in the back of the crowd screamed out. Then everyone broke out into boos and hisses and hurtful profanities about Weller and his mother. He even heard something about his dog. He didn't even have a dog! His rage went from zero to sixty in half a second. He pulled out his Sig and pointed it at Stupid-Haircut.

"Okay, you fucking fucks! How about this?" He was yelling now. "How about you get the fuck out of here and find something useful to do, or I shoot as many of you as I can in the fucking face? I bet I can get half of you before you even touch me!" He followed this up with a maniacal laugh, swinging his gun back and forth across the crowd. "I was front-page news last week! I believe the headline was 'Crazy Cop Causes Chaos'. You don't want to fuck with me! I'm ready to die!"

Weller and the four astonished uniforms watched the crowd disperse in fear, running in all directions, many of them yelling "Fuck the police," as they did.

"Well, that takes care of that," Weller said, smiling and putting his gun back in his shoulder holster. Of course he wasn't serious. His finger hadn't even been on the trigger. But sometimes people needed tough love. If now wasn't one of those times, then Weller's whole life was a lie.

He turned around and looked up at the precinct building and felt pride swell in his heart. *It's good to be back*, he thought while walking up the stairs to see what kind of fresh hell was coming next.

It was all-hands-on-deck inside the building. While all seemed quiet at the main entrance, through which Weller had just walked, the rest of the building was more alive than he'd ever seen it. During the last week he had become quite infamous, and he found that despite the terrible tragedy that was currently befalling his state and quite probably his country, people still found the energy to stop what they were doing and leer at him.

He gave those he didn't know personally a big, toothy smile. Those he did know got the finger as he passed by, many of them scoffing in disgust before resuming whatever bullshit they were doing. To Weller, any time spent inside the police precinct was a waste of time. He thought that the whole point of being a cop was that you were out in the city looking for dirtbags to assault and innocents to protect. Paperwork and politics were unimportant. Co-workers were to be tolerated when they couldn't be ignored. The brass were to be heeded when they were right, and disregarded when they were wrong. But still, he had made some friends during his many years working out of the old, dirty building.

Weller boarded the elevator with a mess of other people and pressed the button for his floor. Stepping into the bullpen a few minutes later, he smelled industrial cleaner mixed with sweat and coffee. He gazed up at the buzzing halogen lights and couldn't help but feel a little better about everything. The first person he ran into when he got off the elevator was Ralph Hardiman, an old-school detective a month away from retirement. He hadn't seen Weller yet.

"Hardiman, what the fuck do you know?" he said as he put a stiff finger in the middle of Hardiman's back.

"I know you put that finger in my ass or we're gonna have problems."

Weller laughed, shaking his head. "You sick old fuck. It's a date."

Hardiman laughed right back, his big white teeth bearing through under his bushy mustache. Then, Hardiman got serious. He placed a hand on the back of Weller's neck and pulled him close.

"What's this I hear about the shit you pulled last week? You really do that?"

"It's not what you think, Ralph. I'm getting fucked slowly by you-know-who. She's been trying to get rid of me for years. She would have, too, if the world hadn't come to an end."

This seemed to remind Ralph what he was doing. Kurt watched as the man's face fell, thinking that the sense of unreality was everywhere. People just couldn't believe what was happening.

"You think it's really that bad?" Ralph asked, still talking close.

"It ain't good. I'll be surprised if we survive the month."

"Jesus H. Christ on a cracker." Ralph looked much older all of a sudden. "Do you have any more info? You talk to her yet?"

Weller shook his head. "I'm headed there now. If she tells me anything new, I'll tell you. Alright, brother?"

"Alright." With that the two men parted ways, each clapping the other on the back as they went.

Weller made his way through the old and fraying cubicles, the squeaky office chairs, the worn linoleum, and the piles of paperwork. Through the coffee stains, the strange smells, and the air pumped through dusty vents. People were running around everywhere. Detectives, beat cops, volunteers, family members, and perps in handcuffs led by officers. Phones rang on empty desks, computers dinged with notifications, the PA system crackled with inaudible announcements, everyone assuming someone else heard it, hoping it wasn't important.

It all served to lift his spirits, despite everything that had happened and everything that was currently happening. He even managed to forget about the one that got away. Giovanni Linori, head of the Linori crime family. Not a day had gone by that he hadn't thought about that large, laborious piece of shit, although it had been months since he'd finally been forced off that case. It was one of the reasons why his suspension had landed so hard on him. Linori was unfinished business.

Weller's good mood shattered like a Molotov cocktail through a window when he caught a glimpse of someone he hadn't seen in a while, far off down the corridor, coming out of the captain's office. He immediately balled his fists in fury. Before this moment he'd thought that maybe he could gather enough civility to let the man pass him by— or all the better if he didn't see him. But he did. And he suddenly found civility in short supply, whereas testosterone and rage were as abundant as stale, recycled air.

Internal Affairs Detective Ray O'Shea had once been a good friend to Kurt Weller. In fact, they had been more than friends. They had been partners. For seven years. Weller felt— no, he knew— that O'Shea and Captain Shellbourne had acted together to try and get Weller out of the way. He just couldn't prove it. Not yet, anyway. He didn't know why, either. Nothing made sense to him.

Ray hadn't been the same in the years since he transferred to IA. At first Weller thought that it was just the inevitable separation that happens when a person is no longer in your life every day. When you no longer have the hours together to talk about everything and nothing. When you no longer depend on someone to watch your back, to keep you from getting killed. He had experienced something similar when he and his wife split up, not too long ago now. A drifting apart.

But over the last week Weller had been going over and over his recent interactions with Ray, trying to get a clue as to what he was after, and why it would involve getting his ex-partner out of the way. He had come to the conclusion that the man had changed in more ways than a simple drifting apart could explain. Every theory he came up with pointed to "Dirty Cop," but that wasn't a term easily levied. The guy had been beyond reproach in all the years that Weller had known him. Plus, in order to get the pay raise that came with a job in IA, you had to be squeaky-clean. The IA headhunters were so thorough that people in the station joked about getting turned down for the job if you hadn't wiped well enough during your morning dump. But something didn't add up. *And I'll be damned if I don't figure out what the fuck it is*, Weller thought, showing his teeth as Ray walked toward him.

The man was a mess. But that had always been the case. Not that he was overweight, because he wasn't. He was a gym nut, but that didn't stop him from somehow dropping half of every meal he ate down the front of his shirt. He wore an expensive gray suit that had dog hair, lint, and dandruff on it, all in equal amounts. He had coffee stains on his white collared shirt and what looked to be a marinara stain on his striped tie.

O'Shea and Weller were almost exactly the same height. After arguing about who was taller endlessly, they had come to a consensus back when they were partners. Each one would get to claim the title of "tallest" every other day. And not a day went by when the two worked together that they didn't remind the other of this fact.

"Your turn to get coffee, shorty," O'Shea would say on his days.

"I'm taller, so it's my turn to breach first," Weller would say on his day. And on and on. It was part of their routine, and it worked out well. They still held the record for most arrests in a single day— a particularly crazy Halloween some five years back. But they also held the record for most complaints filed and most perps walked because of improper conduct— which was almost always something Weller had done. But still, on most days they would have more perps walk free on some technicality than other detectives had total arrests. They had come to be known around the city as "The Machine" by perps and other cops alike.

Instead of yelling "six-up" or "five-o" people would yell "Machine's coming" and whatever heinous activity the criminals were engaged in would be dropped and they would scatter like cockroaches. In the station, people would see the two walk in from a shift and say to each other, "You hear about The Machine's day? Fifteen arrests," while shaking their heads in wonder.

All that was but a distant memory now as O'Shea approached Weller, smiling like they were still friends. Weller couldn't take it. He rushed forward and grabbed O'Shea by the jacket, slamming him back against a cubicle, knocking down someone's framed pictures and knick-knacks.

"You got some nerve smiling at me like that. I know what you did, you sonofabitch bastard."

O'Shea was taken aback. He didn't resist and wore a shocked look on his face. It was almost genuine, Weller thought. He's good. Too damn good.

"The fuck are you talking about, Kurt?" He sounded hurt.

"Whatever you got me into, it didn't work. I'm still here. And I'm coming for your ass, motherfucker."

"Kurt, I don't have a goddamn clue what you're talking about. And haven't you heard the news? We're under attack. And we're getting some really strange reports coming from all over the city. People are losing it. People are dying. When we get this shit settled down, you come find me and we'll clear this up. You're my friend, man. We're The Machine, yeah?"

"Fuck you. Machine's broken. I'll come find you, all right. Soon." Weller released him with a shove and stalked into the captain's office, oblivious to all the people who had stopped to watch the office drama.

The meeting with Captain Shellbourne wasn't much better, although Weller managed to keep himself from lunging over her desk and strangling her, mostly because there were other people in the room. But also because her betrayal wasn't much of a surprise to him. He had never really liked her to begin with. She had always been cold and almost feral in a way, like her thoughts were never fully on the people she supervised. He got the impression that she was always looking upwards, toward the glass ceiling that she would inevitably encounter. It was no way to be a good boss, he thought. She was competent, but nothing more. He could think of a handful of other people that could do the job better, himself included. Not that he wanted the job. No fucking way. Not worth the stress. He wanted to slide back into his detective duties and get to work on proving his innocence. But he soon learned that she was taking that away from him, too.

At first he thought it was strange that he was in the room with only uniformed officers. Beat walkers. Not that he didn't respect them, but he had put his time in. Been there, done that. As the meeting continued it became clear that she expected him to go back to kicking rocks.

"Weller," she said, after telling the other officers what was expected of them. "You're going to be under Kilgore, working with his squad to set up a perimeter as far north as you can. From Delta to Rockaway. I need to know what's salvageable and where the looting is taking place. We're getting all kinds of strange reports from 7th street and further on." As she said this she took Weller's badge out of a desk drawer and tossed it to him.

Weller was too tired to put up a fight. The cocaine had worn off, and the ordeal with O'Shea had been the brick that broke the detective's back. It had been a long goddamn week. He would do what she said and play the good little cop. He didn't think she would kick him out again, but he didn't want to take the chance. Not yet. Yelling at her on the phone was one thing, doing it in a room full of subordinates was another entirely. It would almost force her hand. Plus, he was happy to have his shield back. It felt good.

At least he was headed to his old stomping grounds. He knew the area well, and something dawned on him: he also knew a drug dealer who lived off of Delta. A guy who, during their intersecting careers as cop and criminal, he had come to know fairly well. There was a begrudging respect there. The guy was good at getting out of hard time. Weller decided he'd pay the man a visit while he was there. He told himself it was to let the guy know that Weller hadn't forgotten about him, but really he just wanted more cocaine.

He felt his wall of sanity slowly slipping, and his energy flagging. It was funny, but before getting unjustly suspended he never would have even considered doing drugs while on duty, but he was on the tail end of a bender and would be useless if he didn't get something to keep him going. His emotions were running high even before the city started going to shit. So, he told himself that once the night was over and order was restored, he would never do cocaine again. Probably.

He headed down to the motor pool and signed out an unmarked cruiser. Once out of the garage and on the road he called Lt. Kilgore. "Hey, Gene. It's Weller. I'm headed up to Delta and 7th to check things out. Who do you have out already?"

"Good to have you back, Kurt. I've got people up there. Should be five cars in the area, setting up a perimeter. Give me a second and I'll tell you their numbers. Shit— let me call you back." The line went dead. Weller shrugged and kept driving.

Most everyone in this part of the city had cleared the roads, and the ride was fairly smooth. Streetlights were still on, and there were a few people hanging out on stoops and talking on sidewalks. Otherwise, it was pretty quiet. But the further north he went, the worse things started to look. Broken windows, cars on fire, figures darting in and out of shadows. But, so far, nothing that couldn't be handled by a few uniforms. He reported what he saw to dispatch and kept going.

Reaching Delta and 9th, he pulled over and double-parked with his hazards on. The block was quiet. No one on the street. There were a few broken windows, but that was it. Weller ducked into the drug dealer's building and started up the steps to the guy's apartment on the third floor. There was an elevator, but Weller wasn't about to risk getting stuck in there. For all he knew, the power could go out at any minute.

By the time he got to the third floor, his "cop sense" was tingling. There was something in the air that didn't feel right. The fact that the guy's door was opened didn't help. What self-respecting drug dealer leaves his door open? Especially when the world's going to shit in the worst way possible. The apartment building wasn't fancy, but it wasn't run-down, either. Solidly middle-class. Probably rent-controlled.

All the other doors in the hallway were closed. Weller pulled out his pistol and stalked forward. He pushed the door open all the way and it squeaked on its hinges like doors often do. Not loud, but loud enough for someone inside to hear. *Fuck it*, Weller thought.

"Bertrand? You there?" he yelled down the short entryway. He could see half of the living room from where he stood by the door, but that was it. No one there. He thought about announcing himself as a cop but didn't really want to do that since he was here to score drugs. Better that any witnesses think he was just some anonymous visitor looking for his buddy Bertrand.

He stood and listened, and heard movement deep in the apartment. Someone had been startled and was making moves in there. He'd been in the apartment a handful of times, usually serving a warrant, so he knew the layout. The kitchen was off to the right and would be the first room he would have to clear. Which he did, moving through the hallway and the kitchen like a wraith in cheap leather shoes. Then he cleared the rest of the living room, the only sounds his controlled breathing and the whisper of cloth on cloth as he moved.

No sign of anyone, but there was stuff strewn about on the floor between the leather couch and the big screen TV. Someone else must have had the same idea as Weller: score some sweet sweet nose powder. Weller padded back to the entryway, where he could see the living room, kitchen, and hallway to the bedrooms all at once. He yelled again.

"Bert, it's me. Come on out."

He hurried over to the couch and knelt behind it, hoping that whoever was back there would think he was still in the entryway. He heard movement again and poked his head and gun over the couch at the same time. Bullets started flying from down the hallway, some striking the couch, some the walls, and some the floor. They were firing wildly in his direction. Weller hit the floor and got as flat as possible behind the couch. It was a semiautomatic weapon and whoever was firing it was a terrible shot.

Early in his career, Weller had kept count of how many times he had been shot at, but it proved a futile effort. He had lost count long ago. It used to scare him, now it just pissed him off. His adrenaline always spiked, though. No stopping biology. But he could have done without it. It always left him feeling drained when it inevitably trickled off after the danger had passed and Weller had proved victorious. You do things enough and you start to get used to them.

It was things that he had never handled before that truly scared him. Like the dead-eyed psychos from earlier, or the fact that millions of people had probably died in the mysterious bombing that he was finally accepting as reality. Another reason he wanted drugs: he felt his composure starting to slip. And not in a good, controlled, pissed off way that had made him such a good and ruthless cop.

The firing stopped. Time to reload, he guessed. Weller jumped up and ran down the hall in a mad dash. He passed a bathroom on the right. Empty. Only two options left: a bedroom-turned-study on the left or the master bedroom on the right, both at the end of the hall. He took a guess, based on the glimpses he got of the bullet holes in the walls and floor. He was right.

Just inside the door of the master bedroom was an average-sized man in a ski mask, head down, sliding a new clip into his pistol. Weller dropped his own pistol on the floor without slowing down. He lowered his shoulder and drove it into the man's midsection, just like he was taught in football as a teenager. Weller kept pumping his legs, driving the guy backward— and straight into a window overlooking the street. Weller stopped himself from falling out by grabbing the wall on either side, but the burglar tumbled three stories to the empty sidewalk below, landing with a crunching thump near Weller's car. The jingle of broken glass rang in the detective's ears as he looked down at the black-clad figure, smelling air tainted with fire, death, and destruction.

*Well, that guy's dead. Oops.* Only it hadn't been an accident. He had dropped his gun because he didn't want a slug in the guy leading back to him. He saw the window and could have avoided it, if he had really wanted to. He was angry. Mad at the guy for shooting at him. Mad at the world for having changed. Mad at himself for coming to this place at all. But he was already here. Might as well do what he came here to do. And do it quickly.

He pulled on a pair of latex gloves from a handful he had grabbed out of the unmarked cruiser. So far he hadn't really touched anything from which fingerprints could be pulled but the walls around the window. He picked his gun back up and holstered it before ducking into the master bathroom and finding some cleaner and a rag, with which he wiped down the frame. Then he went directly across the hall and found Bertrand. Dead on the floor. Two bullet holes in his chest.

The masked intruder must have shot him before he found out where the drugs were because the place was ransacked. That narrowed it down for Weller. It wouldn't have taken him long anyway. He had seen almost every conceivable hiding place there was. In fact, he had helped search this very apartment several times. Somehow the guy always knew they were coming. They never caught him with so much as a joint. Weller suspected the guy was paying off a cop, but he was never able to figure out who. It didn't matter anymore.

After about five minutes Weller found the stash behind a false-back in the fridge— a plastic panel that popped out if you pressed it just right. It was a good spot, but he'd seen it before. He found a backpack and stuffed what he judged to be about two kilos of cocaine in it. He was headed for the door when he heard a sound coming from down the hall. Like someone was moving down there. Impossible.

He drew his pistol again after pulling on the backpack. This time he didn't call out. It was a cat, maybe. Or a breeze coming through the broken window. There was no way someone else could have gotten into the apartment. He would have seen them. He walked slowly down the hall as the sound issued again. From the bedroom-turned-study.

Something was wrong. Weller's pulse pounded in his head and his adrenaline was ramping up again.

As he crept closer to the room, he heard a low groaning sound and a slow, subtle scuffling sound. *You've got to be fucking kidding me. This is not happening right now.* Before he saw it he knew what he would find.

But that didn't make it any easier to see. Bertrand had gotten up and was shuffling toward the hallway, leaving his blood on the floor behind him. Weller froze when he saw the corpse walking toward him, the eyes cloudy, the fresh bullet holes in its chest. He didn't know what to do.

The impossibility of it all washed over him with the realization that this wasn't a one-off. It all came together in his mind as he stood there in the hallway, his gun out in front of him, a dead drug dealer groaning toward him. The part of the city where he had first encountered these dead-eyes (he didn't know what else to call them, certainly not zombies) was far from here. A couple of miles toward downtown. The implications made him dizzy. If dead people were waking up to walk around, and bombs were falling around the country, they were all screwed. Certainly the two were related, but that didn't really matter right now, did it?

He snapped out of it as what used to be Bertrand grabbed clumsily at his outstretched arm. Weller slapped him away. "Stop it," he said while backing up a couple of steps.

"Ugghhhh," Bert said, as if in reply, and kept coming.

It was all too much to take in. All of a sudden Weller wanted badly to find a place to do some of the coke he had strapped to his back. Bertrand grabbed at him again, this time he came at the detective with his mouth open, looking for a meal.

"Goddamnit," Weller said. He leveled his gun at the dead guy's head and pulled the trigger. He was no longer worried about a slug leading back to him. The city was about to have bigger problems than a dead drug dealer. Bert collapsed in a heap, a bloody sludge leaking out of the large hole in the back of his head.

Weller kept checking on the twice-dead Bertrand as he gathered supplies to do some coke: a CD case, a lighter, a 20-dollar bill and credit card from his own wallet. By the time he left the apartment, about ten minutes later, he was fairly certain that the bullet to the head did the trick, which was some good news, at least. When he got outside on the street, headed for his car, he noticed that the dead guy in the ski mask wasn't there.

"Goddamn it," he said again. He looked around and spotted a figure in the distance, limping slowly away.

"This is such bullshit," he mumbled to himself as he headed after the figure.

\*\*\*

Diirek was taking his time getting back to his lair. Okay, it wasn't really a lair. It was a windowless basement in an old apartment building. But lair sounded cooler. And before you start conjuring images of a dusty coffin in that basement, don't. Diirek sleeps hanging upside down from the rafters.

No, not really. He sleeps in a bed. Stop stereotyping already.

Anyway, Diirek knew his girlfriend wouldn't be there until just before sunrise. They only spent a couple of nights a week together out and about. It wasn't so much the fact that they'd been together for a century— they truly did love each other— but something about being a vampire made alone-time a necessity. At least it did for Diirek and Lidia.

So, after his embarrassing little incident with Bertrand, and the fact that bombs were dropping around his current city, Diirek didn't feel like going back to that bed in that basement. After all, he only had so many hours of darkness before he had to be snuggled out of the reach of the sun.

So, he decided to wander around the city. It was strange, really. For the most part, people were heeding the authorities' advice to stay inside. At least in the parts of the city he had seen so far. As he made his way from shadow to shadow, as was his habit, he was startled by the sound of glass shattering across the street. He crouched in a dark doorway and saw a man falling backward out of a third-story window. He knew the masked man was dead as soon as he hit the ground. What he didn't know was that the window belonged to Bertrand, who he had almost drained a few hours earlier. Had he known Bertrand's fate, his mood would have lifted considerably.

Diirek looked up at the silhouette of another man framed in the broken window. Diirek zoomed his vision in, just out of curiosity. The man had dark skin, a shiny bald head, and an angry but somehow friendly face. He looked like a cop. But cops don't usually throw people out of windows. Not in this century, anyway. Much easier to shoot people. Diirek shrugged and waited for the cop to leave the window. Then he continued on his way. When he got a whiff of blood from the dead guy on the sidewalk, he changed his mind.

He usually wasn't one to scavenge, but this guy was freshly dead. Plus, he had been so close to a meal back in the shitty alley next to the bar. He hadn't been hungry before that, but now he could eat. Might as well not waste some good blood.

He waited a minute to see if anyone would be drawn out by the commotion, but it looked like everyone was serious about minding their own business on this night. He watched as the cop came back to the window and wiped it down with a spray bottle and a rag. Then he listened as the guy started rooting around in the apartment. Diirek would be able to hear him walking to the front door, so he flashed across the street and knelt by the dead man in the mask. But something was off. The guy's blood didn't smell good anymore. Like it had gone sour almost immediately. That never happened. It usually took an hour at least for the blood to smell this rotten, but it had only been a few minutes. Sure, some people's blood smelled pretty bad even when they were alive. Usually if they had a far-gone terminal illness or ate lots of fast food (which is pretty much the same thing). But even then, the blood of the living never smelled like this.

Diirek decided to pass on this particular meal. He looked up at the broken window above and wondered if the cop had done something to this guy before he threw him out the window. He was tempted to head up there and ask the guy, but as a rule he tried to stay as far away from cops as possible. After all, he did need to drink people's blood to live. Cops generally don't smile upon that kind of thing. He stood up, sighed at the wasted blood, and headed for the nearest shadow to continue his skulking.

He didn't get very far before he heard glass shards scraping on the sidewalk.

He spun around and saw the stinky dead guy getting unsteadily to his feet. His first thought was: *That is not my doing. Not this time.* He had learned early in his life as an undead that the fewer people he turned like him, the better. People usually didn't like being undead, he found. He liked it. So did his girlfriend, and a few of the others, but many people didn't. Even if they swore they would beforehand. The grass is always greener on the other side of life, apparently.

This night was full of never-befores. First, the bombing. Although the city proper didn't get bombed, the surrounding areas were destroyed, and he didn't think that there were many people alive outside the city.

He had already made his way to America by the time war broke out in Europe in the middle of the 19th century. He had barely missed the bombing of Japan, having spent a few years there before things really went downhill. During the first world war, he had been living in the jungles of South America, helping give rise to legends of jungle creatures who crept into the cities at night to feed on locals. Before that, there were no bombs. Not really. Not like today's.

The second never-before was the failure to perform. He had never been that close to feeding and not gone through with it. The surprise of the falling bombs just took him out of the mood. It was a never-before that he hoped would be a never-again. Super embarrassing.

Lidia would never let him live it down. Not telling her wasn't an option. They told each other everything. He could accept that. As long as the others didn't find out. He had a reputation to protect.

Finally, there was this dead man getting up and walking around, seemingly of his own volition. Not normal. Diirek wasn't sure what to think of it. He was curious. He started stalking the stumbling figure down the sidewalk, staying in the shadows as he did so. They hadn't gone far when a single gunshot sounded from inside the apartment.

The dead man turned around at this sound and headed back the way he came, moving slowly on a clearly broken leg. Diirek kept watch from the shadows, trying to figure out what the hell could have caused this anomaly. After a few minutes, a door slammed down the block and the dead man turned again and started in the direction of the slammed door. Diirek noted this with interest.

Another few minutes passed before the vampire heard footsteps coming down the stairs of the apartment with the cop inside. The front door opened. Diirek watched the cop from deep shadows as he noticed the missing dead man. The guy cursed to himself, spotted the man he'd thrown from the window, and started after the walking dead.

Diirek let him pass and then stalked him to see what he would do. It wasn't hard for him to follow humans unnoticed. He had been doing it for a very long time. He could move fast and stay quiet easily. Plus, he wore the blackest of black clothes. He much preferred the clothes of this century than any other. They were far more comfortable than those of previous generations. He wore all black everything, but only the best. His entire outfit sold for a couple of thousand dollars, easy. Not that he'd actually paid for it. He had no need for money. Not really.

Diirek was about twenty feet behind the cop, watching as he caught up with the dead man. Without hesitation, the cop tackled him to the ground from behind and got handcuffs around his wrists. He hauled the drooling and groaning dead guy up and perp-walked him back to his car.

Diirek watched the plainclothes officer struggle to get the dead man in the back of his car without getting bitten. When he finally got him in and was about to close the door, his phone rang. He reached for his phone and slammed the door at the same time. But he didn't notice that the dead guy had lunged out at his hand on the door, trying to bite it.

Diirek uttered a small sound of surprise as the dead guy's still-masked head was lopped off by the closing door. The cop made a much larger sound of surprise as the head came to rest by his feet, chomping ineffectively at his scuffed shoes. His phone rang in his hand as he stared at the lively-as-ever head on the ground.

"What the fuck?" the cop said.

"What in the world?" Diirek said.

Finally, after five or six rings, the cop answered his phone.

***

"Weller here," he said, distracted, staring down at the severed head. Its eyes were rolling, teeth snapping.

"Kurt, where are you?" It was Lt. Kilgore.

"Delta and 9th. Where do you want me?"

"Get up to 6th. I've lost contact with James and Ricco. That's their last known."

"Copy," Weller said and hung up the phone.

He stared down at the masked head for a long moment, deciding what to do. He needed to bring it back to the station. This wasn't a one-off thing. It was happening all over the city. The brass had to know about it, so they could make some sort of plan. He didn't have the faintest idea of what that plan would be, and didn't envy those who would have to come up with it.

Something moved off in the shadows. Weller snapped his head up in time to see a dark figure with a pale white face rushing toward him faster than he thought possible. A split-second later Weller was on his back on the concrete, a man on top of him, holding him down. He seemed impossibly strong. Weller couldn't move at all.

"What did you do to that man?" the pale face said to him, gesturing at the head a few feet away.

"Get the hell off of me. I'm police." Weller kept struggling, breathing hard, while the guy didn't seem to be working all that hard to keep him down.

"I know. Detective Weller, right? What did you do to him to make him like that?"

The guy's accent was vaguely European, Weller thought. But he couldn't really place it. It was just a faint whisper at the end of his words.

"All I did to that asshole is toss him out a window after he tried to kill me. He got up and walked off on his own. I didn't do shit. It's something to do with the attacks. Gotta be."

"You've seen this before? When?"

"Earlier tonight. Whatever it is, it's happening other places, too. So if you want to stay safe, you'll let me go. I've got to get that head back to my boss."

The strange, dark eyes in the pale face narrowed in thought. Then he adjusted, placing his forearm across Weller's collarbone, rummaging through his pockets with his other hand. It was hard for Weller to breathe, but his arms were now free so he started to pummel the guy with his fists. It was like punching a human statue. The blows had no effect whatsoever. Finally, Weller reached across his body for his gun, but the guy had found what he was looking for; a business card. He grabbed Weller's wrist with one hand and pinned it to his body. He waved the card in his face.

"My name is Diirek. I will be checking in on you, Detective Kurt Weller. I want this problem solved as much as you do." Diirek released Weller, who sat up and looked all around. There was no trace of the man.

He rubbed his collarbone and his wrist. *What the hell was that? This is getting ridiculous.* He got up and looked down at the head again.

"This is such bullshit," he said for the tenth time, carefully picking up the zombie head so as not to get bit. He had a sudden and barely suppressible urge to punt the masked head down the road. He figured it was a natural response to holding a severed human head that was trying to bite you. After a few moments of contemplation, Weller decided that he might injure his foot or destroy the only evidence he currently had that would prove he wasn't going insane. Not to mention a host of other problems that came along with the dead walking around biting people. No, he needed to show this head to Captain Shellbourne if there was to be any chance of saving the city.

He looked into the back seat at the headless body. It wasn't moving. He popped the trunk and tossed the head in, closed it, stepped around, and jumped in the driver's seat. He looked in the mirror at the black-clad body through the plastic divider as he started the car. It creeped him out, but it wasn't moving at all.

As he raced down Delta to 6th, he promised himself that, if he ever came across an animate severed head again, he would kick it as hard as he could away from him.

He saw the lights from the squad car as he approached 6th and Delta. It didn't look good. The black-and-white was parked on the sidewalk to his left, both front doors were opened. No sign of James or Ricco. Figures darted in and out of a store halfway down 6th. Those coming out had their arms full. Maybe five people in all. Looters.

Weller pulled out his Sig, which he had reloaded in Bertrand's apartment after doing a rail of coke. He jogged down the sidewalk, past a few burning cars, over broken glass from store windows. The streetlights here had been shot out, the only illumination coming from the burning vehicles and a few lighted windows in the buildings lining the street.

"Police, shitbags! Stop now!" Weller yelled when he was close enough to startle them but far enough away that he could take cover if they fired on him. They looked to be teenagers, piling loot in a crappy van facing away from Weller in the road. His voice startled them and they scrambled, the driver taking off before all his buddies were inside, causing one of them to run after the van. Weller watched as they rounded the corner down the block, making no move to follow.

He ran into the store— a new and used musical instrument shop— to see if either of the missing uniforms were in there. Finding nothing but a half-empty store, he jogged back out to the sidewalk and looked around, deciding what to do next.

A man's piercing scream sounded from above Weller. A scream filled with terror and dismay. A final attempt at rescue, it was the sound of a man screaming for his life. Weller looked up, thinking that the sound came from the roof of the five-story building next to which the black-and-white was parked. He was halfway there when another scream issued forth, followed by a man— a uniformed man— flung from the roof. Only this man didn't fall. Not really. He sailed high above the street like he had been thrown from a catapult, smashing into the building across the street, one floor down from where he started at the other building.

The man hit the building face-first, his upper chest and head smashing into brick just above a window, the rest of his body breaking the glass. The force of whatever threw him was enormous, the result was like that of a ragdoll, the momentum of his lower body carrying him in a gainer through the window. Another figure followed him, this one graceful and deliberate. It was really no more than a shadow traveling through the air. A dark spot that landed noiselessly through the window that the cop's legs had broken.

Weller knew that the cop was dead as soon as he saw him hit the building like that, but it didn't stop him from running as fast as he could.

The outer door of the office building was locked so Weller had to shoot it to get in. When he made it up to the correct floor there was only the body laying in broken glass. No sign of anyone else.

The officer's head had been torn off and thrown into a wall, where it was wedged face-first in the drywall, deformed and badly damaged. Weller didn't know James or Ricco by sight, but the name tag on the headless body said James. Weller looked out the window at the building across the street. *What kind of thing could throw a man that far?* He thought. *Nothing. Not possible.*

Weller called Lt. Kilgore back and told him what he had found. He left out the part about seeing the man flung impossibly from building to building. One thing at a time. There was no sign of Ricco, but he feared the worst.

As soon as Kilgore arrived Weller took off for the precinct. He had to get the zombie head back to headquarters so they could formulate a plan. Time was most definitely of the essence.

# CHAPTER FOUR

# AN INTRO TO VAMPIRE POLITICS

O ld subway tunnels sat like hungry catacombs beneath the city, some still in use, some abandoned or used for storage. Trash and all kinds of debris had a way of sifting ever downward from the city above, coming to rest in the tunnels, like carcasses of dead whales finding their way to the ocean floor. While city workers routinely cleared the active tunnels of trash, the abandoned ones were ignored, the trash left to pile up, attracting bottom feeders that scavenged for tiny morsels of food. That is, until the vampires took up residence.

While it's true that there are all kinds of vampires just as there are all kinds of humans (after all, *most* vampires used to be humans), it's also true that vampires as a whole are notoriously anal. Usually the slovenly vampires you come across haven't been vamps for long. Given a couple of centuries of living in filth, even the most enthusiastic of disgusting slobs will grow tired of such an existence. Plus, when you're trying to get laid— whether by vamp or human— a dirty lair (or home) is a turn-off for most. As a result, and to the detriment of city rats, cockroaches, flies, maggots and a host of other creatures, a couple of the abandoned subway tunnels had been cleaned up. In fact, they looked kind of homey, in a dark and creepy sort of way.

The brood of vampires hadn't been in the city very long when the end of the world came. Only about 5 years. But in that time they had done wonders with the place. They had turned it into a mini-city of sorts. They called it "The Underground" not only because those in charge lacked imagination, but also because they thought it was funny. Technically, they were dead and so belonged underground anyway. There was also a rebellious connotation to the name. Most of the vamps in charge thought of themselves as better than humans, and as such they fancied themselves warriors in a war between races, even if they knew that they needed humans to survive. In reality they did all they could to stay hidden from the human world above, which was why they moved cities fairly often.

The small vampire bureaucracy, or Vampaucracy, as they called themselves (see? a severe lack of imagination) learned long ago that the best way to keep from getting killed by vampire hunters was to stay under the radar. This wasn't done by living in large castles near small villages where the victim pool was almost nonexistent. No, that was just asking for trouble. You've got to learn from the past, after all.

They stayed under the radar by limiting the number of kills per vamp, per month. That number was different in every city and was determined by the total population of the city they were living in (or under) and the average murder rate of said city. If local law enforcement got wind of something funny going on and started to suspect the supernatural, it was time to find another city.

Of course, not all blood-sucking fiends adhered to the rules. There were outcasts scattered around the world who did their own thing, in whatever way they deemed fit. Diirek, who had recently left The Underground after finally growing sick of the drama, ineptitude, and pow-er-trips that seemed the never-ending bane of his existence, was missed by many. Plus, there were a few individuals that he had never gotten along with, and who seemed to be out to ruin Diirek's life— or lack thereof, if you want to get technical.

He felt that they had won an important battle when he finally decided to strike out from the group. Sometimes he felt angry at himself for letting them drive him away, but most of the time it was a relief to not be living in a vampire soap-opera.

Lidia stood by Diirek (bless her cold, black heart) and lit out with him. Lidia, or Lids, as Diirek called her, had been undead for only a few centuries, whereas Diirek had been a vampire for a very, very long time. Although they came from different parts of the world, their experiences as vampires had been similar and they had fallen in love almost instantly.

They were almost polar opposites in every conceivable way. Where Diirek was as white as white can be, Lidia's skin was of a sepia tone, more brown than red. Diirek preferred to read and Lidia preferred to watch movies. Where Diirek liked time alone, Lidia had many friends in The Underground with whom she visited regularly. She was also a talker, whereas Diirek never had much to say— unless it really needed saying.

There were certain things he gave up when he left the Underground and the relative comfort and protection that had come from strength in numbers. For years vampire societies had been hunted by some un-known foe. Initially, this was the reason for the Vampaucracy to form in the first place. In his many years on earth, Diirek had never seen this vampire hunter. Nor had anyone he'd ever talked to. There were many names for this ruthless monster— so many that Diirek began to feel it was some sort of urban legend meant to teach vampires not to get too big for their fangs, so to speak.

Currently, Diirek's thinking was that the whole thing was a ploy to form vampires into a society that could then be taken advantage of by its rulers. It was one of the reasons he'd left. He didn't think he was in any danger from a vampire-killing monster. Most other vampires he knew felt that this so-called monster (or monsters) was simply lore based on a particularly ruthless vampire leader that had gone insane and killed his brood.

Of course, there *were* pesky vampire-hunting teenagers that did their best to eradicate the blood-sucking fiends, but they were pretty easy to dispatch. They always seemed to be skinny little blond teenagers, which was kind of strange. But, they hadn't been around since the early 2000s. So, he wasn't really worried about that, either. They'd had a nice run, as far as he was concerned.

The fact was that the Vampaucracy had the hook-up on blood in the city. Standard operating procedure was to find a blood bank and grease the wheels before the bulk of the Underground ever even got to whatever city they were moving to. At least, that had been S.O.P since blood banks first started springing up in the middle of the 20th century. Before that, groups of vamps had to move cities quickly or seek out war zones where their insatiable appetites would be hard to notice. Of course, living in a war zone came with problems of its own.

The bottom line was, if they couldn't find a decent blood bank, they wouldn't move to the city. The reason being that it was just easier to do things that way. While drinking blood from a plastic bag wasn't great, it did the trick. If every vampire in the Underground went around finding victims every time they were hungry, a good portion of the population would die pretty quickly.

People would start to catch on. Then came the pitchforks, torches, and tactical assault weapons. It was messy— not worth it when modern society had a never-ending supply of blood available for the right price.

So, since going out on his own, Diirek had gone hungry more often than not. Lidia was still welcome in the Underground and she would get a blood bag every so often. Once in a while, she would bring half back to

him, but it wasn't enough. Of course, he realized the sacrifice he would
have to make before ever leaving the Underground.

But the Vampaucracy just wasn't his bag. The blood banks in the city
were wrapped up tight by Elena, the current head of the Vampaucracy.
Diirek had tried to approach a couple, only to be refused with indigna-
tion and mock horror. So it was either go hungry for a while or put up
with Elena's bullshit, which he was done with.

When Elena first took power, it was on promises of free blood bags
for everyone, infrastructure in which to live comfortably, and relative
freedom for each vampire to do what he or she pleased. But, like any
typical politician— vampire or otherwise— those promises were never
truly filled. At first, Elena and her small, sycophantic crew would 're-
quest' favors in turn for blood. Small favors in the beginning, gradually
increasing over the years. The last time Diirek had requested a blood bag
Elena told him to bring her a human baby. When he asked what for she
threw a fit and Diirek had to fight two of her idiot followers off. He left
the next day.

There had been a few vampires over the years that had plotted against
her and conveniently disappeared without a trace. Diirek's theory was
that Elena killed the last ruler— a charismatic young vamp by the name
of Teddy— and his crew in order to take power. He got the feeling
that, were it not for his immense popularity in the Underground, he
would be dead, too. He still felt that she might try to get rid of him, but
he had to risk going back to the Underground to talk some sense into
the Vampaucracy. Diirek knew how Elena operated and knew that they
were in a very precarious situation as a species with the recent events.
The sudden existence of what could only be described as zombies was
troubling, to say the least.

The world had shifted under his feet when Diirek saw the zombie
get up from the sidewalk and trudge away. He hoped wildly that it was
some sort of freak occurrence. A one-off, an anomaly. He thought briefly

about traveling around the city, looking for zombies, but decided against it. Lidia was no doubt heading toward their sparse apartment now. Plus, he knew that most of the Underground would be above ground for the night, doing their bloodsucking or partying thing. Surely they would be regrouping momentarily. Bombs falling and dead people walking around (present company excluded, of course) trumped all other issues, for now. He had to find Lidia and they had to go talk to those imbecilic vampires who comprised the Vampaucracy.

He knew that Lidia could take care of herself, so he wasn't too worried. After the initial shock of the bombs dropping outside the city, he calmed down somewhat when it seemed that the city itself had been spared. Of course, it was always possible that another barrage would rain down destruction on them at any time. If so, there was nothing he could do about it.

Up until coming across the zombie, he had been enjoying his limited time outdoors. But with the new information he had, it was time to find his best friend and partner. He and Lidia had a long-standing plan to meet at their place if disaster struck. And if not there, then back in the Underground.

Diirek headed for their shared basement apartment using his preferred method of travel when he was in a hurry. It took three effortless jumps up the side of a building to reach the rooftops. From there it was smooth sailing. He soared between buildings, silent and graceful. He used each rooftop as a launching pad, gaining speed to the edge and then jumping through the air, enjoying the breeze and the feel of the city around him.

Something bad was happening, but once he found Lidia they would deal with it together. There wasn't much that they couldn't figure out. Not much that they couldn't do. No ordeal they couldn't survive, if they were together.

CHAPTER FIVE

# SUBURBAN ZOMBIES AND HEAD-KICKING

John Simpson, Jr. had started his day like any other. He woke up groggy, his only wish to crawl back into his warm bed and slip into the oblivion of unconsciousness. Unfortunately, he had to go to work.

As always, his wife was already up, seeing to the children. She was a saint, and he only wanted to strangle her on occasion, which was pretty good, he thought. When they met they had both been 29, and her energy and vitality had seemed endless. Now, twelve years later, Cindy Simpson was verily bubbling with purpose while John struggled to make it through the day without falling asleep at his desk. All he wanted to do was sleep. It was the elusive goal that would never be attained. At least not until his children of 8 and 10 were out of the house.

John showered, shaved, dressed, and brushed his teeth, bleary-eyed and in a foul mood, as was his ritual. Working his way toward the door, he said goodbye to his wife and two kids, wishing them a good day the same way he did every day. He left to catch the train on time, chomping a croissant sandwich fresh out of the microwave on the way.

Work was much the same as it had been in the fifteen years he had been employed in logistics for an industrial chemicals company. He joked with male co-workers and harmlessly flirted with those female workers he had known for years. He had a salad for lunch, proud of himself for resisting the urge to get a burger or a burrito. He had finally begun to heed his doctor's warnings. His not inconsiderable girth was a testament to the many urges he'd given into over the years.

He did good work and left at the appointed time. He headed to the gym for an hour of slow, laborious cardio, and then he met up with his best friend from college for their once-weekly beer session at a sports bar halfway between the suburbs and downtown.

It's impossible to say whether or not John would have lived if the events that followed had never happened.

John was finishing his second beer, his friend Mark was already on his fourth, when the bartender changed the TV they were watching from baseball to a news channel. This was met with grumbles from some in the crowded bar. But the grumbles turned to gasps when people realized what the news anchor was saying. Pretty soon every TV in the place was turned to news channels, the previously loud patrons were deathly quiet. The country was under attack. Missiles flying, bombs falling, people dying.

John felt dizzy and lightheaded, then he felt a sharp pain in his left arm and chest. A blackness slid over his vision like a curtain closing after a lengthy and not-very-interesting play. The aftertaste of beer in his mouth was the last thing he thought of before coherent thought left him. Instinctually he knew he was dying and he had never liked the taste of beer. He'd liked the effects, but never the taste. Not really. He silently asked God why he had to die with the taste of beer in his mouth. He got no answer.

John Simpson, Jr. collapsed from his barstool onto the floor and was dead three seconds later. It wasn't long before John's body was up and walking around again, to the shock and confusion of everyone who hadn't left the bar in a rush to get home to their families.

Mark, who had been attending John's dead body, at first trying CPR and then giving up and waiting for an ambulance, was the first to be bitten. When John's newly-dead corpse struggled to its feet, Mark was there at once, his mind reeling at the miracle he was witnessing. He momentarily forgot about the end of the world and was happy to have his friend back. Happy that he wouldn't have to explain to John's wife what had happened.

He went to wrap his friend in a teary embrace, and his joy turned to pain and confusion as John's teeth sank into his shoulder. And then his neck.

After that it was inevitable. The two zombies turned into four, then eight, then sixteen, and so on. They spread out through the suburbs, the chaos and confusion of the nearby attacks only serving to assist the rise of the undead.

Nor was John at the epicenter of the zombie crisis in the city. When the news started coming in that the country was under attack, a rash of suicides all across the city added fuel to the drooling and stupid undead fire that was in full splendor by the time Weller found himself holding a severed zombie head on the sidewalk.

Roving pockets of chaos, be it by looters, zombies, or run-of-the-mill apocalypse-inspired lunatics, sprouted all over the city. Some areas were deathly quiet, where people stayed inside and waited to die with their family members or, in some sad cases, their cats. (Who, by the way, were still unwilling to provide comfort or affection to their owners in a time of great crisis. And don't think they didn't know what was going on. Cats can sense the apocalypse. It's science.)

Other parts of the city were alive with the screams and hysterical laughter of broken minds. For some unknown reason, the chaos spread swiftly toward the suburbs. Much of the downtown area— where our brilliant and harried detective lived— was left untouched. As it so happened, the Underground was situated in the downtown area, as well.

What would become known as the safe zone (aka downtown) was situated on a wide peninsula that bulged out into the waters of the lake. This fact made it possible for the rest of our story to happen in the way that it did. If it hadn't happened the way it did, it would probably be super boring. So, yeah. Think about that while you're reading this. Are you not entertained?

Anyway, moving on.

\*\*\*

Not long after John had died and came back to eat his good friend Mark, Lidia came upon him and kicked his head off. It was a first for her, and she had to admit that it felt good. She'd always wanted to kick someone's head off, she supposed, but it wasn't something she ruminated on or anything. Although, back before she had been a vampire, she'd been a little girl in France during the Reign of Terror.

She was in a crowd with her papa one day when a guillotine was in heavy use, and it left quite the impression on her. She would never forget the spectacle even if she lived to be 1,000 years old. The way the blade sounded when it sliced through a neck— the popping sound it seemed to make when passing swiftly through spine. The thump of the head falling to the basket beneath and the gushing fountain of blood that always ensued from the liberated neck. Since she'd become a creature of the night, it made her hungry whenever she thought about it.

She didn't start the night aiming to kick a head off. She and Diirek parted ways outside of their building shortly after the sun went down.

While Diirek went off into the city, Lidia headed toward the suburbs. She needed to feed.

With her special abilities, it didn't take her long to find prey. She wore a comfortable but tight short gray skirt with a white blouse and a black jacket. She looked like a stylish, successful 20-something who'd had a long day at work but still somehow managed to look immaculate. The combination of her smooth, sepia skin, wide, dark eyes, and incredible physique meant that there was plenty of attention directed her way as she walked into the half-full club.

A couple of men came up to her, asking to buy her a drink, but they didn't have the right feel, so she politely told them no. Her instincts were finely honed, and she could sense the kind of man was looking for. Soon enough, he found her.

Lidia pretended not to notice the drug he slipped into her drink before walking back from the bar, smiling a soulless smile at her. The drug had no effect on her, but she was a good actress. After an hour, she let him guide her out of the bar and to a nearby hotel he had already paid for. The guy was good. He'd done this before. She kept her anger under control until they were alone in the room, where she slipped out of her character.

"How many times have you done this?" she asked him when he came out of the bathroom in his underwear. He looked from the bed, where he'd lain her face-down only minutes before, to where she was standing, blocking the exit.

"What do you mean? You wanted to come up here. You all want to."

"I don't remember you asking me. In fact, I know you didn't. You drugged me and took me here. So, I'll do you the favor you never did me. I'll ask you: Do you mind if I drink your blood? I'm very hungry."

"What the fuck, lady? You can go, alright. We don't have to do this. I thought you wanted a good time."

"I'm about to have a great time. You, not so much."

She was upon him before he had a chance to move, her jaw clamped tightly on his neck, the blood flowing quickly out of his body and into hers. He struggled wildly at first, but her strength was too great.

When she was done, she dropped his lifeless and empty body to the floor, licking her lips in satisfaction. She stepped into the bathroom and made sure there was no rapist-blood on her nice white blouse. As she stood there in front of the mirror (yes, she could see herself reflected there) she had a sense that something very wrong was happening. Sirens wailed outside, which was nothing out of the ordinary in itself, but they kept wailing. More and more streaming past on the street below.

Lidia stepped out of the room, her meal already forgotten, and made her way outside and into the chaos awaiting. Cars were speeding by on the road, swerving around others pulled to the curb, the people craning their necks, trying to see over the buildings. Lidia sent her hearing out and heard what could only be a massive explosion several miles away.

She ran back into the lobby and into the room where breakfast was served. There was a TV bolted to a wall, and several hotel employees staring at it, their eyes wide, mouths open. She stayed there for less than a minute before starting back to meet Diirek at their shared basement apartment.

She wanted to travel by rooftop, but in this part of the city the buildings were too far apart, and too short by far, so she ran. She took off her pumps to run because it turns out even vampires can't run in heels.

Lidia was arguably the badassest of vampires. Diirek certainly thought so and told her as much on several occasions. Even before she was turned, she could handle herself very well. Her skills only grew in the years after she became immortal. She outran many of the cars in the road, dodging past people who were looting, people who were in a daze, and people who had just plain lost it. About halfway to her destination, she noticed something very strange.

There was an ambulance parked in front of a sports bar, its lights flashing in silent warning, clashing with the neon beer signs in the establishment's windows. But that wasn't what caught Lidia's attention. It was the man that threw himself through one of the front windows, screaming something about bees, she thought. Lidia watched the man land on the sidewalk, bleeding profusely from dozens of cuts. He lay there, dazed, before seeming to remember why he jumped out the window in the first place. His eyes went wide and jumped up and ran past Lidia, leaving much of his blood behind. He said nothing more about bees, and Lidia walked toward the bar to see if there were, in fact, buzzing insects in the place.

She heard screaming and saw a woman jump out of the now-broken window and run down the street, relatively unharmed. The woman looked wildly at Lidia and screamed, "Run! Zombies!" before continuing away, her hair a mess, and her sanity cracked. *Ahhh, not bees. Zom-bees,* Lidia thought, as if it made sense. Then she stopped. *Zombies? No way.* She continued a few steps and looked inside the bar.

A man was sprawled out on the long table by the window, his intestines being pulled out like spaghetti by— sure enough— a zombie. It was the eyes that solidified the realization for Lidia. They were cloudy, dark, dead eyes.

Further inside the restaurant there were a dozen people running around the big square bar in the middle of the place, several zombies trailing them like a morbid game of duck, duck, goose. Inside the double doors at the entrance were two more zombies. But evidently they were trapped between the two sets of doors that made up a waiting area. They couldn't figure out how to open the doors to get back into the restaurant, where all their attention was on the people running around in circles. The people weren't even screaming. They just looked tired of running away from the surprisingly nimble zombies.

Lidia dropped her expensive pumps on the ground and opened the first set of doors. One of the zombies turned around and looked at her for a moment as if unsure of what to think. It started to turn back around when Lidia gave it a shove, propelling the thing into the glass of one of the inner doors, shattering it and sending the zombie flipping over the metal push-rail and into the bar.

The other zombie turned around then. The zombie was a man who had previously been John Simpson, Jr., and Lidia, with a beautiful roundhouse kick, removed his head and sent it bouncing along the glossy wooden bench like a deformed soccer ball, finally coming to rest next to the outer doors.

The people inside saw their chance and came streaming out the doors. Lidia stepped aside and let them pass, and then faced off with the zombies following. She went to town, punching holes in their chests, ripping off their limbs and using them as bludgeons, poking their eyes into their rotting brains, throwing them and smashing them and pulverizing them. It was the best time she'd had out on the town since the nineteenth century. And that was saying a lot— that century was crazy as hell.

When all was said and done, Lidia stood amid a pile of zombie corpses that would have made Michonne proud.

She made her way back outside, picked up her pumps, and was about to run off when she saw something wiggling on the sidewalk. The head she'd kicked off was moving around little by little with its tongue. *Clever zombie*, she thought before smashing it to pieces with a single stomp. *This could get really bad for us.*

## CHAPTER SIX

# NO WAY TO GET A HEAD IN LIFE

D etective Kurt Weller got back to the precinct in record time. Teams of city workers and police had been out clearing the roads of obstructions, working from downtown out. This not only let them have confidence in maneuvering around the city, but also gave a sense of order to all those people who had been told to return to their homes.

The airwaves had been overtaken by a message telling the citizens in no uncertain terms to seek shelter, hug their loved ones, and hope they didn't die. Anyone on the street not in an official capacity would be treated as hostile, the friendly female voice said, in between the sharp and insistent tones of the emergency broadcast system.

Below the city seal on every station on every tv, there scrolled the words, "Stay in your homes or the nearest habitable structure. This is not a drill. Those individuals found on the street will be arrested and prosecuted. Stay tuned for further instructions." Most of the law-abiding citizens had found their way to their respective destinations after the initial chaos, but there were still some with nothing to lose wandering the streets. Almost without exception, their interactions with nervous police were not pretty.

Weller was glad that order was slowly being restored. It would make the coming tasks much easier. He thought about the animate head in his trunk and the superhuman feat he had witnessed. The uniformed officer being thrown from building to building, a dark shadow following it without a sound. Plus his little interaction with the incredibly strong and incredibly pale movie-star-looking freak that questioned him about the severed head. He weighed the dangers. It didn't take long for him to come to the conclusion that dead people walking around and attacking citizens was more worrisome, for now.

"This is. Bull. Shit," he said. He stopped at a barricade at the block before the police plaza and showed his I.D. card to the uniform that approached his window. Another three officers pointed automatic rifles at him, and he figured there were probably snipers perched with their crosshairs trained on him, hidden by night and distance. The uniform handed his I.D. back and waved him through while the other three men relaxed and lowered their weapons.

Weller drove through the dogleg barricade and pulled into the parking garage. They'd been busy. He hoped roadblocks and manpower would be enough to control the situation that he figured was spiraling out of control not more than a couple of miles away.

Weller parked, popped the trunk, and went to grab the severed head. He found a plastic grocery bag in the trunk and maneuvered the head into it, careful not to let the bastard bite him. Carrying a severed head through the police station would surely raise some eyebrows, but a severed head that was still moving would cause more chaos than he could deal with.

As he was turning to head for the elevator, he remembered the body in the back seat. He was pretty confident that it was no longer a threat, but didn't want anyone walking by and seeing it. He opened the back door and pushed the body down into the footwell. It offered no resistance. *Good enough*, he thought as he walked briskly toward the elevators.

He was hopeful as he rode up in the elevator alone, the muzak playing softly through the speakers a strange contrast to what the world had become in the last few hours. If the body wasn't moving without the head, then that was the way to kill the zombies. *We could arm everyone with swords*, he thought. *Someone dies, cut their head off. But then we'd probably have people cutting heads off all willy-nilly. Can't have that. After I show this to the captain we'll have to put a bullet in its brain, see if that works.*

He didn't even think about going over the captain's head for this. Even if he hated her with every fiber of his being at the moment, he still had the chain of command ingrained in him. You just don't go over your superior's head. Plus, he wanted her to let her guard down, and treating her with some respect would do the trick. He wasn't about to forget about the betrayal she surely perpetrated on him. No matter how strange things got. As long as he was drawing breath, he'd find a way to make her and Ray O'Shea sorry for what they did to him. But he had to prove it first.

The ding of the elevator brought back his focus on the task at hand. He looked down at the plastic bag in his right hand, its contents bulging as the head's jaw opened and closed and its eyes blinked slowly through the oval holes in the mask it still wore.

There were far fewer people milling around than before. He supposed they were all out in the city erecting roadblocks and restoring order. No one paid him much attention as he hurried to Shellbourne's office. He knocked on the closed door and without waiting opened it to find Captain Shellbourne alone in the room with her head in her hands, her elbows propped on her desk.

"What is it now?" she said without looking up.

Weller said nothing. He walked up to her desk and upended the bag. By some freak happening the masked head landed with a moist thunk directly on its ragged neck, facing Shellbourne.

The noise caused her to raise her head. Her eyes went wide as she sucked in air and pushed herself away from the desk. The back of her chair hit the wall and her gaze stayed on the head, its eyes rolling, lids blinking, tongue lolling in the slowly opening and closing mouth. She looked at Weller, back to the head, and then under the desk, as if to make sure it wasn't some sort of trick. Like someone could have sawed a hole in her desk and crawled under it while she was sitting there, all without her noticing. Weller had to suppress a smile.

After a long moment the shock on her face faded and she looked resigned.

"So it's true. Damn it all to hell."

"Not the first you've heard about this?" Weller wasn't really surprised. After all, he now knew that the druggies he encountered earlier in the night were, in fact, zombies. "Where else is it happening?"

"Everywhere," Shellbourne said with a sigh. He'd never seen her like this. It produced a strange mixture of delight, pity, and empathy. Delight was winning out, though.

"Well, then. I guess we've got a big fucking problem. What's the plan?"

"Same as before," she said. "Barricade the city as best we can to protect against invasion."

"That's not going to help against these bastards." Weller gestured at the head on the desk.

"Oh no? And why's that?" There was the old captain. She hated being told she was wrong, even in so many words.

"Because, from what I've seen, these things come to life when people die. You think someone's dead, you just wait a few minutes to watch them get up and walk around." He paused to let it sink in before continuing. "So, do you have a way to keep people from dying within the barricades?"

\*\*\*

Lidia and Diirek stuck to the shadows on the way to the Underground. Not that they really needed to. Even the active subway tunnels were silent. Everyone had been told to go to their homes. It was true that a few of the major underground stops had been used as bomb-shelters of sorts when the attacks first started happening. But it had been a while since the last explosion was spotted, off in the distance, seven or eight miles away from the city. So the subway stations had been cleared, and the two lovers had the place to themselves as they made their way to their previous home.

City workers had long ago sealed the doors to the abandoned stations, God-forbid squatters or drug addicts find a free place to live. Inhabitants of the Underground left the doors sealed, essentially ensuring no human could get in. Instead, they chiseled the grout from the wall of bricks above the door. While the bricks were too heavy for a single human to move, they were like nothing to the undead that lived behind them. Diirek jumped up and found the finger-holes. He pulled out the large, jigsaw formation and let Lidia leap through before replacing the makeshift door behind him.

Lidia landed elegantly on the fine plush carpet that signified the home of the city's vampire lair, followed shortly by Diirek. Not long ago, when they'd called this home, the two often removed their shoes to enjoy the feeling of thick carpet under their feet. Like most other vampires as old as them, carpet was a reminder of how far they— and the world— had come. They had both spent their youth walking on stone, dirt, and wood floors. Even though carpet was everywhere now, it had yet to lose its novelty for the couple.

This time, however, they both left their shoes on. There was an urgency behind their cool eyes and blank stares. Anyone who had been alive as long as they had didn't have to practice the thousand-yard stare. It was a byproduct of living through so much. But tonight it was apparent that they were witnessing events that no one had ever lived through.

The walls of the service hallway flickered with candlelight. Not real candles, though. Ever since the invention of battery-powered candles that flickered like real flames, there had been no turning back for the Underground. Diirek remembered when a friend of his, Isabelle, had first discovered them. She came back to the Underground (this one in Paris, Isabelle's hometown) and proceeded to gush, telling everyone how long they would last, and turning them on to demonstrate. She had picked up a fake candle by its imitation flame, the look on her face one of sheer joy and wonder.

Everyone liked Isabelle. She had been turned when she was fifteen and had never lost her teenage optimism, even after almost 100 years. So it was that the Underground used fake candles from then on, even though some of the others wanted to stick with regular candles. This was no surprise to Diirek, since those set in their ways often resist change, even if for no apparent reason.

As it happened, Isabelle was the first to spot Diirek and Lidia as they entered through the service door at the end of the hallway, walking into the station that served as a communal living area. She flew over to them, squealing as she came, and wrapped an arm around each of them, forming a three-way hug. There was an old ticket booth and a line where turnstiles used to be, otherwise the place held no resemblance to a working subway station. There were couches, cots, tables, and chairs. Carpets covered the concrete floor. Bookshelves were against almost every wall, filled to the brim. Laptop computers were strewn about, as well as a flatscreen tv complete with an expensive sound system. Not much had changed since they'd been gone.

"Oh my goodness I've missed you both so much!" she said in her still-heavy French accent. "Mes amours!"

"Oh, my sweet baby. It hasn't even been a week since we've seen you!" Lidia said, pulling the girl back to look into her brilliant green eyes.

"It's good to see you, too, Is. Have you been out tonight?" Diirek was trying to be polite, but he couldn't take his mind off the changes happening above them. Lidia had always been better at keeping her worries at bay.

With the question, Isabelle's face changed from joy to consternation.

"Yeah," she said. "It's pretty bad, huh?"

"We think so," Lidia replied. "But it'll be okay. That's what we're here for. Where is everyone?"

"Les cochons started a meeting a while ago and tried to keep everyone out." Diirek couldn't help but smile at Isabelle's nickname for the Vampaucracy. *"Pigs" is right,* he thought.

"But everyone demanded to be in on it," she continued. "I was even in there. But all they're doing is arguing. Like always. I got bored with it. They never listen to me anyway."

"What do you think we should do, Is?" Lidia asked.

"I say give the humans a chance to figure it out. We shouldn't get involved unless we have to."

Diirek and Lidia nodded at this. "Pretty good idea," Diirek said. "You want to head back in there with us?"

"Okay, sure," Isabelle was perking up again. They headed down the stairs to the station proper, where meetings were always held.

***

Weller would never have gotten into the meeting had it not been for captain Shellbourne's disgust with the still-moving severed head. She tried half-heartedly to stop him from coming, but Weller kept pushing. Insisting that he could explain it better first-hand than she could second. She looked exhausted anyway, and gave up without much of a fight. Weller put the head back in the plastic bag and the two of them (three if you count the head) took an elevator up to the top floor of the police plaza.

The wood-paneled conference room was full. It was set up like a miniature amphitheater, with a fan of stadium seating narrowing down to a wide area at the bottom where a speaker would stand. There was a large tv on the wall facing the seats, used for presentations to the top brass of the city's police. Weller had given a speech or two in there, back when he was full of piss and shit and baking soda and vinegar. At one point he had his sights set high in that organization. If pressed, he wouldn't be able to explain exactly what happened to dim the light that had once burned so brightly inside him. That want to thrive, not just survive.

Not that he was trying to remember as he walked into the room of mostly white, mostly old men who were even more out of touch than he was. No, his mind was on how to best stop the wave of undead that was surely forming in on them, surrounding the city like a medieval siege, if they were lucky. If they were not, and the people in this room were too senile to figure out a sensible solution to this most fucked-up of problems, then they would all be dead within a month, tops.

Weller saw all the big dogs in attendance. The mayor and district attorney were in the front row. Plus the superintendent, first deputy superintendent, chief, deputy chief, commander, and all their respective assistants and lackeys and suckerfish and hangers-on and ass-kissers, and even a mistress or two. He nodded to most of them, whether they acknowledged his presence or not. He knew that they all knew who he was, especially with the front-page news that had kicked up a shit storm a week before. Even before that, though, they knew him well. He had helped a few of them get where they were today. The rest of them he had either pissed on or elbowed or jabbed in the kidneys during their mad and violent scramble up the ranks. Such was the nature of things. He'd taken his beatings, as well. It was part of the rat race. The cost of doing business. You didn't get to the top without a few scars. If you did, you wouldn't stay there for long.

The briefing started shortly after Weller and Shellbourne found seats. Weller wanted to break the news first and foremost because it would impact everything else, but Shellbourne stopped him. Even in times such as this, there were protocols to be followed, politics to heed, and bullshit to swallow. Once things got started, though, he was glad for it. He listened intently to figure out what exactly was happening to his city.

First and most importantly, no one had heard from Washington D.C. Dead air from everywhere outside the city. For all they knew, the rest of the country had been fried to a crisp. The governor was missing, presumed dead. Everyone who was left alive to matter was in this room.

They could keep the power and plumbing running for the foreseeable future, according to city engineers. That infrastructure was still intact, and they had enough people to run it— at least to power the protected area. They had a plan for systematically shutting off power to other, overrun parts of the city. But only after they gave people plenty of notice via radio and local TV messages.

Cell phones would soon be useless except for GPS and telling time, which would work for a long time to come, according to the wonks. They didn't know exactly how long phone service would last, but they didn't think it would be very long. Many of the towers in the suburbs and surrounding areas were operating on backup power, which would only be good for 12 hours, max.

The internet was officially down, presumably because servers in other cities had been destroyed. Local servers had survived, but it didn't really matter because they were only pieces of the whole. They could probably do a mini-internet in the city, but that wouldn't be for a long time, if at all. For now, no email, no social media, no porn. Damn.

They had two fully functioning hospitals running at full capacity and initial estimates said that food wouldn't be a problem for at least a month or so, but initial reports said that there was plenty of farmland untouched by the attacks. *Thank goodness for being in the middle of farm country,* Weller thought.

There was no sign of radiation, which was surprising to most of the room. Everyone assumed they had been hit with nuclear missiles, but apparently not. Weller figured that it was something much worse, if that was possible. The bulk of downtown was doing okay. Somewhat fluid perimeters had been established, keeping the chaos beyond downtown from spilling over and razing the only peaceful area left.

Weller listened as the Deputy Chief, a guy named Norman Doyle, dismissed the numerous reports of dead people walking around as 'mass hysteria'. It was his cue.

"Actually, Norman, I've gotta stop you there," Weller said, standing up. All the heads turned back toward him as he made his way down the steps to stand next to Doyle, who rolled his eyes.

"What is it, Weller? You hysterical, too?"

"Yes. But only because being in a room with this many white people always gets me on edge." He figured a little comedy would help lighten the blow, but no one was in the mood. Crickets. He shrugged and held up the plastic bag with the head in it.

"I've got proof that we've got a much bigger problem than mass hysteria," he yelled out while elbowing Doyle toward the wall. He dug into the bag and pulled out the mask-laden head, careful not to put his hand near its mouth. He held it with both hands, one on each ear, and leveled it at the audience. A few gasps sounded, but for the most part it was a lackluster reaction.

"What is that? A movie prop?" said the mayor, his considerable jowls shaking with the questions.

"Looks pretty fake to me," said some no-name lackey.

"This is no time for a prank, Weller. Somebody get him out of here!" The deputy chief called from where Weller had maneuvered him.

*I'm losing them! Maybe it's the mask,* Weller thought, and shifted his grip to pull off the ski mask that still adorned the head. To do this he put one hand around the ragged neck and the other at the crown of the head, gathering the rough black fabric in his hand.

Two uniformed goons that had been sitting behind the chief of police were moving toward him, getting ready to force him out. As Weller tried to pull off the mask, his other hand slipped and he had to grope to keep the head from dropping. The last thing he wanted was to have the damn thing stop moving because he dropped it on the floor at a crucial moment.

His hand slipped inside what was left of the neck, the feeling of being inside a person's throat, grabbing spine and sinew to keep it from falling, was sickening. He got it steady just as the goons reached him, grabbing him by the shoulders, one on either side. He yanked off the mask in a quick, desperate movement.

The air left the room. Weller was confused. He hadn't expected such a swift and strong reaction. The crowd stared at the head and then at Weller, and back again. Finally, everyone looked to the mayor, whose blood was draining out of his face, his eyes bulging in disbelief.

"MY BOY!!! OH GOD, MY BOY!" The mayor screamed, groping at the air as he tried to get up out of his seat, his considerable bulk fighting him.

"This is such bullshit," Weller said to himself as he stood there, holding the mayor's son's decapitated and still-moving head like a trophy. One hand was still in the throat, the other instinctually moving up to try and fend off the blow that one of the goons was in the process of delivering.

CHAPTER SEVEN

# VAMPIRES ARE STILL HUMAN (KIND OF)

E lena sat, like always, in the great wing-backed chair at the head of the long, ornate table. All of the chairs, a total of 9, were occupied. Other vampires stood around the table, watching the Vampaucracy argue. All told there were supposed to be 30 of them, including Diirek, Lidia, and Isabelle, who were just joining the group. But a quick count told Diirek that someone was missing. Everyone went quiet and turned toward the newcomers as they walked from the stairs and onto the wide subway platform.

Diirek locked eyes with Elena, the head of the Vampaucracy and, therefore, the Underground. She looked the same as ever: grim eyes always squinting, her blond hair done up with utmost care, her clothes a style two centuries old. She looked tiny in the giant chair, and she was. Her pudgy arms barely reached the armrests, her feet dangled just over the edge of the seat. She sat on a pillow, which sat on a stack of old phone books to help her see over the table.

She was the oldest vampire among them, but she had been younger than any of them when she was turned: 6 years old. Diirek thought of her as his fat little nemesis. One of the main reasons he left the Underground. The vindictive young-old vampire that stared back at him now, her eyes peering out of the fleshy face of a child, had become too much for him. She had gained power fifty years previous, after decades of obscurity. She and her lackeys turned the commune into a cult of sorts.

Diirek knew that by leaving the cult he and Lidia had both made a very powerful, very small enemy. In fact, if the unthinkable hadn't happened this night, Elena's number one priority would probably have been to rid the world of the traitorous two. It couldn't go unpunished. She had said as much before the couple had left for good: "This betrayal won't go unpunished," spoken in her little girl voice. A voice that Diirek and Lidia just couldn't take seriously, much as they tried.

"Look who I found!" Isabelle said, beaming a brilliant smile at the brooding bourgeoisie.

Everyone looked from Diirek and Lidia to Elena, waiting to see her response.

"I'm afraid we don't have any room for you. You made your choice, now you must live with it, no matter what's happening in the world above. You'll—"

"Before you drone on for an hour, I should tell you that we're not here to rejoin the Underground." Elena liked nothing more than to hear herself talk and Diirek couldn't take much of it. Not now. Lidia picked up where he left off, showing their united front.

"We're here to make sure you know what exactly is going on up there. Looks like zombies are suddenly real, and they're going to be a big fucking problem. But I'm guessing that's what you're already discussing."

At that, all of the vampires started talking at once. Diirek and Lidia used the opportunity to share a look with their few remaining friends. In order to save them from the wrath of their little leader, they refrained from anything more than a quick look, saying what they needed to say with their eyes. The others understood and appreciated this.

Elena tried to restore order, which meant that she wanted to be the only one talking. She stood up on her little throne and started jumping up and down, screaming with her eyes closed in true tantrum form. It was a regular sight in the Underground. This accounted for much of why she was able to gain control; she was just too annoying when she wasn't in charge. She would scream and cry and run around making awful little-girl noises until she got what she wanted.

Diirek and Lidia were in favor of killing her little highness, but she had sired too many of the Underground, who wouldn't hear of it. In fact, Elena had turned her mother, father, and older brother shortly after she had been turned. Like they had been in life, they were her servants in death, as well. That was the least of her atrocities. She also seemed to have a taste for torturing little human girls around her same age, although she tried her best to hide this fact.

Finally, everyone stopped talking at once and Elena looked around at them, her face scrunched up and distorted with rage.

"Elena," Lidia said, "what do you think we should do?"

The old little girl glared at Lidia, blank-faced. She clearly didn't have any ideas. Diirek and Lidia guessed it would be the case.

"I say we give it time. Let the dust settle and keep an eye on how the humans are doing. I really do not think that total extinction is a possibility, but we should not assume anything," Diirek said.

"Right," Lidia continued. "No need to risk exposure more than we must. But blood is also going to be an issue. We'll need to start half-feeding so we don't end up killing a bunch of the small number of humans left." As soon as the Underground heard "half-feeding" they all went crazy again.

"Fuck that!"

"I'm not half-fee—"

"No way! We've tried it befo—"

"You can do it but we're n—"

"Are you kidding?"

Diirek and Lidia expected this. They didn't like half-feeding any more than the rest of them, but they knew it was pertinent— at least for a little while.

"You can't tell us what to do. You're no longer a part of the Underground!" Elena was screaming and jumping up and down again.

"Have any of you been up there? We're not going to be able to move to another city for a very long time. If there even is another city left. This is all we've got for at least another twenty years." Diirek managed to keep cool. Maybe, just maybe, they would listen to logic for once. His words seemed to stun some of the vampires seated around the table. It gave him a chance to continue.

"Think about it; there are zombies walking around up there. Everywhere. How many of you were out there tonight?" Diirek asked. Most of the vampires in the room raised their hands. "Then you probably saw zombies. They smell terrible and they don't look right. It's clear that we can't feed on them. I'd rather starve than feed on something that smells that bad. What about you all?" No one said anything.

"All of the surrounding area has been blown to bits," Lidia took over now. "Even if we find out there is another city big enough to house us close by, how would we get there? Chances are there's no infrastructure left. No blacked-out busses to rent. No Sky BNB to rent houses. No way to get anywhere but walk. And hope we find someplace intact to sleep that will keep us completely out of the sun. Plus, there may not be any food along the way. Not if everyone is dead— or walking dead. So, like it or not, we're stuck here. With a dwindling food supply. If we leave people alive by half-feeding, we can stay here indefinitely. But if we go around leaving bloodless corpses, someone is going to catch on real quick. We need to be smart about this."

"But wouldn't half-feeding risk us getting caught, too? What if someone wakes up while we're feeding?" The question came tinged with a thick German accent from Bruno, one of the sycophantic Vampaucracy.

"Good question, Bruno," Lidia said, flashing her brilliant smile at him (she knew he had a crush on her). "That's why it's imperative to hunt in pairs from now on. I know it's strange, but the second vampire can act as a lookout, can make sure we don't get carried away while feeding, and can move quickly to cover the human's eyes if they wake up. This will keep anyone from being spotted."

"It just seems so strange to not hunt alone... so... unnatural," Bruno said, half talking to himself. "Plus, not feeding to completion is like... how you say... blue balls. Is this the expression? Blue balls?"

It was true. Half-feeding was a special kind of torture for vampires, but Diirek and Lidia just didn't see another way. It looked like the Vampaucracy was coming around on it, too.

"I would also suggest we help the humans stay safe from the zombies. They're pretty resourceful, but it wouldn't hurt to take a few laps when we go out, see if there's anything we can do. Apparently, the zombies are pretty easy to kill, right Lids?" Diirek asked, although he already knew the answer.

She nodded her head and smiled. "And fun, too!"

This was something that the vampires could get behind: killing zombies. They rarely got to use their full power, and the thought of being able to do some real damage was exciting for many of them.

"Just, you know, don't get seen by humans," Diirek added. He knew what was coming next.

"The Vampaucracy will discuss this!" Elena said, reaching forward to bang her little fists on the table. "*You two* are no longer a part of the Underground. So get out! Now!"

"Fine. But first, who's missing?" Diirek looked around the crowd, trying to put faces to names, something he'd never been particularly good at.

"Antonio," Isabelle said, her voice sure.

"Anyone know where he is?" Diirek said. No one answered. Vampire shoulders were shrugged. It wasn't a good sign. Diirek knew in his gut that something bad had happened, but he didn't know what. Antonio wasn't one to wander around during the apocalypse. None of them were.

"He'll be back. Now get out!"

Diirek and Lidia were happy to leave. They could tell that their plan had worked, they had gotten through. Even Elena saw the wisdom in the plan, although she wouldn't show it. She had to save face, and they were giving her the opportunity. They left without a cross word, feigning obedience.

Once out, they headed to the rooftops to spend the last few hours of darkness observing the city. They watched as police and city workers and civilians made roadblocks and stopped looters and restored some sort of order to the downtown area. But they could see that chaos still reigned supreme not far from the barricades. They hoped the humans could contain it. If the humans died, so did they.

\*\*\*

Not far behind the two undead lovers, on a rooftop adorned with stone gargoyles, a hulking shadow perched. The shadow had been watching the two since shortly after the end of the world broke loose. He didn't know what had caused the attacks, but he liked it just fine. Couldn't be happier, in fact. After almost one thousand years of life, nothing humans did surprised him anymore.

He hoped, vaguely and instinctually, that it was a global phenomenon. He sensed it was. He could feel the death all around him. It would make his mission that much easier. The normal constraints put on his travel would be lifted. He would be just another monster roaming around the hellscape. But one thing at a time.

He eyed the two figures below him. Now that he knew where the rest of the vampires were, nothing could stop him. He would wait for them to come out and pick them off, one by one, taking his time with it.

The figure waited, hoping for the couple to split up. He wanted them alone. He licked his lips and then tongued something free from between his teeth. He spat it into one enormous hand. It was a piece of a badge. A policeman's badge. The two unlucky cops had come upon him while he was dealing with a vampire he'd caught alone. They had to be dealt with. There was no question about it. After all, what were a couple of human lives in comparison to the eradication of vampires from the world? It was a price he was willing to pay. Plus, human blood was still pretty tasty.

It wouldn't be long now before his centuries-long goal would be achieved. He thrummed with purpose and excitement, watching the two vamps until just before dawn.

## Chapter Eight

# Models, Meet the Apocalypse

"Eww. Oh my god, is this real? No way this is real. It looks super fake."

Robbie rolled his eyes at the fast-talk that Serena engaged in when she was nervous. She was looking over his shoulder at his phone, watching the video a friend had sent him. He would not have rolled his eyes had she been able to see it. Robbie was secretly afraid of Serena. She was a narcissist, for sure. *Thank god I'm not a narcissist,* Robbie thought just before becoming distracted by how good his hand looked holding the phone. *I should talk to my agent about hand modeling... but it would be such a waste of this body.*

"What is it?" Kirri asked from the kitchen, standing at the marble-topped breakfast bar. Robbie glanced at her, not surprised that she still wasn't done with breakfast. She had been eating a single strawberry for the last five minutes, quietly humming to herself.

"Nothing," Robbie answered from the couch. "Just some fake video my friend sent me last night." It did look *kind of* real, he thought. And hadn't he had some strange dreams last night? Like something bad was happening?

"Did either of you guys stay up late last night?" He asked the two women, with whom he had been living for the last year. Serena straightened up as Robbie swiped the video aside and pressed his phone to put it to sleep. For the second time, he failed to finish the whole video. The quality was poor. He had received it late last night. Half asleep, he downloaded it, watched half of it, and fell back asleep, sure it was a prank.

In it, someone was standing on the balcony of a high-rise, filming with their phone. There were mushroom clouds sprouting up in the distance. The camera zoomed in on them, the resolution getting poorer the further the camera zoomed. The sound of wind overcame the exclamations of the person filming, turning them into inaudible blurbs.

"I went to bed right after you," Serena said, walking from the living room to join Kirri in the kitchen.

"I was up for a little while," Kirri said in her perky, no-worries way.

"Well? Did anything strange happen?" Robbie asked, somewhat impatient.

"Uhmmmm." Kirri swept her eyes to the ceiling. She was thinking. Or trying to, anyway. Finally, after much too long, she answered.

"Well, the power went out for a minute. That was about it."

Something was wrong. Everything seemed quiet. Then again, their loft sat at the very top of a high-rise just past the edge of downtown. When you're 70 floors up, everything seems quiet.

Robbie got up from the couch, walked to the floor-to-ceiling windows, and looked down at the city below. There were little figures moving around in the street. Two cars were moving, but it looked like gridlock almost everywhere. He could see two accidents at separate intersections, which were no-doubt causing the backups. Rare, he supposed, but not unheard of.

He glanced at the cityscape, which looked unchanged. Clouds streamed by in the morning sun, pushed by the constant wind off of the lake. The blue waters were barely visible between buildings, bordering the other side of the city. Robbie shrugged and pulled his phone out of his pocket. He opened up IckyGram only to see a dinosaur telling him there was no internet. He didn't have service, either.

"What the hell?"

"Robbieeeeeee? What are you doing?" Kirri, the trio's self-appointed life coach, had spotted him. "I know that yesterday was our social media cheat day. I know because my neck hurts from staring at my phone, and I'm really worried about my posture today. So, please tell me you're not breaking our agreement? No social media today!"

Robbie looked up and into the accusatory stares of the two supermodels. He smiled weakly.

"I know, I know. It's just that something feels... weird."

"Yeah. Probably the fact that you haven't eaten your breakfast and we're all going to be late for today's shoot." Serena said this as she pushed a small plate with an orange, two strawberries, and a hard-boiled egg toward him on the kitchen island. It was double what the women ate for breakfast. Robbie looked at the time on his phone. She was right. Time to get ready for work.

***

Two hours later the trio was waiting at the private elevator in their entryway. The gleaming metal doors opened directly onto the loft and they stepped inside. They took it down to the underground garage where their cars were parked.

Today was Kirri's turn to drive, which aggravated the other two models for several reasons, the first being that the car was two years old. Terrible.

Kirri had come from a middle-class family and still had some bad habits from her days living with 'regular people'. One of these was the fact that she didn't feel the need to buy a new car every year. She even checked her own oil! This was unthinkable for Robbie and Serena, who, when they first saw Kirri pop the hood and begin rooting around in there, screamed. Although the engine wasn't running, they both thought that their friend was about to lose a finger or, at the very least, get dirty. It was a wonder that Kirri could manage to focus on such a task for more than a few seconds. In almost every other part of her daily life, she seemed to get by on sheer luck and sex appeal.

Both Robbie and Serena had been born into this life. The fact that they lived with Kirri was, to them, an incredible act of charity and forward-thinking. Although they liked the girl, to them she would never quite be on the same level, even though she was fast becoming a bigger star than either of them. That was another thing Kirri had taken with her from her old life: a work ethic. Although she would never admit it, she spent years reading books and studying marketing and the fashion world. She worked very hard to get where she was, and continued to do so, in her easy-going, flighty sort of way. In fact, Serena and Robbie both harbored the assumption that Kirri's flighty, dumb-blond persona was a put-on, although they had no evidence to back it up.

Robbie's mother had been a model in her own right, before age ravaged her (something that Robbie was sure would never happen to him). His father was an incredibly successful real-estate broker who, in fact, owned the very building the three of them lived in.

Serena's mother and father were both fashion models. They had made it first in eastern Europe and then broke out into the American scene, subsequently settling in New York and raising Serena and her brother Tristan, who was a college football star.

They had been living the good life, but it was all about to change.

Kirri hopped into the front seat of her "old" Audi and fired it up as Robbie and Serena conducted a silent battle for the front seat. Serena had an uncanny ability to turn her eyes into lasers that bored through Robbie in a matter of moments. But Robbie, to his credit, continued to attempt these little battles of status with his eyes, always losing unless Serena happened to be sick or exhausted. He lowered his eyes from Serena's in an instinctual sign of surrender and folded himself into the tiny back seat of the car.

They corkscrewed up one level and came out onto a one-way street. It was two blocks to the studio. Two city blocks that could have been traversed in five minutes on foot. But walking in the open air often made you sweaty, rogue wind had a tendency to mess up your hair, and 'regular people'— especially men— had a tendency to yell lewd remarks at women. At the very least, people would stare. Whether they recognized the models from magazines and billboards, or they just weren't accustomed to seeing such beauty was anyone's guess.

Never mind the fact that they would probably end up with entirely different hairdos and makeup, the two hours they spent getting ready for the short trip to the studio erased with makeup remover and water. But showing up to work without looking like a model— without looking as good as possible— just wasn't an option.

By the end of the first block, which took about thirty seconds, all three of them knew something was wrong. Empty cars were parked haphazardly at the side of the road. As if people pulled over for a passing ambulance and just left their cars there for some inexplicable reason. They saw no pedestrians that first block. At the cross street, Robbie glanced down the valley of buildings and saw what looked to be a roadblock in the distance, some five or six blocks away. He opened his mouth to say something, but then it was out of sight as they cleared the intersection. The traffic lights were still working, but there was no traffic.

"Is there a parade today?" Serena asked, fighting the feeling that something was really, really wrong. No one answered.

They made it down the second block and stopped at a red light, left blinker on, waiting for the light to change so they could turn. It changed and Kirri let off the brakes, but before she could put her foot on the gas a truck zoomed past them, from left to right, going the wrong way down the one-way.

It was a late-model pickup truck with dark paint. It had two men in the bed, standing with their backs against the cab. They both had assault rifles and as they passed through the intersection they began to fire at six or seven deranged looking people hanging onto the back of the truck, some of them dragging along the ground, some of them clambering over into the back of the truck, reaching for the two men. The truck swerved to miss a parked car in the road, spilling two of the hangers-on from the truck bed, and continued toward the heart of the city, the muted sound of gunfire receding as they sped away.

Each of the three models had the exact same look on their face as they watched this surreal happening: eyes wide, mouths open, astonishment splashed across their perfect features. Kirri, not knowing what else to do, made the left very slowly, heading for their original destination. She was processing what she had just seen, operating on autopilot: car driving mode. But as they turned the corner and came face-to-face with what the pickup was driving away from, she slammed the brakes.

The street was filled with a seething crowd of people, crammed shoulder to shoulder from building to building. In fact, there were so many that as the three models watched, a couple of people in the front got their feet tangled up and fell flat on their faces. The crowd behind them kept shuffling inexorably forward, trampling those unlucky enough to have fallen. Inevitably, more and more tripped over the fallen ones and fell themselves, which in turn caused others to fall on top of them. There was no room to step around them, so others would simply walk over their fallen comrades.

The growing weight on those who'd fallen caused skulls to pop from the bottom up. Legs, arms, and ribs snapped and crunched. Viscera ripped and popped out of rotting skin. Eyes bulged out of skulls. But the crowd kept coming.

The result was much like watching a slowly broiling sea. Some waves were big, some small. Some rose and fell quickly, while others built up like mountains, only to reach their tipping point, people walking stupidly on a pile of bodies so big that they simply fell off the edge to crush the stumbling figures below, the disturbance momentary before the pile fell over and was assimilated. Those that were still able to move got up and kept walking, or limping, along.

It seemed like the supermodels had been mesmerized by this ghastly scene, watching the wave move slowly toward them as they sat in Kirri's car. Serena snapped out of it first.

"Kirri! Move! Go back go back." This startled the driver into action and she threw the car into reverse and slammed on the gas. The tires screeched as the three were thrown forward against their seatbelts.

Kirri's pulse was pounding. She was sweating through her makeup. A foul stench was coming off of the human sea ahead of them. She wished desperately that she wasn't driving. Everything felt out of control, and the fact that she had two people depending on her to save them added to her spiraling fear.

What had they just seen? It wasn't possible. She couldn't get the image of a woman's skull being crushed out of her head. It played over and over again in her mind's eye. What was wrong with those people? Could this be a bad dream? Just then Robbie screamed at her to stop. She looked into the rearview mirror and saw a parked car coming at them fast—the same one the pickup had swerved to miss. She turned the wheel and applied the brakes, but too late. Instead of hitting the car with the rear bumper, they hit on the driver's side passenger door.

Windows shattered, metal tore, and fragile bodies were snapped around inside the car. And then it was over and it was hard for Kirri to believe that it had even happened. Nothing seemed real.

They checked themselves, telling each other they were alright, the airbags having done their job. But the human wave was closing in on them. Kirri tried starting the car, but nothing happened. Serena got her door open and was helping Robbie out of the back.

"Get out, Kirri! Let's go! Leave your old car, it's totaled." Even in a situation like this, Serena still had to give little jabs.

Kirri crawled over the center console and out of the front passenger side. She could smell the rotting mass of humanity bearing down on them, now only about ten yards away. Once the crowd cleared the bottle-neck of the buildings and got into the intersection, they began to spread out. It left only one way for the trio to head: toward the city center. They ran, unsteady, helping Kirri along, who had a shallow gash in her left leg. Robbie and Serena found themselves with only superficial injuries from the crash.

***

"What's happening? What's going on?" Kirri's words were barely audible as she sobbed and cried, ruining her makeup further. Neither Robbie nor Serena attempted to answer her questions. They had no answers.

Kirri's crying wasn't helping anything. In fact, it was getting on Serena's nerves. She had never seen Kirri cry before and was surprised that such a pretty girl could make such an ugly face. It made Serena want to leave her in the street, although she didn't fully understand why.

Ever since she was little, Serena had been surrounded with only the most beautiful things and people. Her parents had started this trend, wanting to give their little princess the best life possible, and Serena continued it into adulthood, albeit unconsciously. Seeing things that she perceived as ugly, like Kirri crying, or a dirty homeless man, made her want to escape from them as fast as possible.

Fortunately, this very trait helped to keep her wits about her as she quickly escaped from the ugliest thing she had ever seen: the human wave of what were most definitely zombies. She couldn't think of anything uglier. She wondered why it had to be zombies. Why couldn't it be something sexier? Like the vampires from those Sunset movies? Little did she know that ten blocks away, Diirek, the most charming and sexiest of vampires in the surrounding area (by popular vampire opinion) slept soundly underground. Not only were the zombies uglier versions of regular people, but they seemed to be clumsy and they didn't even say "brains" like in the movies. Not that she'd heard, anyway.

"This is some sort of parade, right?" Robbie asked, his voice high and tight. "I know it's not Halloween, but that could be a Halloween parade right? Right?"

"They're zombies," Serena said simply. Robbie laughed shrilly and shook his head.

"No, no, no. They're probably just zombie fans. Like those people who identify as animals. It's some sort of crazy flash mob that went too far. That's all. Yeah. That's it."

Serena didn't say anything this time and Kirri was too busy crying to worry about Robbie's tenuous grip on reality.

The models came up to a corner and decided, by some unspoken consensus, to turn.

They didn't know it at the time, of course, but if they had gone on straight toward the part of downtown that was surrounded on three sides by water, they would never have died. At least not for some time. While by that time of the day (Z-Day Plus 1, people called it later, the first day of the changed world) there had been a few roadblocks set up to keep monsters and people out, the three models wouldn't have had any trouble finding a way to safety. Those people lucky enough to have been inside the perimeter after the bombings found themselves, for the most part, unharmed and unharried.

But the models didn't go that way. Nor did they discuss turning left before they did it. All three of them could sense the mass of rotting corpses behind, moving inexorably toward them, and they didn't want to keep going straight. They wanted to get out of sight, at the very least. So, after trudging for one city block away from the totaled car, they turned left on Washington street. And walked straight into men with guns, muscles, and drugs.

The two groups almost collided at the corner of Washington and 4th. The three models met three men that looked like they were straight out of central casting for a prison movie. Serena thought she saw disappointment in one of the men's eyes, and lust in another's as they looked the women over.

Two of the men were carrying assault rifles and sporting vests with spare clips in them. The third was toting a duffle bag filled with who-knows-what, and smoking a blunt. The skunky smell was pungent and the brown paper looked moist.

"Can I have some?" Serena asked, and, without waiting for an answer, reached out and grabbed the blunt out of the guy's mouth. Not only did she actually want to calm her nerves, but she knew men and how to deal with them. She knew that anything could happen to her and her friends and that the risk these men posed to them was small compared to whatever was coming down the street they had just left.

She took a puff as Robbie and Kirri stared at her in disbelief. Taking a moment to savor the familiar smell and taste of the weed, she looked over at the three men, who seemed somewhat dumbstruck, as well.

"Boys," she said in as calm a voice as she could muster. "We need to go somewhere else. This way is no good." She handed the blunt back to the shorter of the three, from whom she had taken it, as she pushed her way between him and the man next to him.

After a moment, Robbie, who had a dazed Kirri hanging from him, headed after Serena. None of the men said a word until the models were out of earshot. At which point they huddled together and whispered— one of the men doing most of the talking. After their little huddle, one with an assault rifle walked to the corner and looked down 4th. He immediately turned around and hurried back to the other two, shaking his head.

Presently, the heavily-armed men followed the models.

The two groups formed one, turned into a parking garage a couple of blocks down Washington, and introduced themselves. The leader of the crew (at least that was the vibe Serena got) was tall, dark, handsome, and said his name was T. The one that had been smoking the blunt said his name was Ryan. He wore a smirk and had the kind of nervous energy that small, wiry guys often have. The tallest of the three, and biggest, said his name was Sly. In fact, that was all he said. Just "Sly." That was it. He kept looking around, his rifle at the ready, his muscles bulging through colorful tattoos poking out from under his t-shirt.

T and Sly headed to the top of the parking garage to get some perspective while Ryan stayed behind with the models. He set his large bag down and unzipped it, pulled out a pump-action shotgun, and set it next to him. He rooted around some more and found a first-aid kit and went to work on Kirri's leg.

"So," he smiled as his practiced hand cleaned her wound. "You guys saw the zombies, too? Pretty fuckin' crazy, huh?"

"There's no such thing as zombies," Robbie snapped. Ryan looked as if he didn't even hear him.

"What do you think, babe?" He was addressing Serena who figured she had endeared herself to him with the whole blunt thing. She had no doubt that her looks played a part, as well.

"I don't know. I feel like I just want to wake up from this nightmare." Serena had been holding vigil, but now sat down with a sigh, finally able to let her guard down. They were on the second floor of the garage, sitting in an empty space, cars on either side. Surely they would be able to hear something coming. The shotgun on the ground made her feel much better.

"There's no waking up from this one, babe. The only way out is death, and even that I'm not sure about. I've seen some wild shit in the last twelve hours." He spoke as if everything was funny, and it was beginning to get on Serena's nerves.

"She going to be okay?" Robbie asked Ryan.

"The fuck do I know? I look like a doctor?" He swung his blue eyes to Robbie, no longer a smile on his lips. Then he laughed out loud.

"Just kidding, man. Y'all need to lighten up. It ain't the end of the world." He laughed even harder at this one. "But seriously? She'll be fine. At least physically. She don't seem to be all there right now." He shook Kirri's uninjured leg. "You hear me, babe? You'll be fine. Snap out of it. Ryan's here to help you."

Kirri, who had stopped crying and started staring into space, brought her vision down to Ryan's face. She looked down at her bandaged leg and then back up at Ryan. The next thing anyone knew, Kirri was hugging Ryan around the neck, dragging him toward her. Ryan looked like he thoroughly enjoyed this, his head pressed against her breasts, her smell wafting into his nostrils, her heart beating into his ear. When Kirri finally let go, Ryan couldn't help himself: "All it took for a girl like you to notice me was the end of the world. I'll take it." Serena and Robbie both laughed at this. Ryan smiled big, showing his teeth.

***

T and Sly couldn't see much from the top of the parking garage. They saw the zombie wave heading toward downtown, with small groups breaking off here and there. They had been trying to get back to their own neighborhood. But now it seemed almost impossible. They had spent too long gathering supplies. Now they were cut off. They would have to wait until the wave passed and try again.

"So, what are we going to do with those girls, T?" Sly asked.

"What do you mean? And there's one guy with them. They look like models. I swear I've seen the blond one before."

"I mean," T continued, "are we going to kill them?"

T looked at him. "No, Sly. Why would we do that?"

"It just seems like we've killed a lot of people lately. That's all."

"Yeah," T sighed. "I guess we have."

***

The six of them came together and formulated a plan. For the models, the plan was to stay safe under the watchful eyes, loaded weapons, and bulging muscles of the three men they now found themselves with. For the men, aside from Ryan, the plan was to get back to the familiarity and implied safety of their neighborhood. Ryan wanted nothing but to hang around these two women, with whom he felt he had a shot— with at least one of them, anyway. To his credit, Ryan recognized the ridiculousness of thinking about getting laid at a time like this, but he could do nothing to overcome it. T and Sly had decided on the roof that they would help the models as best they could, but it wasn't their top priority.

The plan wasn't so much a collective effort as it was T telling them all what they were going to do, and the rest of them agreeing readily. The models had tried making calls to their friends and family, but to no avail. The network was down. Ryan told them as much. He said that the last time a call went through was in the early hours of the morning, but they tried anyway. None of their phones could find a WIFI signal, either. They were cut off.

Kirri seemed to have snapped out of her daze. Where her eyes had been glazed and blank, they were now lively and curious. She didn't say much but could be heard humming softly from time to time. It was a good sign.

Although they didn't voice the notion, all six of them felt better for having found each other. There was strength in numbers. Twelve eyes were better than six. So they started on their quest to reach a part of the city known as Freebrook, which was only about a mile away, but in the direction from which the mass of the undead had been coming. They had a few hours of sunlight left, and plenty of ammo in Ryan's duffel bag. Leaving the relative safety of the parking garage was an exercise in paranoia, but once in the sunlight and the familiar sights of the city, things started looking up.

And then things went to shit.

In an attempt to skirt the zombie horde, they decided to walk north, parallel to the horde with a buffer zone of a few blocks, traveling in the opposite direction. Eventually, they thought they would come to the tail end of the zombies, at which point they could cut west and then south to Freebrook. Then they could hole up in T's place until they figured out what the hell was going on.

T and Sly led the way as they turned north on 7th after putting a few blocks between themselves and the zombies. Posh clothing shops lined the road, most of the windows unbroken. Sunlight glinted off the few abandoned cars along the stretch. They saw no movement, no figures, and very little damage ahead. The buildings housed offices and shops exclusively, and hell had broken loose after the close of business the night before. As a result, the group let their guard down. Here, away from the zombies and all those reminders that the world was ending, it was easy to pretend everything was hunky-dory.

T made a sound like the air had been punched out of him, and half a second later they heard the gunshot echoing off the man-made valleys of stone, glass, and metal. Their de facto leader went down on the sidewalk, clutching his chest, sucking in a ragged breath, blood pouring from between his fingers.

Sly immediately stepped forward and began to open fire, spraying bullets wildly, unsure where the shot came from. The shooter clearly waited for him to run out of bullets, which he did quickly, and then fired on Sly, too. The back of the large man's head exploded, showering the rest of the group in blood, skull fragments, and brains.

It was Ryan's turn to pull a trigger, but he made no attempt to find the shooter. Instead, he fired a booming shotgun blast at the floor-to-ceiling window of the women's clothing store they found themselves next to on the deserted sidewalk. Cracks shot out from the large hole in the window. Ryan jumped through the fractured glass, knowing he would be the next target. This caused the whole window to tumble down, glass showering him and cutting him enough to bleed, but not enough to concern him, given the circumstances.

Robbie, in an unusual act of kindness, shepherded Kirri and Serena over the low threshold and into the store. The sniper's third shot caught him in the neck just above the collarbone. He collapsed on the sidewalk, his eyes wide in terror, staring at his two roommates as he died. Down to three, the survivors huddled against a wall full of neatly organized and expensive clothes, at which Serena and Kirri barely gave a glance.

***

"What the hell are you doing?" Travis Victor's voice was high with horror as he dropped his binoculars and grabbed at Joseph's rifle. "Those are civilians!"

Joseph, whose first name Victor had never learned, let him take the rifle out of his hands as he feigned surprise.

"How can you tell?" he asked Victor.

"How about the fact that they were carrying weapons? Or the fact that they ran into the store like that? You ever seen deadheads do that before?"

"The hell should I know? I've only seen a handful of those fuckers. I'm not taking any chances. Fact is we don't know what the hell is going on."

The two men stood facing each other at the edge of a ten-story building. They both wore police riot-gear and were sweating under the warm afternoon sun. They had been on the roof for twelve hours without food or sleep or any sort of action whatsoever. At least until the group had come into view, down on the sidewalk.

"Orders were clear. Observe and report," Victor said, still shocked at what he had seen. The image of the second guy's head exploding stuck in his mind.

"Why? So they can get to the safe zone and do god-knows-what? They looked like bad news to me."

Victor thought that Joseph was the worst kind of cop: the kind who joins to kill. He had never laid eyes on the guy before all hell broke loose the night before, but he had known a handful of guys like Joseph in his few years on the force. He had assumed, back before he knew better, that there would be some sort of psych eval that would weed these guys out, but his first six months on the force had told him he was wrong.

Everything was all messed up, with headquarters scrambling to set up a perimeter. So Victor had ended up on this damn roof with this killer in a cop's uniform. Victor thought it more important than ever to hold the public's trust, and guys like Joseph would make that a problem. He saw no other option but to report the incident.

He walked away from Joseph, shaking his head. He set the rifle down on the roof's edge and pulled out his radio, his back to the man that had just killed three civilians.

"This is Victor on lookout at—" He heard the rushing footsteps coming at him and had just enough time to turn. Before he could make a move Joseph was upon him. A single shove sent Victor toppling over the edge of the building. The ten stories flashed by him as slow as the longest minute of his life. A life that came to an end as he hit the sidewalk. He made not a sound on the way down.

***

Joseph didn't know whether the annoying little bitch Victor was going to tattle-tale on him or not, but he wasn't about to take the chance. Not when his fun was just getting started. Plus, he had always wanted to shove someone off a tall building. Check that off the old bucket list. Without so much as a second of preparation, Joseph brought his radio up.

"Officer down, officer down! Oh god, he just jumped. He jumped off and I couldn't stop him!"

Just as he expected, they had no one to spare to come investigate the death or to provide him with backup. Joseph smiled at the thought of more fun to come. The end of the world was proving to be just his kind of party. Who knew?

***

Kirri couldn't stand the sight of Robbie's body on the bright sidewalk outside the window. She knew there would be a rear entrance for deliveries that doubled as an emergency exit.

Ryan was inching forward on his belly toward the broken window, trying to clear glass out of his way as he went. He was going to try to locate the shooter. Serena was talking to herself in a low voice, staring at Robbie's body. Kirri couldn't make out the words.

She headed to the back of the store and found the back door. She pressed the bar and the door opened— about three inches. Something was keeping it from opening all the way. She put the side of her head against the door and gazed out into the alley. There were cars filling up every available inch, one of which had been parked against the door.

What she couldn't know was that there had been a terrible car accident on the street adjoining the alley when news spread of the attacks. As a result, people, expecting the worst, had abandoned their cars. While most did this to try and get home, a few decided to join in some looting and partying like it was the end of the world.

When the police came in force several hours later to restore order, they brought two tow trucks. They moved the cars into the alley as a way of getting them off the street and clearing a path for maneuvers. Unfortunately, they would have been better off piling them up as a barrier on the street. Many of those cops— and the two tow truck drivers— were overtaken by the horde not long after clearing the street. At the time, they didn't believe in zombies. Their thinking turned around as they were dismembered and devoured.

Hindsight's a bitch.

Kirri headed back to the other two. She found Serena in the exact same spot, sitting on the floor against a shelf of clothes, muttering under her breath, staring at Robbie's prone body.

Ryan had made his way to the corner of the window. He had removed his baseball cap and was looking down the deserted street from his position on the floor. He didn't see the shooter. What he did see was Sly and T, about five feet away from him on the sidewalk, lying in front of the next store over. A few feet to his left was Robbie's body.

"Ryan, the back door is blocked. We're stuck in here. Do you see him?"

Ryan backed away from the window into cover and looked back at Kirri. His face no longer held a knowing smirk. He was dead serious.

"I can't see him. I can take a guess where he fired from, but I don't see anyone. He's either waiting for us to come out or heading here to finish the job." Knowing he had no other options, he inched forward again and looked out the window— to find T standing up on the sidewalk.

Ryan knew better than to say anything. He had seen this happen before. It had been a long night for him and his now-dead friends. He slid back into cover and got to his knees. He had left his shotgun by Serena. It was no good over long distances and would have made his crawling even harder. He moved quietly toward the shotgun. Then everything seemed to happen at once.

"Robbie!" Serena cried out in surprise and relief. Ryan spun around to see Robbie's corpse staring at them from the sidewalk.

"Shit," he said as he lunged for his shotgun. Kirri was staring, unbelieving, while Serena was getting to her feet and Ryan was hefting his shotgun off the floor.

Kirri saw Ryan level the menacing weapon at Robbie, who had started walking stiffly toward them, crunching on the broken glass. Something seemed wrong, but Kirri couldn't put what she had seen earlier together with what she was seeing now. To her, Robbie was miraculously alive, and needed help. And Ryan was about to shoot him.

"No!" Kirri screamed and lunged at Ryan, knocking his shotgun away just as he pulled the trigger. Serena, who had been making her way to Robbie, oblivious of the other two, caught the errant gunshot in her side. The large slug severed her right arm above the elbow and continued through her ribcage, tearing her lungs apart and narrowly missing her heart. She died a few seconds later.

Kirri screamed again, seeing the carnage that the shot did to Serena. She was vaguely aware of Robbie coming toward her and Ryan staring blankly at Serena on the floor.

Robbie's teeth sank deep into the flesh of her neck, the sensation was a pain like nothing she had ever experienced before. Reflexively she recoiled, effectively helping sever the muscle and tendon that kept the mouthful of flesh attached to her. She came away with a large chunk missing in an almost perfect bite-shape, like she was something as simple and fragile as an apple. She backed up and bumped into a dress rack. Robbie stumbled toward her, hungry for more.

Ryan chambered a new cartridge and fired at Robbie, hitting him in the shoulder, the force knocking the dead model down in front of Kirri, who used the opportunity to retreat back into the store, her hand to her gaping wound. She started to feel dizzy from the loss of blood, which had been leaving her in spurts with the pumping of her heart.

Ryan sensed a figure behind him and suddenly noticed the sound of crunching glass. He spun around to see his dead friend T towering over him. Ryan pulled the trigger. Nothing happened. He hadn't reloaded. T grabbed him by the shoulders and leaned toward the smaller man to bite him. Ryan raised the shotgun between the two as a shield. T took a bite from Ryan's right hand, an index and middle finger coming off in his mouth. Ryan screamed and dropped the gun. The next bite came down on Ryan's nose. After the third bite— this one taking out one of his eyes— Ryan passed out. He wasn't conscious to feel Robbie join T in feasting on his flesh.

Kirri collapsed behind the checkout counter, leaving a trail of blood behind her. She bled out within minutes. Ryan lived a little longer, but not much. His heart stopped beating exactly sixty seconds after Kirri's.

When the three models were together again, they didn't look quite the same as they had. Their eyes had changed, and they had gaping wounds and drying blood all over. In death, however, there was one similarity as in life: they were hungry. But this time, they wouldn't put a cap on their appetites. After all, for zombies there is no such thing as self-control.

# CHAPTER NINE

# CONVENIENT REMEMBRANCES

Weller was unconscious. But, by definition, he didn't know that. In his mind he was reliving the worst day of his life in vivid, accurate detail. Meanwhile, around him in the real world, his fate was being decided by a room full of mostly white, mostly old cops.

He would have laughed had he been awake to see the mayor picking up his son's head, which Weller had dropped after getting hit in the face. But his joy would have only been momentary. Because, if he had been awake to see it, he would have yelled for the mayor to stop before the politician put the animated zombie head to his chest in a gesture of loss and sorrow, cradling his adult son's head to his considerable left man-boob.

Unfortunately, Weller wasn't awake to stop the mayor. He wasn't awake to witness the teeth sinking through the mayor's shirt and into the flabby skin around his pink, hairy nipple. He didn't hear the screaming that followed as the head latched on to the three-term mayor's left areola. He didn't see the somewhat comical sight of the mayor's aid yanking at the head not once, not twice, but three times before the mayor's nipple came off in his ersatz son's mouth.

No, Weller didn't see any of this. Instead, he saw a deep betrayal that he had lived through only a week earlier. It was a special sort of hell that he was experiencing, but another one waited for him whenever he managed to gain consciousness again.

*\*\*\**

Dirty cops are nothing new in any big city. They were nothing new in Weller's city, either. While Weller was known for being a little overzealous at times, he was nowhere close to being a dirty cop. But, thanks to his gruff demeanor and fuck-you attitude, he was often mistaken for one. He had been investigated more times than he cared to admit, but little more than wrist slaps ever came out of all the unpleasant ass-crawling he'd endured as a cop.

Weller hated corrupt cops as much as the next guy. They made his job harder to do by eroding the public's trust in the police. They killed unarmed and innocent civilians, robbed people, and dealt drugs. Plus, Weller felt that dirty cops as a group were generally assholes. And that was coming from a cop... so yeah... pretty bad.

Despite Weller's hate for his corrupt brethren, he never felt comfortable dropping a dime on one of them— unless he felt it was absolutely necessary. Being a rat was almost as bad as being a dirty cop. That being said, he didn't hesitate to take matters into his own hands when he saw some cop doing some bullshit that crossed the line. It's one thing to break an arm or a hand to teach a guy to not fuck around, it's another to go crying to the captain. The latter wasn't acceptable, the former was. Yeah... cops are weird.

So, Weller was hesitant when Captain Shellbourne summoned him to her office where she waited with his old partner and Internal Affairs Detective Ray O'Shea. The two explained to a wary Weller that a gaggle of new cops belonging to a neighboring precinct was suspected of being dirty. But they were careful. Too careful to get caught by IA. They wanted Weller to get "transferred" over and ingratiate himself with the group of dirty cops, to find out if they were, in fact, dirty.

The fact was that stories about Weller made their way around the city. Almost every cop had heard a story about him at one time or another, even if they couldn't pick him out of a lineup. Cops, like anyone else, had workplace gossip that facilitated the spread of rumors and stories alike, whenever anything of note happened. As a result, all different kinds of cops read into those stories about Weller what they wanted to.

The by-the-book cops secretly wished they had the balls to go over the line like Weller did when he dispensed his own brand of justice. To them, he was a hero to be looked up to, if not emulated.

To the stick-up-the-ass cops, obsessed with following protocol no matter what, he was a hated figure for breaking the rules they so cherished. When they looked in the mirror, holding a ruler up to their mustaches and sideburns to make sure they were within regulation, it was cops like Weller that they used for fuel in their self-righteous fires. Those same fires, by the way, made them the intolerable assholes they were.

And for the corrupt cops who were sure they would get away with all the heinous shit they did on the job, the stories about Weller served as proof that they would never be caught, as long as they were smart. They knew, in their small black hearts, that Weller was a dirty cop. The fact that he'd never been busted was a testament to how smart he was. At least that's what they would tell themselves as they planned their next robbery or extortion or murder. After all, everyone needs a role model.

But Weller wasn't dirty. Not like many people assumed. He didn't deal drugs, sit on people's necks until they suffocated, participate in extortion rings, fraternize with criminals, or shoot people in the back. In fact, in all his years, Weller had only shot three people. And those three were absolutely, 100%, without a doubt trying to murder him or someone who needed protection. They did have one thing right, though. He *was* smart, but mostly he was one lucky bastard.

So Weller had to admit that he saw the logic in the plan O'Shea and Shellbourne had. The plan to bust a bunch of dirty cops not a year out of the academy. But he didn't feel good about it. In fact, he refused it twice, as he had refused other such requests in the past. He didn't want to get involved. He had no desire to be an Internal Affairs detective. It was only after O'Shea leaned on him hard, calling in an old and almost-forgotten favor from their time as partners, that Weller finally caved.

"Fine," he said. "But after this, you guys leave me the hell alone."

They agreed and a month later Weller found himself approaching a small, unkempt house in a part of town that belonged to his new precinct. He recognized the car numbers and knew that he was walking into a house full of the suspected cops.

His transfer to Vice in the new precinct was accompanied by rumors of sexual harassment, to make it seem believable. There had to be a logical reason for his transfer to make the sting work. In his month "undercover" he had come across a few of the uniforms at various crime scenes but hadn't seen an opportunity to gain their trust. He figured today would be the day. From the looks of it, four of the six were inside the little house.

He parked his unmarked car and headed inside. From what dispatch said, shots had been fired when the police arrived and one perp was down. As he stepped onto the tilted front porch, he heard another black and white pull up at the curb, followed closely by a news van. Weller directed the two uniforms exiting the newly-arrived squad car to keep the press back. His detective-sense was on high-alert and he took note of everything as he walked inside.

The porch had two rusty metal folding chairs sitting on the side that wasn't slanting toward the ground. Above the chairs was a large picture window, the glass cracked but still intact, half-broken blinds made of flimsy plastic drawn shut inside. On the other side of the porch was a smaller window, probably belonging to the kitchen, Weller thought. The siding was covered in chipped blue paint. He figured the place had probably been built in the sixties.

A single-story A-frame, he thought it was one of the better-looking trap houses that he had ever seen. It had recently been vacated according to the eviction notice still taped to the front door, the date clearly visible on it. The outer screen door was barely hanging on by the bottom hinge, the wooden door behind it was open. Weller could see the shapes of men milling about, heard them talking in low voices, but couldn't make out the words.

He stepped inside and the whispering stopped as three of the suspected dirty cops looked up at him. They seemed on edge, which wasn't uncommon following a shooting. But there was also something else there, in the way they looked at him. Dust motes floated in the waning afternoon sunlight, the uniformed officers inside cast in shadow. Weller flipped a switch on the wall. Nothing. Power was out. The place smelled of fear-sweat, dirty cash, and gunpowder. All the makings of a textbook crime scene. Weller opened his nostrils wide and took it in, smiling a little.

"Detective," Jones said in greeting. He was the tallest of the group. Corn-fed looking. Blond hair and blue eyes. Probably played football in high school. Weller nodded at him, then trained his gaze on the other two in turn. Balzen had dark hair and eyes. Half white and half Hispanic, if Weller had to guess. Little had pockmarks from teenage acne on his face, which couldn't have been long ago. None of them were over 25.

"So? What we got here?" Weller said, looking at them. Something was wrong. "And where's Pratt? He call in sick today?"

"He's in the back, next to the perp," Little said, gesturing toward the living room. Weller noticed that every single one of the men had their holsters unbuttoned. As Weller turned away from them to head into the living room behind him, he reached under his tan suit jacket and unfastened the leather clip on his shoulder holster.

The living room had a ratty old couch and matching coffee table inside. The plyboard table was covered with piles of money, most of it wrapped up nicely in stacks of one or five thousand, depending on the denominations. It looked like close to $75,000, all told.

Weller looked left, through a gap in the half-broken blinds covering the picture window, and noticed that there was another news van parked outside, cameramen and anchors clamoring for the first statement and maybe a shot of the dead perp. *Slow news day*, Weller thought, absently. To his right was an open door leading to a bedroom. Pratt was there, looking back over his shoulder at Weller as he crouched in front of what looked to be a dead lowlife. Pratt had blue surgical gloves on and had been searching the perp. There was a gun on the floor next to the guy's limp hand.

Weller saw his opportunity. He thought that the uniformed officers were nervous because of his presence there. He wanted to put that to bed. He looked around and then stepped up to the coffee table. He picked up a couple of stacks of bills and put them in his jacket, making sure that the others saw him do it.

"Did you already count this?" he asked Pratt, who was getting up from the floor, looking at Weller like he was crazy.

"What are you doing?" Pratt said, too loud. "Put the gun down, detective!" He was practically yelling suddenly, pulling out his gun and leveling it at Weller's chest. Weller's Sig Sauer remained in his shoulder holster.

"Detective! Don't do it!" This one came from Little, to Weller's right, who also had his gun out. The other two were following suit.

"Are you guys fucking crazy? There are reporters outside." Weller had no idea why it was happening, but he was pretty sure he was about to die.

"They can't see shit in here." Pratt was talking low. "Now, very slowly, pull out your gun."

"Fuck you."

"Jones, help him out."

Jones came from Weller's right, stepped behind him, and put the barrel of his 9mm to Weller's left temple. With his right hand, Jones grabbed the back of Weller's hand and guided it toward his shoulder holster. Weller let him. He grabbed the gun with Jones still guiding him, like some sort of twisted version of the famous pottery scene in Ghost. Only Weller was Demi Moore and Patrick Swayze was about to facilitate his murder. Jones guided his hand down so Weller held his gun pointing at the floor.

"You move that gun up you'll die. We don't want to kill you, just get you off the force for a while," Jones said, his breath sour with coffee and fear.

"This is such bullshit," Weller said, rolling his eyes. Jones stepped away from him but remained close enough that he wouldn't miss Weller if he squeezed the trigger.

The whole situation seemed unreal, and Weller knew Jones was lying. They were going to kill him. But they needed it to look beyond suspicion, which was why they had him pull out his gun. He had moments left, at most. His mind raced.

Weller shifted his grip on the gun, holding it by three fingers at the very bottom of the grip. Not a single finger near the trigger. No threat.

"Fine!" he said. "You want me to drop it? I'll drop it." While he was speaking he did an exaggerated shoulder shrug, like he was pissed but giving up. Then, in one quick motion, he flung his gun backward through the blinds, shattering the picture window, sending the weapon onto the dry grass of the front lawn. Pratt's eyes went wide and Weller could see the debate on the guy's face. It could have gone one way or the other for a moment, then he thought better of it and dropped his gun slightly.

Weller turned and put a fist through the wall. He started screaming and throwing money all around the place. The four uniforms stood back and looked at each other in confusion. Then they looked a question at Pratt. He shook his head in response.

"Fuck," Pratt yelled before tackling and cuffing Weller. Outside the cameras were recording, as Weller knew they would be. He was perp-walked to a squad car in handcuffs, yelling and screaming obscenities. He pleaded with the reporters to hand him his gun from the grass, talking crazy, and fighting the uniforms the whole way. It wasn't too hard to act upset about the whole situation. He was pissed. But he knew it wasn't over.

Pratt and his friends were told to kill him. He was sure of it. He didn't have any dirt on them and they didn't know him well enough to want him dead yet. So the question was, who ordered the hit? And why? What was he into that someone would want him out of the way bad enough to risk a murder like that?

Of course, he understood that it probably would have worked. As soon as he had put the money in his pockets— to try and gain their trust— they had seen their opening. Pratt went right to work yelling about him wielding his gun. Their story would have been easy: '*We saw him taking the money from the crime scene and let him know that that kind of stuff doesn't fly around us. We don't tolerate dirty cops. Then he pulled his gun out and started threatening us. He fired at us, so we had to put him down. You know... the guy has a reputation for being a little crazy. He just snapped I guess.*'

Pratt knew that Weller would need gunshot residue on his hands in order to sell it. Otherwise, there would have been too many questions. He would have had to fire first. They wouldn't have had time to get the scene right. Not with those reporters and other uniforms outside. Plus, you can't get away with killing a cop the way you can a civilian. Just doesn't work that way. But still, it seemed a little risky to have Weller pull his gun out like that. It was the only thing that saved him. He figured that if he had lifted it to point it at any of them, he would have been dead, whether he fired his gun or not.

All this he thought about in the back of a squad car, waiting for word from on high about what to do with him. He figured he would be okay—until he heard the call over the radio telling them to bring him in for processing. Weller was going to jail. Such bullshit.

*** 

Weller awoke alone in a jail cell. He immediately recognized it for what it was: his precinct. All at once, everything came back to him. The end of the world, the zombies that were the icing on the apocalyptic cake, the crazy superhuman figures he'd seen, and the unfortunate occurrence of having been seen with the mayor's dipshit son's head in his hands by a roomful of cops. Speaking of hands, Weller brought his up in front of his face and looked at the dried blood caked on them. He made to get up but his head felt like it was splitting in two, so he laid back down on the concrete slab that served as a bed. How could they really think that he had killed the mayor's son? Well, he kind of had, but only because the guy was shooting at him.

What was his name... Fucktard Jr? No.... Prince Asshat of Shitland? No.... Jon? That was it. Jon Westin. Mayor Westin's son.

Everyone knew that Jon was a wannabe criminal, and a poor excuse for one at that. Almost every cop in the damn city had collared him for something, only to find out later that it had never officially happened. Apparently the dumbass was free to buy drugs from a narc, or solicit an undercover lady cop, or get caught with an unlicensed firearm, or rob and kill a well-known drug dealer and then open fire on a police officer and then get himself killed and then become reanimated somehow and then get his head chopped off by the same cop who killed him and then... well, you know the rest.

At least Weller was alone in the cell this time. Last time wasn't pretty. But, to be fair, he should never have been put in with career criminals, anyway. The only thing he could think was that Shellbourne had been called after his arrest at the trap house and she was the one that had told the officers to do what they did. To almost get him killed. For the second time that day. He figured some palms had been greased at the jail to facilitate the 'mistake'.

Now, despite his anger about it, he started dozing off again, unable to keep his eyes awake in the dim jail cell. Before he fell back into dreamland, he uttered a proclamation to no one at all: "This is such bullsh..." And with that, he was asleep again.

***

The intake team seemed reluctant to process him, but they did it nonetheless. After trying to explain himself to the guard that had him take off his clothes and spread his cheeks, Weller gave up. There was no stopping it. He just let it happen, sure that they wouldn't be so dumb as to put him with general population. Putting a cop in with career criminals was asking for trouble. Surely, they wouldn't do it.

They did.

That's when he knew beyond a framed silhouette of a doubt that someone up high was setting him up. *Shellbourne.*

He was shoved into a cell with ten pairs of bunk beds and nineteen scumbags to occupy them, plus, now, one cop. The room was long, one central corridor running between the bunks, five to a side. From where he stood Weller could see straight down between the bunks to the guard's observation room opposite the door he'd just been pushed through. He saw no guards there.

All eyes looked at the fresh meat, standing there in his white prison garb with blue letters on the back, holding his bedding in both hands.

Weller looked around, trying to find the empty bed, when his eyes landed on someone he knew. Someone he had arrested not two days earlier. The guy looked like Charles Manson's older, crazier brother. Instead of just a swastika on his forehead, like little bro, he had an intricate tattoo of the Nazi eagle there, holding onto a swastika with its racist eagle feet. The man was bald and bulging with muscles from excessive steroid use, and his tiny blue eyes were set in a head that stood a foot taller than Weller's.

The guy had been busted while trying to kill a black shop owner that had told him to fuck off when he walked into the store. But first, in an inexplicable act of either masturbation, self-loathing— or both, the Nazi bastard grabbed milk gallons and started smashing them into his own crotch, giving the store owner a chance to call the police. Weller happened to be around the corner and took the call, arriving to find the Nazi bastard breaking down the bulletproof glass that surrounded the shopkeeper and his register. It had taken a taser, pepper spray, and a knock to the head to get the guy subdued. If he hadn't decided to pound milk into his crotch (drugs are bad, mmmkay?) before going after the shopkeeper, he probably would have gotten through the glass and popped the guy's head like a grape.

Recognition dawned cartoonishly slow in Nazi Bastard's eyes. A smile formed on the big man's face as the implications of Weller's presence there finally seated themselves stubbornly in his head.

Weller stood in the aisle, bedding still held in his hands, and watched as Nazi Bastard reached his hand into the back of his prison pants, dug around for a minute with a strange but satisfied look on his face, and came out with a toothbrush shank. Weller wasn't concerned so much with the stabbing part, but more with where exactly that shank had been, and the literal shit that was probably on it.

"I just got finished with your mother," Weller said, casually. Nazi Bastard stepped into the walkway between the bunk beds, five sets on either side. "She says hello. She asked about your racism. You know, to see if it was still going strong? She'll be here tomorrow for a conjugal with me, I can tell her all about it then." Weller was looking right at the guy, but it was like he wasn't being heard. Nazi Bastard looked around at the other inmates, who were all staring between the two men.

"Yes, I'm talking to you. Did you not hear me? I said I made sweet love to your mother. Me, a black cop, had sex with your mom." With the word cop, all heads turned toward Weller. *Oops*, he thought, but right then he had bigger things to worry about. Nazi Bastard finally understood, it seemed, as he took a moment to picture the aforementioned act in his imagination. A long moment later his face changed into a look of horrible hate and he charged down the aisle, straight at Weller.

Although outmatched in size and strength, Weller had a leg up on the guy. He had seen him in action before. He knew there was no finesse, just brute force. The guy would attempt to bowl over Weller, maybe swinging a roundhouse right or wrapping him in a bear hug and crushing his ribs— but that wasn't going to happen. Weller dropped all of his bedding but the scratchy, stiff wool blanket, which he let unfold to the floor, gripping one side of the rectangular piece of fabric. Then he flipped the other side of the blanket up and grabbed it, folding it in half lengthwise.

Nazi Bastard was at full speed and almost upon him when Weller sidestepped to a bunk on his right and launched off the bottom bed with one leg. He timed it perfectly. Nazi Bastard turned toward him slightly, trying to grab him, but his momentum was too great. Weller turned in midair and landed behind NB, who was just slowing down short of the metal door, his back to Weller. Taking two steps and jumping toward the giant Nazi, Weller flipped the blanket around the guy's face and planted his knees in his back at the same time, letting the full weight of his body drive through his knees.

Weller held onto the blanket with his hands, propping himself against the giant's back, as their momentum ran them into the metal door. Nazi Bastard hit face-first because his hands had gone instinctively up to his face when Weller had blinded him with the blanket. Weller, however, was ready for the impact and he absorbed it easily. As Nazi Bastard started to topple backward, Weller jumped down and gripped both ends of the blanket in one hand. He pulled hard on the blanket, and by proxy, Nazi Bastard's head, helping gravity and stepping out of the fall zone all at once. The sound of the guy's skull hitting the concrete floor was sickening, but Weller figured he'd be alright after he remembered who he was. Which, hopefully, was never.

Immediately Weller looked around at the eighteen other men in the room, waiting for one of them to make a move. He unhooked the blanket from around Nazi Bastard's face and held it at the ready. Two guys came at him from either side at the same time, but one arrived just before the other. Apparently, the little show with the giant Nazi wasn't as much of a deterrent as he had hoped, but Weller figured this next one would do the trick.

He stood in the middle of the aisle, watching each of the attackers come at him. It would have been easy for the one on his left to wait a moment or two, giving the other guy time to get out from between the beds and travel a few steps down the aisle, but he didn't. It was a mistake.

He came right up to Weller and jabbed at him once as a distraction, then let loose with what he thought would be a knockout punch. Weller held the blanket down around his waist, his hands at his sides like he was waiting in line. He feigned back at the jab and then ducked down under the punch. Pushing from his heels, Weller led with the blanket as he jumped under the guy's swing, wrapping the fabric under his outstretched arm and then around his neck. Weller ended up on the other side of the guy, with his back to him. He pulled the blanket tight and used his body to flip the convict over his shoulder, and straight into the second guy that was coming down the aisle.

The two of them ended up on the floor in a pile. Weller put a knee to the first guy's head as he tried to get up. He stood next to the second guy until he was almost on his feet, then sent him back down with a crushing elbow to the temple.

No one else came at him. He had made his point. Picking up his sheets from the floor next to Nazi Bastard, Weller chose a bunk next to the door, in the corner. He stripped the existing bedding off of it and threw it on the floor.

When the guards came rushing in, conveniently late to stop anything, Weller was laying on his new bunk, his hands behind his head and his feet crossed. They manhandled him up and out the door to his very own cell, like it should have been in the first place. He thanked them graciously with a shit-eating grin and settled in for a long wait. Which wasn't that long after all.

He was released two hours later, without being charged, and taken straight to Shellbourne, who tore into him after watching the clip of his freak-out on the news.

"You're getting off easy," she said. "I have 4 officers who all swear they saw you taking money from a crime scene. They said you pulled your weapon on them? Why they're not pressing charges is beyond me." She was working herself up into quite the fervor, pacing around the room while Weller sat still, watching her performance. She was good. It looked real. But, she could have been equally pissed that the four cops tasked with getting rid of him had failed miserably. It would have been easy to use that emotion to rail into him.

He thought about all the cases he was working. What could he have gotten into that would piss off career cops so bad? Nothing rang a bell at the moment. He was doing his normal hyper-effective-cop thing, collaring more criminals per month than a lot of detectives did in a year. If there was a connection to any of his recent or current cases, it had to be a pretty big one to get such a reaction.

His only guess was that someone's money was getting fucked with as a direct result of Weller's actions. He would have to go through his case files. Dig up some dirt. He loved being a detective, and his nipples got a little hard as he sat there, thinking about unearthing the case and getting payback on whoever had put the hit on him. Oh, yes, it would be sweet. All he had to do was get to his case files.

"You hear me, goddamnit Weller?!" Shellbourne screamed, bending over and getting in his face.

"Huh?" he said. He hadn't heard her.

Shellbourne's face went from red to purple. "You're suspended! Without pay! If I have anything to say about it you'll be contacted by the DA within the week. Now, get the fuck out!"

"Gladly," he said, and got up, threw his badge on her desk, and slammed the door behind him on his way out.

Instead of waiting for the elevator, he headed straight for the stairs in a mad dash to get to his desk and scoop up the case files before the captain came to her senses and had him thrown out of the building. She could stop him from getting paid and using company property, but not from working.

He got to his floor sure that he had a few minutes to gather up his stuff, but when he rounded the corner he saw two uniforms standing in front of his desk. One of the cops spotted him and nudged the other. They both started toward him. Weller had two options: go quietly or cause a scene and try to get some of his files so he could figure out what the fuck was happening. Really, it was no hard choice.

"Fuck you!" he said and took off running away from them in the maze of cubicles. He dodged past plainclothes detectives and uniformed officers while running away. When the guys chasing him started yelling for him to stop everyone around paused their work to watch as Weller led the two of them on a chase around the wide room. Twice he tried to dodge back to his desk, but they headed him off. They were quick learners, these two. They would make great sheepdogs— perfect for rounding up crackheads and drunks. Finally, Weller gave up and headed to the elevators, his hands up in the air to show surrender.

"Alright fellas, I'm done. I'll leave quietly." But they weren't done. He had pissed them off good and plenty. The look on their faces told him everything. He was about to get a beating. They ran right up on him.

When the elevator doors opened, Shellbourne was there. Apparently, she had decided to come down and make sure that Weller hadn't managed to take any work home with him or cause a further scene. The first thing she saw was Weller— directly in front of her— standing over two uniformed police officers, both of whom were on the floor groaning and bleeding. Weller was admonishing them for their poor behavior when he heard the elevator ding. He looked up and smiled.

"Oh, hey captain. I was just leaving," he said to her, stepping into the elevator. "Going down?"

Shellbourne stepped out of the elevator, her face a mask of murderous rage, her arms shaking slightly as she balled her fists. Weller smiled at her as the door closed between them. He whistled a happy little tune the whole way out. Nothing like delivering a good beating to lighten the mood.

It wasn't until the next day that the reality of the whole thing hit him and he spiraled into a pit of despair. A junkie without a fix, Weller was nothing without his work. He was just getting started with his self-destruction when the apocalypse happened.

You could say that, in a strange kind of way, the end of the world saved Detective Kurt Atticus Weller's life.

# CHAPTER TEN

# WITH GREAT POWER COMES A BUNCH OF ZOMBIES

W eller awoke to a visitor outside his cell. It was the Chief of Police, William Roan. Weller never had much interaction with Roan. When the former was still pounding the pavement, the latter was already way up the ladder. Far enough up that their paths never really crossed. Like almost anyone with any sort of authority, Weller was inclined to skepticism about him, but overall he seemed like a decent chief and had been a good cop.

Weller had no idea how long it had been or what time of day it was. There were no windows in his cell and they had taken away his mostly-useless phone. He felt a little bit better, although he probably shouldn't have slept, what with the head injury and all. Oh well. Life's full of little mistakes.

Roan sat on a folding chair outside of the cell. He was a large man, al-though not as large as the mayor. He looked like he could be of Mediter-ranean descent, with an olive complexion and hazel eyes. He had on his face a look of patience and exasperation, as if he were just waiting to die, but very, very worried about how it would happen. As was required by official decree, he wore a bushy mustache and was almost bald. Weller didn't think there had ever been a chief of police that wasn't losing his hair and sporting a 'stache. Otherwise, he had on a rumpled suit and a tie loosened and hanging at an angle above a sweat-stained white shirt. He wore a striking ring on his right hand. A black ornate band held a large, deep-blue gem.

Weller's awesome detective prowess told him that the chief hadn't changed clothes since the world started blowing up, so he figured it couldn't have been more than a day since Weller presented the severed head to the most influential people in the city. In reality, it had been a little over 24 hours. The chief had been busy.

Roan waited while Weller sat up, rubbed his eyes, and got his bearings. When he was relatively sure that Weller was awake enough, he spoke in his slow, deep voice, pronouncing every word expertly. The result of hundreds of press conferences over the years, Weller figured.

"What do you know about this... this—" he struggled with the word— "zombie business?" Weller gathered his thoughts for a moment. He had to make this good. "It's not just people who get bit, like in the movies. I think it's everyone. If we die, we get back up and walk around. It's gotta have something to do with the missiles or bombs or whatever they were. Something airborne maybe.

"That's the biggest thing to worry about. We can barricade down-town, but we can't keep people from dying inside the barricade, can we? Old people, sick people, injured people, suicides. Then, if they kill people just by biting them? I mean, if we don't do this right, we're all dead. I just hope we're not the last of the human race..."

"They do kill people just by biting them," Roan said, casting his gaze toward the concrete floor.

"Who?"

"The mayor. Right after you got knocked out, the idiot grabs his son's head and brings it to his chest and starts sobbing. Of course, the goddamn head bites him. He died about an hour later. Poor dumb bastard."

"So... Did he get anyone after he turned?"

"No. By then we had some idea of what was happening. He's locked up down the hall, groaning away. There's some political power grab going on now. The mayor's people say he's not dead, just sick. While many of the aldermen are arguing the same, many are saying that Brendan Reed should take over because he's President Pro Tempore. But really, in the event of an emergency, it's the Emergency Operations Board who makes decisions. Of which I am the chairman. So—"

"Hold on, hold on," Weller interrupted, holding his head. "You're giving me a headache. This sounds like way too much information. I don't know jack about aldermen or emergency operations. What exactly did you want from me?"

"You really are a piece of work, Weller... Damn, I miss being like you... It was nice while it lasted." Roan looked wistfully into space, as if remembering times when he could freely be an asshole.

"Yeah, well, I'm the one in the cell. Don't miss it too much."

"Grass is always greener, eh? Anyway, you're right. It's not your job to worry about who runs the city. It's your job to figure out what exactly to do about these..."

"'Deadeyes?'" Weller suggested. He didn't like saying zombies, either.

Roan looked at him. "Hey, that's pretty good. 'Deadeyes,'" he said, trying it on for size. "Yeah. I like that better than the other word. It's kind of problematic, grammatically, but what the hell? See? You're already making progress." Roan smiled under his black mustache.

"So, we're going to let you out and give you command of a few officers to see what you can learn about these deadeyes. How to kill them, how smart they are— everything you can. Meanwhile, we've got some wonks working on the scientific side. You need to focus on keeping the remaining citizens safe. You'll be reporting directly to me on this one.

"We've got to find a way to tell all the citizens about this that doesn't cause mass panic. For now, the barricades are holding, but we've got to get on this fast. We've got police stationed every other block inside the barricades. A message is playing on repeat on all TV channels, telling people to stay calm and to find the nearest officer if anyone dies. Cell phones still aren't working. Probably won't for a long while."

"You're going to let me out?" Weller couldn't believe it. He had many questions, but that one seemed the most important. "What about the whole thing with the mayor's son?"

Roan shrugged. "Everyone knows that he was a shithead. Plus, I saw the look on your face when you realized who it was. You had no idea. It was just a dead scumbag to you, right?" Weller nodded. "Okay, good. So you'll write up a report and that will be that, for now. Really, the only person who wanted your head was the mayor. And he's one of *them* now."

Weller thought about this for a long moment. His natural distrust of authority was making him skeptical, but everything seemed to check out. Of course, he would have to find the sycophant that knocked him out and return the favor, but that wouldn't be too hard. He smiled a little and prepared his next questions. "Okay. So, we still have tv, and power? What about internet?"

"No internet. But, yes, the city engineers think that we should have power and tv for the foreseeable future, if nothing else changes. Our main power plant was miraculously unharmed and the tv infrastructure is intact. It all seems a little too perfect. Like this is some kind of experiment on us or something. Almost none of the surrounding farmland was destroyed either. As far as we can tell, all the little towns surrounding us were destroyed. Somehow, we were missed. We can survive, provided we don't all turn into deadeyes."

"And we still don't know who hit us? Or what's happening around the country?"

"No," Roan said, shaking his head. "We haven't had contact with anyone outside the city since it happened. But we have people trying to establish contact by radio. We'll keep trying."

"Shit."

"Yeah." Roan paused then, playing absently with his black and blue ring. "I want to be clear on something, Weller. If I let you out of here, I expect you to devote your full attention to the matter of protecting this city from this new threat. Understand?"

Weller looked Roan in the eye. "Yes," he said, after a moment.

"So, whatever you were working before— and that business with you taking money from a crime scene— is over now. It's a changed world out there. I need you to look forward. Your old cases will be handed to other detectives, and they will do with them as they see fit, whenever we get this under control. Do we have an agreement?"

"Yes, sir," Weller said, thinking this whole conversation strange. But, then again, what wasn't strange these days?

"Okay," Roan said. "Good. Glad we see eye to eye on this."

"Alright, well, let me out of here so I can kick some deadeyes ass."

Roan looked at him. "Don't make me regret this decision, Weller."

# CHAPTER ELEVEN

# BUCK'S IMPROBABLE DEATH

B uck recounted the story of his death to his friend Charlie at the bar. Big Dick Bill hovered just in earshot of the small red-haired man to hear the crazy story, failing to make himself look busy as the tale went on. If Charlie hadn't been drunk, the reaction he had to his friend sitting there telling him how he died would have been different, but not by much. In the day since the apocalypse began, Charlie had seen some crazy shit, and it just kept coming.

While he was a functioning alcoholic in the world as it had been, after the bombs dropped and everything went to shit, he drank to medicate. To deal with the shit that came up that seemed improbable, or downright against the laws of the universe. The story of Buck's death seemed like the latter to Charlie. It went something like this:

\*\*\*

Instead of staying in the "safe zone" as it became known, Buck decided to go looking for food, weapons, money, or anything that could possibly be of value. It had only been 30 hours since chaos erupted across the city, so it was probably the most dangerous thing you could do, but Buck had always survived by walking a razor's edge of stupidity, inebriation, luck, and confidence. Why should the end of the world be any different? Besides, the way he saw it, there was no longer any such thing as a safe zone. He doubted if there had ever been one in the first place.

He saw some weird shit as he wandered around in the bombed-out suburbs, evacuated buildings, abandoned housing projects, and empty shopping centers that lay outside the safe zone, but nothing that he would label as impossible. Dressed in a flannel shirt and holey jeans, he looked like a grunge wraith in the dark, silent enormity of the abandoned area.

After that first night, it seemed, nearly everyone was either dead, hiding, or in the safe zone. In the first hours of his late-night jaunt, Buck saw a couple of groups of people wandering around with weapons, no doubt looking to do bad stuff to people. He was small and quick and good at hiding— which is what he did whenever he saw or heard anyone. From his hiding spots, he determined that those people who decided to live out of the safe zone were trying to fulfill some fantasy that dated back to the first time they saw *Road Warrior, The Book of Eli*, or *The Road*. He even saw a few people pretending to be zombies.

It would have been funny if it wasn't so sad.

Word around the safe zone was that people were acting very strangely in the outskirts. Those who had made it inside the barricades spoke about people with cloudy eyes eating other people. Buck didn't believe in such things. He had shrugged it off as PTSD or hysteria.

Before he died, Buck decided to investigate a fairly intact drugstore about three miles into the outskirts. He had spent an hour outside the building, getting slowly closer, stopping to listen for any movement inside. He was a few feet from the front door when he heard a strange sound. A sound he had never heard before. It was a guttural moaning mixed with a scraping sound. Like a large group of people all groaning and dragging their feet at once.

He scrambled back to one of the many abandoned cars in the drug-store parking lot and got in the open trunk. The moon was bright, and Buck's vision had always been good, so he saw the group coming from a ways off. He kept the trunk cracked a couple of inches, and looked out in growing amazement. At first, he thought that it was another dumbass outskirts gang, but a series of events changed his mind. Literally.

It was a large group— he lost count at sixty-three, and by that time they were almost to the car he was hiding in. He had a decision to make: stay in the car and hope they didn't find him, or run for it. Then something happened that provided Buck with new, startling information.

Up until that point, he'd only seen stragglers that he believed were pretending to be zombies. He thought these people were asking to get killed, as they didn't carry any visible weapons. They didn't even do anything but walk around looking dumb.

One member of the blank-faced, slow-moving crowd was suddenly slung into the air by a snare. The wretched-looking woman ended up swinging from a cable by her leg under a commuter train platform about fifty yards from where Buck was hiding.

Triumphant screams sounded from nearby. There had been a trap set, just not in the drugstore. Three leather-clad idiots jumped out of a minivan next to the train platform, all three of them sporting automatic weapons. All heads turned toward the trio.

Nothing happened for a second.

The three gang members stared at the crowd of somewhere around 100, obviously expecting a reaction other than blank stares. They were expecting fear. As one, the crowd slowly turned and began their lazy shuffle toward the trio.

"Okay you fuckers, freeze right now or you're all dead!" yelled the top idiot.

They didn't freeze. There was no reaction. The crowd kept slowly closing in on them.

"Uh, they're still coming, Fred." This from the only woman in the trio as she backed toward the open minivan.

"Yeah, I can see that, *Linda*. Check this out!" Fred leveled his weapon at the slowly swinging woman hanging from the snare. He fired a short burst and missed. Another. Missed. Finally, on his third burst, he hit the lady in the head, which exploded like an overripe melon.

"Whoooo—" Fred's war cry was cut short when he saw that none of the crowd had registered the shot. No heads even turned toward the slowly swinging headless corpse. They just kept closing in, moaning softly. The three idiots opened fire then, spraying the growing crowd with bullets. The sound of hot lead striking soft flesh filled the air.

Buck kept expecting screams but heard none. Not until the crowd of dead-eyed post-humans started in on Fred and Linda, who both screamed in pain and terror. The third, as yet unnamed idiot managed to get back into the van and shut the door. Buck watched as those in the crowd who weren't busy with Fred and Linda surrounded the van. As two screams died out, Buck heard glass breaking, more gunshots, and then a third and final voice began its death throes.

He couldn't stay in the trunk any longer. He had to see what the crowd was doing to the people. He had a pretty good idea, but he had to see for himself. His pulse raced and his breath turned shallow in anticipation. Was he really, truly, witnessing the first real zombie apocalypse in the history of the world? He couldn't believe his luck. It felt like Christmas morning as he lifted the trunk lid, praying that the springs wouldn't make any noise.

His pessimistic mind worried that this crowd was just another gang of fucked up humans playing out their favorite movies. That they made themselves up to look like the walking dead and went around eating people for fun. *That wouldn't be cool,* he thought. But then he remembered that none of them had made a noise as they were shot with automatic rifles. If it was a group of people playing a part, they deserved a Zombie Oscar.

Now out of the trunk, Buck moved toward the crowd and the sounds of painful screams, careful not to make a noise. Most of the crowd's backs were to him, and those who were in a position to see him were busy with Fred and Linda, the poor bastards. Buck found a good vantage point behind another abandoned car and watched as several zombies (yes, he thought of them as zombies now) tried to yank Third Idiot out of the minivan. Only there was one problem: teamwork isn't a zombie strong suit.

They had yanked him by the legs out of two separate broken windows, each leg being pulled out of one. The zombies couldn't understand why he wasn't coming out all the way, and so just kept yanking on his legs. The guy screamed as his crotch was slammed again and again against the door jamb between the front and back seats. Buck snorted laughter and slapped a hand over his mouth. More Zs joined in the leg-pulling, and what happened next stopped Buck's laughter cold. There was a sick, wet ripping sound as Third Idiot's right leg came off, sending the four Zs that had been yanking on it sprawling to the ground with their prize. The screaming stopped then as the guy lost consciousness. For the better, Buck thought. This allowed the others yanking at the guy to pull the rest of him fully out of the van and go to work on him on the blacktop.

"Holy shit," Buck said softly as he sat down against one of the back wheels of the sedan he was hiding behind. He couldn't believe it: zombies were real. And they were roaming the outskirts! He couldn't wait to get back and tell Charlie. It was like a fucking movie!

Buck looked up then, seeing movement in his peripheral vision, and saw a dark figure with a ghostly white face standing not three feet in front of him, staring at him. It was a woman, and something in her face made him feel warm inside. But that warmth turned quickly to the steely cold of fear as she moved toward him. Buck made to get away but before he knew it the woman had him by the throat with one hand, holding him off the ground.

A gurgling sound escaped Buck's throat as he looked into the eyes of his aggressor. It took him a moment to realize it— and if he hadn't been so close to her he never would have— but there was a small blood-red circle around her iris. Her skin reminded him of the type of glossy coffee cups they have at hotels and restaurants. Before he really began suffocating, Buck had a moment to think that the woman looked *hungry* in a horny sort of way. He gurgled a question at her, which she ignored.

Buck's brain slipped into survival mode and he began to squirm and kick and try to scream. It only served to make the cold, vise-like grip around his throat tighten. The pale woman brought Buck closer to her, unhinging her jaw as she did so, revealing four sharp teeth that seemed to be *growing*. He decided that the horny/hungry assumption was correct just before he stopped squirming. He was about to be eaten. Lame.

He supposed it was better than having your leg torn off and eaten by a bunch of zombies. Barely.

As the teeth sunk into Buck's neck a strange peace came over him. It wasn't so bad, really. It didn't even hurt. It just made him tired. So very tired. His eyes began to close for the big sleep when he remembered his knife. It was in his back pocket. Buck fought the sleep off and used his left hand to dig the knife out of his back pocket. He pressed a button and the blade flipped out, clicking into place. Buck lashed out blindly at the monster— that's what she was to him now, a monster. At first, there was no response. Like she didn't even feel it. He kept at it, slashing and cutting. Finally, Buck decided on a stab. He sunk the knife into the soft flesh between the monster's shoulder and neck. It got her attention.

Buck hit the ground with a thud, his knife still sticking out of the looming figure. He felt weak but much less sleepy now. The monster made a growling sound and pulled the knife out. Then she lunged at Buck, who opened his mouth to yell.

It just so happened that blood spouting out of the monster's wound ended up in Buck's mouth. For some reason, it tasted good. Very good. But his mind was quickly distracted by two things: something taking a bite out of his leg, and the cold, strong hands of the monster around his neck. Again. But the hands didn't stay there for long.

The monster looked around in panic at the zombies that had gathered around the two. She let go of Buck, who had his shoe in a zombie's mouth, fending him off. Before Buck could register what had happened, the monster was gone. Like she had disappeared.

Buck got to his feet just as the crowd was closing in on him. Luckily they were still near an abandoned car. He jumped onto the hood and then the roof, followed closely by grabbing hands and snapping mouths. He inspected the bite on his ankle, surmising that it meant his imminent doom. But he didn't feel like he was dying. In fact, he felt pretty damn good. But things were getting weird. His vision blurred as he stood on the car. Pretty soon, his equilibrium was trashed and the top of the car rushed up to meet him.

Buck awoke to a hunger like nothing he'd ever experienced before. A hunger he imagined that starving people in third-world countries experienced. If there was any such thing as countries anymore. He thought about the state of the rest of the world. Communication was impossible. Phones had stopped working except to tell time, and the internet was down, which was a bummer. Not that Buck was ever really one for Snipchit, Failbook, or Ickygram. But he loved watching "movies" on NutFlix, his favorite porn site. They were all things of the past, he figured.

He realized that his mind was as meandering as ever. He was still him, so that was good news, he supposed. But underneath and around his usual thoughts there was something... else. He couldn't place it yet.

He began to gather his bearings. He knew he was very hungry, but he was surprised to find himself also very upside-down.

He was swinging slowly about half-way up the cable snare that Fred, Linda, and the other idiot had gotten killed for. What was 'up' to him was the headless zombie corpse still hanging from her leg and, beyond that, the ground. 'Down' was the bottom of the train platform and the starry night sky. He looked around, expecting to see the small horde clamoring below him, but there was no one in sight. No scary, bitey monster. No stupid, bitey zombies. No dumbass wannabe apocalypse-movie gangsters.

He wasn't sure how much time had passed during his blackout, but it couldn't have been long. He looked down— up. It was peculiar. He didn't *feel* like he was upside down. There was no extra pressure in his head from blood being forced there. No weird feeling in his stomach. Plus, he wasn't trying particularly hard to stay upside down. His legs were wrapped around the cable, and his hands held fast, but he wasn't straining. It didn't really feel like he was using any of his muscles at all. *Sweet*, he thought. *I'm immune to gravity.*

"Fuck you, Newton!" he said as he unwrapped his legs and let go of the cable— and fell. The ground met him with as much force and enthusiasm as it had on any other day of his life. The only difference was that the crushing impact didn't hurt. Okay, it hurt, but not as much as he would've thought. "Okay, sorry. I take it back," he said as he gathered himself up on the street, checking himself over. His face was scratched up and a bone seemed to be sticking out of his flannel shirt at the collar— a collarbone perhaps— but they didn't really hurt. Much. "Hmmm," he said.

Somehow the bite mark on his neck was gone, but not the one on his ankle. For having been attacked by two different monsters, he felt suspiciously good. He brought two fingers up and pressed them underneath his jaw, like people did in the movies. Nothing. He pressed harder, sure that he would be able to feel the steady rhythm of his pulse. Still nothing. He pressed even harder and heard more than felt his skin give way and his fingers slide into the tendons and muscles of his neck. *That's not good*, he thought, unable to stop himself from digging around behind his jaw, feeling his insides.

He remembered someone once said to him that peace was simply the lack of pain. What if that was why he felt so good? Because he was no longer able to feel pain? Pleasure he wasn't sure of yet. If he were somehow dead but conscious, wouldn't it be possible for him to mistake a lack of feeling for a 'good' feeling? He supposed it would. Buck began to philosophize about this but was interrupted by intense hunger pangs, triggered by a smell on the wind.

All other thoughts left his mind as something took over. He dashed through the streets as swiftly and silently as a grunge-ginger-jungle-cat stalking its prey. It didn't take him long to locate the source of the smell: a pair with shaved heads and baseball bats and jackboots. Buck did not give a second thought as to why they smelled like dinner. He gave no thought to the fact that not three hours ago their smell would have probably made him gag. He didn't even have an internal debate about whether or not he should eat the two men. Nope, one thing was for sure: he was going to kill and eat the shit out of these idiots.

Justifying his startling actions later, as he made his way back to the safe zone, Buck would attribute this to the fact that they were probably from one of the particularly bad outskirts gangs. Anything they had coming to them, he told himself, was surely deserved. The truth was, though, that he didn't have the capacity to do any logical thinking in the moments before he attacked. If it had been his own mother (may she rest in peace) walking around in the outskirts instead of the two gang members, he would have eaten the shit out of her without giving it a second thought. He was just so hungry, and they smelled so damn good. They never had a chance.

Buck was on them with all the ferocity and speed of a combination Jaguar/Shark/Piranha. The first thing he did was to keep the two men together. Literally. He picked the smaller of the two up with newfound strength and, before the poor bastard had time to react, jammed his head through his buddy's midsection. The result was two grown men screaming like whiny little bitches. One of them screaming into the dark night, the other screaming into the first's chest cavity. Buck bit into the bigger guy's neck, taking a huge chunk out and sucking it dry like a juicy piece of steak. Then he moved on to the smaller of the two, yanking him out of his friend and digging in like he was trying to win a pie-eating contest. It was too easy.

By this time both men were either dead or unconscious, so Buck finished his meal in relative peace. When he walked away, the casual observer would be hard-pressed to tell the two men apart. What was left of them was mostly bone and gristle, tossed aside like the remains of a chicken wing meal. Only, you know, human-size.

The bones were located and picked clean twenty minutes later by a particularly cliquish group of three high-fashion zombies. These zombies, who had once, not long ago, been supermodels, had a startling and eventful journey to the world of the undead. But of course, you remember that.

Buck made his way into the city proper with a minimum of harassment. (He didn't kill anyone else, if that's what you're wondering.) He did reluctantly break a man's jaw who tried to ensnare him in a poorly-designed trap. A trap he would have normally avoided. But his thoughts were elsewhere in this instance. He was having a hard time with the fact that he had killed those two men at all. Let alone in the gruesome and delicious way that he had. It was as if he was in a fugue state when it had happened. Like some hideous instinct kicked in when he smelled their musk on the air. He found solace in the fact they had undoubtedly been up to no good. *They were bad, bad, bad men,* he told himself. *Bad, bad, flavorful men.*

And that was another thing: he still remembered how damn good they tasted. How it felt like a man dying of thirst drinking cool refreshing water when he swallowed their blood. So it couldn't be a complete fugue state. It had to be somewhat under his control, if, in his present "normal" state, he still had an appetite for human flesh. The whole thing worried him to no end. How could he have eaten two whole men? The physics didn't make sense. Sure, he was a little bloated and gassy, but that was it. He didn't feel heavier. Usually, a meal that big would give him heartburn. Not this time.

So, considering, it wasn't all bad.

But by the time his bar was in sight, he was feeling pretty down about the whole ordeal. Wishing it hadn't happened. Wondering how it would affect his friendship with Charlie and the other fellows who were still, presumably, living. He hoped that he wouldn't want to eat his friends or his favorite, big-dicked bartender. But most of all, he thought as he walked through the door to see Charlie sitting at his usual spot, he hoped that he still had the ability to get drunk. Otherwise, what was the point?

# CHAPTER TWELVE

# ZOMBIE POLICING 101

"For the last 48 hours, we've been rounding up deadeyes and experimenting on them." Weller stood, once again, in the conference room. This time he wasn't holding a severed head and, instead of the city's upper echelon, he was addressing all uniformed police officers. Grunts. Beat walkers. The first line of defense against an outbreak within the barricades. The room was packed. "As some of you may know, we found no evidence that there is anything resembling a human left inside these deadeyes. The scientific findings confirm this. They—"

"Excuse me, sir?" A young officer called out from the front row. "Are you saying 'dead-eyes' or 'dead-ites'? Because I've heard it both ways. Personally, I like 'deadites' better. I heard it in a movie with that guy with a big chin, I think."

Weller stared at him. "How about this. Let's just hold the questions until I'm finished up here, okay? Great. Now. You may run into people who aren't willing to accept the fact that their grandma or child or brother or sister or aunt is a deadeyes. They may believe that their loved one is still in there, behind the chomping teeth and creepy eyes. This may cause them to act in a hostile manner when you try to dispatch their former-loved-one with a blow to the head. If it is possible, remove them from the room before dispensing with their deadeyes. Do not. I repeat, DO NOT try to move the deadeyes. If you find yourself in a situation where you have to move one of these things, make sure you have someone else with you. Your first priority in these situations is to neutralize the threat. To help this sink in, we have some video for you to watch." He gestured at the screen behind him.

"Some of you may know the officers in these videos. You may know that they are now dead. We show you these only to underline the serious-ness of the situation. You let your guard down for one second, and you're dead." Weller looked over at a young female officer who had a remote in her hand. "Trina, play it." Trina nodded at him and hit a button on the remote, which she then handed to Weller. The giant TV on the wall lit up. On it came footage taken from a cell phone camera.

The cameraman was in the back seat of an SUV, which was racing down the street, bright sun streaming through the windows, throwing the contrast off as the phone was moved around. There were three other people in the vehicle, all of them in police uniforms. Outside of the SUV, abandoned vehicles could be seen littering the street. Behind them were broken shop windows and bodies here and there on the ground. As the SUV came to a sudden stop, the cameraman jumped out but stayed back as the other three headed toward a small group of zombies. Weller paused the video.

"Okay. Right away these officers made a mistake. Can anyone tell me what it was?"

A hand went up in the audience. "They approached too large a group of deadeyes, sir. The rule is two to one, for safety."

"Right. There were four officers and four deadeyes. They should have found a group of two or less. Let's keep watching." Weller pressed play.

On the screen, three of the officers were cautiously approaching the four zombies, who had started to make their way toward them, groaning and drooling. One of them looked like it had recently been on fire, its skin blistered and raw. Each of the officers went for one, trying to tackle them to the ground, leaving one for the cameraman, who apparently thought his job was to stay back and record.

Two of the officers managed to get zip ties around their target's hands and sacks around their heads, but the third was struggling. He had gotten the zip ties around one of the burned zombie's hands, but the scorched and rotting skin served to allow it to pull its hand out of the restraint, leaving behind skin and muscle. It used the free, skeletal hand to push off the ground and turn around. At which point the cameraman was yelling for them to look out because the fourth zombie was approaching. He didn't move to help his fellow officers.

The two other cops jumped off their respective zombies and headed toward their buddy, but it was too late. Two zombies attacking him was too much. He jumped up to defend himself from the one on its feet, which gave the one on the ground a chance to take a bite out of his calf. The scream was brutal and piercing through the speakers set around the meeting room. Finally, the camera operator was forced into action. But, for some reason, he kept filming, leaving only one hand with which to defend himself.

Weller stopped the video again. On the screen was a frozen shot of the burned-up zombie grabbing the unlucky officer by the leg, its teeth sunk in on its second bite— this one on the guy's thigh. The two other officers were frozen in time, trying to subdue the fourth zombie, but one of the officers had looked back at his buddy when he heard the scream. He left his hand on the deadeye's shoulder, which everyone in the room could tell was a mistake. Weller had frozen the footage while the zombie's teeth were a half-inch away from the officer's hand.

"Okay. What's wrong with this picture?"

"The guy recording should have helped. He didn't do anything, just watched." This came from an officer in the back.

"Right. And what's the proper protocol when someone is bitten by a deadeye— uh deadeyes? Deadeyed? Fuck it. What's the proper protocol when someone is bitten by a zombie?"

"Restrain, Resist, Realize," the whole room said in unison.

"What's that mean," Weller asked. "You, in the middle."

"Restrain the subject, resist the urge to go near them, realize that they're already dead."

"Right. This may seem harsh, as whoever is bitten will probably plead with you, insisting that they are okay. But these protocols can save your life. We've found that the turning happens fast. Somewhere between five minutes and over an hour, depending on the person's injuries and other factors we have yet to identify. There is no cure that we know of for a person who has been bitten. If you have the means to quickly remove the appendage that has been injured and try to keep them alive— while practicing the three R's, then do so. We've yet to see this work, but there's nothing to say that it won't yet.

"The scientists working on this seem to think that it's an infection. If you're around someone who is bitten and they ask you to end it for them, I would suggest you do so as a mercy. I know I would."

Weller, despite the subject matter, felt pretty good at center stage. He had donned what Trina had called his 'professor voice' after their first briefing together. It was something he did unconsciously, but he found that she was right. It was the same voice he had used on Z-Day when he tried and failed to inspire the small mob in front of Police Plaza.

He had always been comfortable in front of crowds, which was a dichotomy of his natural introvert tendencies and his unconscious need for validation. A captive audience was something that seemed to feed his ego and bait his arrogance.

He pressed play on the remote and the video continued. Sure enough, the zombie bit the officer's hand.

The cameraman started cursing as he ran up and yanked the zombie off of the other officer's leg by pulling it backward with one hand. Its jaw was firmly on the guy's leg and when the cameraman pulled it back, stubborn strings of muscle and tendon tore away. The officer screamed anew and then passed out.

The cameraman started to stomp on the zombie's head with his heel. At first, his boot just bounced off, but after a few tries the skull cracked and brains started splattering out with each footfall.

There was suddenly more screaming offscreen and the guy stopped stomping and looked up, but he didn't lift the camera up.

"Oh fuck," he said before dropping the phone on the ground. It landed next to the head-smashed zombie in such a way that the legs of at least twenty other zombies were visible. More screaming issued from offscreen before a fresh-faced young officer fell down in the camera's frame, his throat torn out. This had to be the camera operator.

The screaming stopped and all that came out of the speakers in the meeting room were the sounds of wet flesh being chomped, and a low, guttural groan.

Weller pressed stop on the remote and the flatscreen went black. He looked at the gathered officers. So many young faces stared back at him. If he didn't instill in them the danger they were in on any given patrol, many of them would die needlessly. Some of them would, anyway. There was no way around it. And he knew this was only the beginning.

There were still people out in the suburbs and those parts of the city that weren't within the safe zone. People who decided to stay out there and eke out their existence while committing unspeakable acts. It really was a hell-world out there in the outskirts, as people had started calling the area outside of downtown. It wouldn't take much to tip the scales and let the chaos flood past the barricades. Then they would all be fucked. Weller didn't like to think about it much, but he had started to assume that they were the only people left in America. Maybe even the world.

"What would you have done different? How would you have handled the situation, had you been there?" he asked the crowd of blue uniforms. "You," he said, pointing to a young officer in the middle.

"I would start shooting. Why didn't they use their guns? Doesn't a bullet to the head kill deadeyes?"

"Yes. Destroying the brain does kill them. And I'm not going to tell you that you can't use your gun on deadeyes. But they can still hear and see you. A gun going off can be heard from a long way off and will bring more deadeyes. Plus, these officers were under orders to bring one back. For research. Although I will say that things might've turned in their favor if they had started using their weapons as soon as one of them was bitten. At least three of them could have gotten away."

"Damn, that's cold," the same officer said. "You would've just left him there to die?"

"I guess you haven't been listening, have you— what's your name?"

"Rigald."

"Okay, Rigald. Where were you five minutes ago when we were talking about the three R's? Let's go over it. Once he was bitten, if they had used their weapons to kill the other deadeyes there, did they have a way to restrain him? Keep in mind that they would have had to move fast because the gunshots would have attracted more deadeyes."

"Well," said Rigald, "they could have put him in the car and buckled him in. Or put him in the back."

"A seatbelt is not restraint enough for one of these. Restrain means they are unable to move their arms and legs. At all. If they had had a divider in the back of the SUV, they could have put him in there, but they didn't. Even if they did, they would have gotten to safety only to have it unrestrained in the back seat. At which point their only course of action would be to kill it quickly whenever they got to safety. Trust me, you do not want to be wrestling an unrestrained zombie out of the back of a car. That's asking to get bitten.

"And the other two R's. Resist the urge to go near them. That one's out the window if they're traveling with one in the vehicle. Realize they're already dead. If they had realized it, they would have left him as soon as he got bit, so they could save themselves."

Weller looked at Rigald, who seemed to be getting it. "So the correct answer to my question is this: you wouldn't have allowed yourself and your team to be in that position in the first place. Because of the 2 to 1 rule. Which really should be a 3 to 1 rule, but we don't have enough manpower for that. There should always be at least one person whose only job is to look out for incoming deadeyes. Whenever you go out you need to designate a spotter. You all need to be crystal clear on what your job is and what your objective is and what your escape route is, at all times.

"Now, you've probably heard rumors and speculation about what caused this. The fact is that we don't know. Smarter people than me are working on it right now. Best guess so far is that it was some sort of airborne weapon that was included in the explosives that dropped in the surrounding areas. Maybe the whole country is infected. We don't know. Whatever the case, it's likely that we will all turn into deadeyes when we die." The crowd let out an exasperated murmur at this. Weller knew it was coming because he had heard it before, in earlier groups. He waited for it to die down.

"We've had enough reports to suggest that this is a probability. Police officers around the city— some of which may be in this room— have confirmed shooting suspects and having them come back to life. Once again, this change can take anywhere from a few minutes to upwards of an hour. We've also had reports of drug overdoses, suicides, homicides, fatal accidents, and old age causing deaths that turn people. So, pretty safe bet that we're all headed that way.

"Now, in deaths where certain parts of the brain is destroyed, they tell me there is less of a chance of transformation. Or, if there is transformation, and the part of the brain that controls movement is no longer intact, they can't move around to hurt anyone." Weller pulled an index card out of his back pocket. "The cerebellum and the primary motor cortex," he said, reading from the card, "are what they think need to be destroyed. But they're not sure. Which is why we have teams collecting deadeyes for the science guys and gals to study.

"Anyway, the point I'm trying to make here is that anyone who dies has a damn good chance of coming back to bite you. Literally. So, what does that mean for you as law enforcement officers?" Weller hoped he wouldn't have to spell it out for this group, too. He waited. No one answered. Confused looks all around. "Let me put it this way: what does that mean for you as law enforcement officers— in a city with historically high officer-involved shootings?" Still nothing. Rigald looked like he was about to say something, but his brow furrowed and he looked down at his feet. Weller sighed.

"It means that you need to be careful to not shoot anyone while on patrol. Not only is it a bad idea in the first place, with all that's going on, but shooting a perp can lead to the end of the city. Of civilization as we now know it. You may be shooting a dangerous criminal, but by doing that you're creating another deadeyes that we have to deal with. So, we need to stop shooting people. Got it?"

A chorus of boos and curses came from the crowd. Balled up papers rained down near Weller, who took several steps back. Something yellow came flying down from the back of the room. Weller caught it. It was a banana. "Thanks," he said. "No tomatoes? Anyone?"

When the commotion finally settled and Weller finished telling them they had to pick up every single piece of paper on the ground, one uniform, a guy in his early thirties, raised his hand and spoke. "So, what are we supposed to do instead? I mean, that's the job, isn't it?"

"Instead? That's the job?" Weller asked, rhetorically. "Christ in church, what the hell are they teaching you people in the academy? You're supposed to keep the peace. Arrest them if they break the law. You'll be armed with plenty of non-lethal options." he paused, looking around. "Your job is not to kill people. It's to protect them. That's what you signed up for. You don't like it, fuck off."

"What do we do if someone is trying to kill us?" This from the same uniform.

"That depends on if they're really trying to kill you or if you just feel threatened. Like they could kill you *if* this or *if* that."

"What if we kill them by shooting them in the head. You know? De-stroying the brain like you said." This from another officer who looked like he spent his patrols with his face in a box of donuts.

"You're completely missing the point. You're not to kill anyone. There are only an estimated 20,000 people left alive in this city. You need to know that, if an outbreak happens in the city, it could be a seriously shitty problem. Plus, I hate to break it to you ladies and gentlemen, but we may be alone on this one. We've received no word from anywhere else in the country. None. So if you shoot someone, you could be shooting one of the last American citizens left alive. Not to mention the fact that the balance of power in this city is incredibly tenuous right now. We've had more riots in the last 20 years than any other city in the country. The best way to piss off the population is to start killing their friends and family members in the streets.

"We can't hold off what's outside the city and put riots down inside the city at the same time. It just isn't fucking possible. To that end, we have a recorded message from Chief of Police William Roan." He looked at Trina who nodded confirmation that she had the video prepared. He pressed play and an image of William Roan sitting at his desk in his office appeared. His voice flowed out of the speakers and into the room.

"Hello. This is your Chief of Police William Roan. Due to recent events, we have decided to enact temporary emergency measures for police officers. Obviously what we're living through is unprecedented in world history, and we've got to come together to make it through and continue to live against all odds. This is why any officer who is involved in shooting a citizen of this city will be automatically let go. They will be able to apply for re-employment after an official inquiry is completed and the officer found justified in the shooting. If you are found guilty of an unjustified shooting, you will be prosecuted to the fullest extent of the law.

"As you all know, we are providing basic food and housing to all citizens, free of charge for the time being. You will never go hungry or be forced to sleep on the streets while you wait for word from an investigation. But you will lose your badge if you kill anyone. I prefer that this doesn't happen. I think there is a way that we as police officers can protect our citizens and ourselves without killing anyone. Now is the time we must find that way.

"We have National Guard units at all roadblocks and perimeters, so your job as peace officers is to keep the peace inside the city. Those few officers who will be traveling outside of the safe zone have a different set of rules. For the bulk of you, this should be some of the easiest policing you've done. People are happy to be alive and no one is going hungry in the safe zone.

"You will all be responding to calls where a death has occurred, and you will deal with the result of that death according to the rules outlined by Detective Weller and his team. Abide by the three R's, don't use your weapon unless absolutely necessary, always have a spotter, and stay safe out there. We will get through this together. Roan out."

"Alright, that's it," Weller said. "You have your literature. Or you'll be picking it up off the floor as you leave. Your commanding officers can answer any questions you may have. Or you can ask me in the next ten minutes. Dismissed."

A few officers handed in their badges and guns to their commanding officers after each of the meetings. Weller was happy to see those people go, although he wasn't all that excited about not using his gun. He figured he would need it when he found whoever tried to have him killed. But that was a bridge he'd torch when he crossed it.

# CHAPTER THIRTEEN

# THE RIPPER OF LIMBS AND CRUSHER OF SKULLS

R ichard Klept had seen the woman jogging the night before. And the night before that. He waited for her, sure she would show up right on time. The first time he'd seen her— two nights ago now— there was a strange sense of unreality that accompanied the sight. He was momentarily mesmerized by the pendulum-like swaying of her ponytail and the sound of her footfalls in the quiet night. He watched her from his dark apartment. There was nothing on TV anymore. Nothing but bureaucratic public announcements. And Richard had watched all the DVDs in his collection enough times that he was bored with them. *Once Upon a Time in Hollywood* was good the first five times, but after that it lost its charm. So, he had started watching the street.

When that hypnotic blankness broke, Richard decided that the woman had probably been running the same route nightly for months.

Maybe even years. He'd just never noticed. Not until now, in the midst of the apocalypse.

He didn't understand how she could just go about her normal life when the world was ending like it was. It made him envy her— and want her even more. There was no way he could approach and ask for a date. No way. Not someone like her, with smooth skin, a toned body, perky tits, and blond hair. Not even close to his league. He thought momentarily that perhaps the new state of the world would increase his chances of getting laid but quickly dismissed the notion. He knew nothing about talking to women before the apocalypse. He was certain that he now knew even less.

There was some sort of secret code that he had missed out on some-how. A code that would get him a girlfriend, or a wife, or even just one lousy fuck. He pictured himself going down to talk to the woman— to ask her for a date— and saw for a certainty that she would laugh in his face. She would continue her run, half staggering with laughter, her thighs pumping, breasts bouncing, ponytail swinging away from him. Forever away.

Unless he did something about it.

She would be no different. He could tell just looking at her. Women all treated him like dirt. His one and only time had been by force, years ago. He had regretted it at first. But as time passed, and he realized that he'd gotten away with it, he grew to crave it more. And when the world started blowing up, he knew his chances were dwindling fast. It wouldn't be long before they were all dead. So why not have his fun now?

Of course, there was now zero tolerance for any illegal activity, if the radio and TV messages were to be believed. There were police patrols often now. Once an hour. And he had seen their improvised precinct around the corner and a block away. There were always police there, but it was far enough away... And he had timed their patrols. He would have most of an hour to do what he pleased with her. Of course, he wouldn't be leaving her around to talk. Oh, no. He couldn't risk that. Not again. Not now.

There would be no way to connect him to any crime. Not without a body.

At present, Richard Klept knelt in the shadows at the bottom of the staircase and waited impatiently for her to come. He looked up across the street at his apartment balcony, the angle just right to see it. He was probably a little too close to home, but he had no record. They would not suspect him. Plus, the empty basement apartment he'd broken into would do fine. He would jump out from the stairs and drag her down to the apartment, where he could take his time. His strength and size would finally be a virtue. He had everything ready. The time was near.

***

Corbin watched the man crouching in the shadows from a rooftop down the street. He was breaking the rules by hunting alone, but something told him this man was up to no good. Why not take him out? It would be helping the humans. Corbin knew he wasn't supposed to kill anyone, but this one wouldn't be missed.

He had noticed the man last night and stopped to watch him. His behavior was far from normal. He sat last night where he was now, and when Corbin saw the woman coming, he thought the creep would go after her. But he didn't. He let her pass by and then crept out of the staircase and watched her until she turned the corner.

Now he was back again. Surely, tonight he would make his move. Corbin smiled. *I'll make mine, too,* he thought. There had never been a more perfect victim. Rid the world of a creep and save a silly human in the process. Wasn't one worth the other? He thought so. Plus, he was getting hungry.

He and Johannes had gone out hunting the night before. Corbin did his part as Johannes fed on an old woman who lived alone, stopping him from feeding for too long. They left the woman alive, simply weakened. She never even stirred from her sleep. But when the time came for Corbin to choose his victim, he simply couldn't do it. Not with another vampire around. The hunt was why he enjoyed being what he was. There was something sacred and intimate about the whole thing. Even romantic, in a strange way.

He hadn't put up much of a fight in the Underground, when Diirek and Lidia came down on Z-Day. He trusted their judgment, even if they weren't an official part of the group anymore. Plus, the Vampaucracy had backed them, eventually. At the time he didn't think it would be much of a problem— hunting with a partner, not feeding to completion. But in practice it was different. It felt... wrong.

The truth was that he no longer felt guilty about taking a human life. Mostly because he chose carefully whom to feed on. They were always either near death or terrible criminals. If he was careful, he could keep doing it the way he had become accustomed to. No human would be the wiser. Corbin knew how to make a feeding look like a run-of-the-mill, garden-variety murder. Moving the body so authorities would assume the blood loss happened somewhere else. He'd always give them a nice big wound to explain it. The little marks on the neck would be noted but largely ignored. Easy.

Now, Corbin prepared for the attack, moving into position above the creep, who waited in the dark of the short stairwell. Corbin sat four stories above the man, on the roof of the building, waiting for the right moment. He heard footsteps around the corner; the jogger was close.

\*\*\*

A shadow moved swiftly across the street a block away. Corbin didn't notice it, he was focused on the creep below. The shadow made no sound that Corbin could hear. It moved up and across the buildings between it and its prey. When it was ready, the shadow turned into what was once a man. Although he no longer thought like he once had, before he became what he was now, he did have a kind of instinctual knowledge that his name was Merek. It was just there, the word forming foggily in his mind on the rare occasions when he thought about himself.

This thinking wasn't exactly coherent. It was a predatory sort of calculation that weighed him against his prey. But nothing had been able to even come close to challenging Merek since the old days. So, for the last five centuries or so, these calculations weren't all that hard to do. One look at something or someone he wanted to kill was all it took. *Merek victorious* was almost always the answer.

His form slightly resembled that of a human in that it had two legs and two arms and a head. But that was about as far as it went. Merek's skin was diaphanous, revealing black muscle and dark blue veins underneath. His spine was curved at both the top and bottom. The deformations gave him an insect-like gait when he did choose to move in his solid form. Despite this apparent handicap, he moved swiftly, his hips and his head in line while his body followed the deep curve of his back, giving him a hunched countenance. But even hunched he dwarfed every human he'd ever seen.

He was in near-constant pain, but it had become a background noise for him. A noise that helped motivate him to kill his children. Not only because killing them made him feel better, both mentally and physically, but because it was something he *had* to do. At this stage in his long and tortured life, he didn't know why he had to, but he didn't question it.

Muscles bulged on his legs and arms. His back muscles extended almost to the top of the back of his head, making the hunched appearance even more pronounced. His spine was lined all down his back on either side with waves of black muscle and strange bone spikes that poked out of his skin.

He stood at the rear of the same roof on which Corbin sat, behind a line of air conditioning machines and ducts. Merek didn't have to see the vampire. He could hear him. Smell him.

He waited patiently, his entire being humming and taut with an energy otherwise unknown in the world. His lungs expanded and contracted, but more as a function of muscle memory and to facilitate smell than any real need for air. He didn't need to breathe. Not with his lungs. He heard faraway footsteps and sensed anticipation from both the vampire ahead and the human below. It was time.

***

Corbin dropped down, spinning around in the air to land softly in front of the creep, face to face. He paused for a second, savoring the fear coming suddenly off the guy, watching his eyes go wide and his jaw drop. A once-powerful predator faced with an unknown but clearly more powerful force; determination turned to pleading in the span of a moment. Corbin smiled and went to grab the creep but something strange happened then. And it happened fast.

A giant, pale-black and deformed arm reached past Corbin as he stood there at the bottom of the short staircase, getting ready to drink his dinner. Someone— or something— was behind him. How did he not hear them? Impossible.

A massive, clawed hand at the end of the arm grabbed the creep by the top of the head and squeezed. Blood, brains, and skull splattered the concrete and Corbin's chest. An eyeball bounced off of the vampire's chin. In almost the same movement, and before the creep even knew he was dead, the hand grabbed Corbin by his shoulder. With a vicious tug it ripped off his right arm and threw it to the ground. Before this pain even registered, Corbin felt what could only be the monster's fingers punching through the skin and muscle on his lower back like knives through cheesecloth. Fingers wrapped around the base of his spine, tearing through viscera as they went. Then the other hand, having ripped off his arm, was at his throat and he was being lifted, held parallel to the ground by two hands on his spine, one at each end.

Corbin looked down at where his arm used to be to see the grotesque face of an otherworldly creature. Its mouth was around his wound, and its eyes were half-closed and twitching in what Corbin thought to be ecstasy.

The vampire spent the last few seconds of his life— a life that turned out to be 178 years, 4 months, 2 days, 17 hours, and 41 seconds long— staring in shock at the face of a nightmare creature. It had thick black hair on its scalp; it had ghastly yellow-red eyes and a nose. Otherwise, it did not resemble a human. Its skin was shot-through with dark veins, underneath which he could see the black tendons and muscles that controlled the face. The muscles looked swollen somehow, and in the little areas where there was no muscle, he saw what could have only been the creature's skull. But it was a deep red, not white like it would be in a human, or even a vampire.

Before he died Corbin appreciated a final irony. That he, a vampire, was dying for his blood. He felt it drain out of the wound where his arm used to be, and some out of the holes in his back, although those were mostly stuffed up with monster fingers. Corbin knew that simply draining his blood wouldn't kill him, that the monster would have to do something else to finish it. But he wasn't hopeful. It seemed like the creature knew what it was doing.

His suspicions were confirmed when the creature clamped down hard with the hand around his neck and then gave a tug, ripping Corbin's skull off of his spine and dropping it to the ground. His head bounced off the concrete, rolled around a bit, and then came to rest.

Before everything went black Corbin heard a woman scream in terror and surprise up on the sidewalk. The jogger, no doubt. He sensed movement and an empty space where the creature had just been. Then he heard another scream from the woman, only this one died down quickly to a wet gurgling sound. A pretty blond head flew down from the sidewalk, landing not far from Corbin's head. But by then he was gone. The woman's head blinked a few times and gulped like a fish out of water. Then she was gone, too.

It would be almost an hour before her eyelids opened to reveal cloudy, dead eyes that searched in vain for fresh meat to eat.

Corbin's eyelids stayed shut.

***

Merek finished up quickly, consuming the woman's blood and what was left of the man's, although most of it had leaked out of his ruined head to soak the landing upon which his body lay.

The pain had started as soon as the vampire's blood had touched Merek's tongue. His body resisted it at first like it always did. But it was a necessary pain. When it was over he would revel in his accomplishment. The pain was part of the ritual for him now. It was all he deserved. Work before pleasure. Punishment for the sins he had spent a lifetime committing, and now spent lifetimes making right. He needed that pain. It brought him back from the depths of his broken mind, helped him see clearly for a little while.

He realized now that there would be no going back to the days when vampire blood was like a horrible, fantastic drug. That addiction had long since faded, the high gone. The pain was the high now. The blood only necessary to keep him alive. Otherwise, there was only the sense of justice that kept him going, and the staving-off of the insanity that gripped him when he went too long without. Not that he was ever truly sane. He hadn't been in a very long time. He knew the world had changed, but only in relation to him and his mission. Nothing else mattered.

He smiled down at the bodies littered about him. The chaos gripping the world would serve him well while he went about his work. If he was lucky, the human war— or whatever caused the destruction and the dead to rise again— might have done much of his work for him. Perhaps the small group of vampires left in this cesspool of a city were the last of them. The thought thrilled and terrified him.

He turned to shadow and made his way back toward the subway entrance, blending with the darkness of the city, moving quickly. It was no time to rest. There were still hours of darkness left. He would continue the hunt.

## Chapter Fourteen

# REGRETS

"What the fuck is this shit?" Weller said, ducking under the yellow police tape and looking at the body parts scattered around the park bench. "Again?" he asked a bewildered-looking uniform. The uniform shrugged and moved quickly away from the irate detective.

It was a beautiful day in the city. Lush green leaves fluttered in a slight breeze under a clear blue sky. Bees went about their business in a nearby flowerbed. The smell of nature filled the little park. Weller noticed none of this. He had been pissed for the last three days, and this morning was no different.

Birds chirped and danced in the tree above the crime scene, oblivious to the angry detective below who stomped around, grumbling. His head was craned down, his eyes looking sharply at the little details that he was sure would yield clues. He was so involved that he didn't notice the unmarked police car pull up in the parking lot behind him.

"Weller? Oh shit. Please, please. Get. The fuckouttahere." Weller didn't have to look to know who it was. He would recognize that herky-jerk speaking style anywhere. Like a bad Christopher Walken impression. Jeremy Dothan.

"Dothan. Hello, youfuckingasshole. You gonna solve this shit, or what? This is the third time in a week. What'cha got?"

"Oh, no, Weller. I'm not telling you shit. Now getthefuckouttahere. My crime scene." Dothan walked up to Weller, pulling a pair of latex gloves on. "You're not even back in homicide, are you? Poor bastard," he said, shaking his head in mock sorrow.

"You know, we're lucky that this sicko likes to remove their heads, otherwise we'd have some fucking problems here," Weller said, not moving, looking at a pale woman's head lying on the ground. "I just don't get why this particular head didn't come back."

Dothan shrugged. "Maybe the brain was hurt before. So it couldn't turn. That's how it works right?"

"Mmmm." Weller was ignoring him, deep in thought, staring at the head. "Let me know what you find out, eh, Dothan?"

"No can do, brother. Got orders not to share any homicide info with you. Sorry. Cap'ns really trying to fuckyouover. You must have really pissedheroff."

Weller grumbled and took one last look at the head before ducking back under the tape and getting into his unmarked. Someone was killing people by ripping them apart and draining their blood. He had an idea that it had something to with those strange events of Z-Day, which seemed so long ago. The too strong, too good-looking pale European guy that had assaulted him to take a business card, and the mysterious shadowy figure that threw a cop from one building to another. His confidence was holding on by a thread, and his mind insisted that both instances were stress-induced hallucinations. But Weller knew better. He had to keep his head, because as far as he knew he was the only one to know about these other... *beings.*

Dealing with humans he could do. Even the worst of the worst. Zombies? Okay, that was making things a little tougher, admittedly. But it seemed the zombies liked to travel in groups. Or, rather, one large group that people called the horde. So far, the police had been able to keep the horde away from the safe zone, save a few stragglers here and there. All they had to do was keep lookouts posted and when the horde got close, they simply made some big noise in the other direction. Fine. Easy enough. The hard part was getting all the officers back safely. As it stood the roving outskirts gangs were more of a threat than zombies.

But whoever or whatever was doing these murders— *in* the safe zone— was starting to worry him. It looked like the thing did it with its bare hands— if it *had* hands— although the medical examiner refused to believe this. Impossible, he said. If Weller hadn't seen what he'd seen that night, impossible would be his guess, too. *One thing at a time*, he told himself as he headed to police plaza. He had a long day ahead of him and he made a promise to himself that he would go see his ex-wife tonight. Before going into the outskirts.

He'd managed to keep his promise to Chief Roan for a week, but he couldn't let it go. Every time he passed by Shellbourne's office he re-lived that day he was almost killed— once by police and once by criminals. He couldn't let it go. And things were finally calming down enough to give him some time to look into it again. But he had to see JayLynn first. Just in case...

***

"I'm pissed at you, Kurt! I can't believe you're only *now* coming to see me! It's been almost 10 days!" Jaylynn screamed through the door. As soon as she saw his face through the peephole, it was like a switch went off in her. "You couldn't stop by even for a minute to let me know you were still alive?! This is how you treat someone you were *married* to?" Weller was surprised that he could hear what she was saying because she was speaking in an angry moan somehow. He'd never been able to figure out how she did it, but it was a sure-fire sign that she was mad as hell.

But two could play that game. Weller had been silent through this short diatribe, trying and failing to stay calm, his temper rising with every infuriating moan-word that blasted through the wood of her apartment door. He could no longer contain it.

"That's exactly fucking right. We *were* married. Now we're *not*. You don't get to be pissed anymore. We no longer live together, or share a last name, or even want to be *around* each other! Didn't you say you never wanted to see me again? Goddamnit Jay. I just wanted to let you know I was alive. I'm headed out of the city tonight and I was passing by..." What started as a yell trailed off at the end. He was so tired of fighting with this woman. So fucking tired of it. He loved her— always would— but he was done fighting. It was the reason he hadn't come sooner. He knew they would find something to fight about.

Silence issued from inside the apartment. Weller heard a door open and looked over his shoulder. On the other side of the hall, a head poked out of another apartment doorway.

"Hey, Rick. How's it going?" Weller asked.

"Kurt. It's been a while since you've been yelling in this hallway. Good to see you again. Heard you fellas are busy saving those of us left alive, eh?" Rick smiled. He was old as petrified dirt but sharp as a single-use hypodermic needle. Kurt had always liked him, even though their only interactions seemed to occur when he and JayLynn were fighting across the door.

"We're doing our best. We got people working on farmland across the lake and around the city for food. That's the biggest concern now." Weller said.

"Oh? And not the dead people up and walking around?" Rick was still smiling.

"Secret's out, huh? I rallied to get them to make an announcement, but I was outvoted. Something like that doesn't stay secret for long, I guess. Stay inside, will you, Grimes?"

"Psshhh. I never leave this apartment. Especially not now," Rick Grimes said, closing the door.

Weller turned back to JayLynn's door, resting his forehead against the solid wood, looking down at the red plush carpet with wavy pink and white lines. Everything seemed normal here, in this upper-class apartment building. Like the world was going on as it always had outside. Like nothing was fucked.

"Kurt?" her voice came through the door, soft and sweet. The poison moan gone. "I was mad when I said I didn't want to see you again. You know that."

"Okay. So open the door."

She did.

They stood facing each other, neither moving. JayLynn spoke first. "When two people share a life for eight years, they don't just drop out of each other's lives. It's not that easy. Even if we both wish it was."

She was still the most beautiful woman he had ever seen, even as she stood here in front of him with no makeup, in nightwear, with her hair done up in a bun. Her skin was the color and texture of rich chocolate, her eyes light brown with tan freckles, her lashes long and delicate, just like her lithe form. She stood with her left hip cocked out, which raised her short t-shirt up enough to show a sliver of skin just above the waistline of her red pajama bottoms.

"I know," Weller said. He couldn't find anything else to say. He regretted telling her to open the door. It was always this way. If he hadn't seen her in a while, he was always dumbstruck when he did lay eyes on her in person. Always.

Without warning, she stepped forward and wrapped her arms around him. He returned the gesture. "I'll check on you every day or two, okay?" he whispered into her ear. She nodded in return. She had begun to cry. "Do you need anything right now? Food or anything?" She shook her head and sniffed. He pushed her gently away and turned around without looking into her eyes.

He walked down the hall toward the stairs. The sound of her door closing as he walked away was worse than any gunfight or undead mob. It was even worse than his partner and captain trying to have him killed. But it wasn't really the sound of it that got to him. It was the fact that he was hearing it from outside and not inside. He should have been in there, with her. And he should have been there a long time ago, back when it was still possible. When she would've still welcomed him in. No matter her current emotional state, he knew that that time had passed. He had blown it and he knew it. They both did. There was nothing to be done about it.

Weller stepped out onto the sidewalk and into the cool night air. Streetlights stood vigil along the road, their necks craned down, their wide, staring eyes pouring orange light onto the quiet street.

Young London planetrees provided the streetlights with backup, growing out of their little dirt squares at regular intervals and striving to reach the heights at which their metal brethren held sway during the nighttime hours. Weller watched a couple walking their massive, furry dog along the opposite sidewalk, their backs to him. To his right he could just make out a barrier off in the distance, separating the chaos from the order. Protecting massive dogs and regular humans alike. How easy it would have been, he thought, for the chaos to have swallowed up just a few more blocks. JayLynn's place could have ended up in the outskirts.

He stood there, staring into space, thinking about the possibilities, the different outcomes that could have changed things. He cursed and cursed again the mysterious people who did this to his city. To his country. He felt lost without an enemy. He wanted to blame someone, but he didn't know whom.

Looking up at the half-moon poised above the city, visible through a thin layer of clouds, he decided that he would right the wrongs that he could. Here. Now. That was the plan, all along. All his life it had been the plan. Right the wrongs that he could. And maybe, one day, he would figure out who did this to them. Who destroyed the world. And he would get to help right that wrong, too. At least as much as it could be set right.

He set off walking. The barrier set up for letting people in and out was one street over and two down. It took him less than five minutes. Giant lights on tripods shone outward. Half a dozen or so national guardsmen milled around behind them. There were two Humvees parked half on the sidewalk and two armored personnel carriers parked nose to nose across the entrance. Or, in Weller's view, the exit. Two walls had been erected on either side of the road, touching the buildings. These walls were made up of blue barrels stacked on each other two deep and four high. On top of those, there were sandbags piled high. Weller guessed the barrels were full of sand, as well.

On either side of the exit, behind the walls, sat two metal guard posts, their perches approximately thirty feet off the ground. There was a soldier in each sitting behind an M240 machine gun. Altogether the entrance looked well protected. There was only a squad on duty right now, but during the day there were usually two or three squads.

Weller passed an empty intake tent on his right. More sandbags were piled up along the sidewalk to the intake tent. During the day the tent would be in the middle of the road and everyone who came in would have to pass through it. Guardsmen would be positioned on the other side of the sandbags, weapons loaded and aimed. There had been attempts to overrun the entrance, and pretty much every other barricade around the safe zone. The caution wasn't for nothing. As a result, they didn't let anyone in at night. They told them to come back during the daytime. But they would let Weller back in when he was done. Police and military personnel were allowed to come and go with their weapons. As long as they were on the list.

The guys on duty knew Weller. He had been there a few times, although he hadn't left the safe zone yet. He liked to stop by and take a look at the operation. It was a way to help him sleep at night. Not that it helped much. He still couldn't sleep for shit.

A couple of guardsmen milling around behind the lights looked over and nodded at Weller as he approached. Weller nodded back. There was no one in either of the armored personnel carriers, but a man in his late twenties came out from behind one of the Humvees parked near the guard stand. Weller noted the sergeant's stripes on his uniform. He recognized the guy on sight but had never exchanged a word with him. He seemed amiable enough as they shook hands and exchanged names and ranks in their respective organizations. Antar, he said his name was. His cloth nameplate said the same.

"I need to go out for a couple of hours," Weller told Antar when the sergeant asked what he could do for the detective. This statement gave Antar pause.

"Right now? Can't it wait until morning, sir?"

Weller shook his head, sadly. "I'm afraid not. For what I'm doing I need an element of surprise." He didn't see any reason to lie to this guy. What he was doing wasn't illegal. He was simply going into the outskirts to see if he could find any one of the dirty cops who had come within a hair of killing him. What happened after that was anyone's guess. It would all depend on if they would tell him what he wanted to know. Besides, the rule of law in the Outskirts was tenuous at best.

"And... You're going alone?" Antar said this like it was the worst idea in the world. And maybe it was. Weller knew what he was doing was stupid as hell but he didn't see another way. If Pratt and his crew were still alive and holed up where he thought they would be, he couldn't make a daylight approach. He knew they weren't in the safe zone. He'd made sure of that.

It wasn't like he would be able to get help from any of the cops. He didn't know whom to trust. He had to do this thing on the DL. As long as he was careful and quiet, he wouldn't attract any undue attention. Weller simply nodded in response to Antar's question, hoping the look on his face would convey his determination. It did.

"Let me send two of my men with you. They're bored as hell. It'll be good for morale," Antar said, as if Weller cared about their morale.

"Will it be good for morale if they get killed out there? No, sergeant, I'm going alone. Three people will draw too much attention. Make too much noise. Besides, I don't think your CO would be very happy about you sending two guys out at night for no reason. Just let me out, and then let me back in when I'm done. That's all I need from you."

After a long moment, Antar capitulated and called for one of the armored vehicles to be moved so Weller could leave.

# Chapter Fifteen

# A Dumb Way to Die

W eller stepped out of view of the entrance and into the darkness of the outskirts. The power had been shut off after two days of constant warnings for anyone still outside of the safe zone to come to the entrance. A small but steady stream of people had come, but not nearly as many as Weller had expected. The rest were either dead or determined to live on their own, for whatever crazy reason.

After leaving the relative normalcy of the safe zone, the outskirts put him on edge. For the first couple of blocks he saw no movement. Just trashed streets, broken windows, skeletal buildings, and dead bodies. It looked like a war zone. There was really no way to tell which bodies had been zombies when they met their demise, and which had been regular people, brutally murdered in the street. He supposed it didn't matter. They had all started as humans.

Weller paused and looked around. He had the distinct feeling that he was being followed. Usually, he would yell some obscenities, take out his gun, and run toward wherever he thought his stalker was hiding. It had worked before to scare them out of hiding and either send them running or force them to show their hand. But running around making noise in the outskirts wasn't a good idea. He was sure he would be surrounded by deadeyes in no time if he did that. Not to mention any number of other insane humans lurking about, waiting for someone or something to kill.

The stories coming out of the outskirts were horrifying, that was for sure. Survivors who made it to the safe zone were lucky to be alive. Cannibals and rapists and gangs murdering for fun. Turns out the end of the world brings out the worst in people. Who knew?

Weller pulled out his gun and listened hard but heard nothing. No movement. No sound whatsoever.

Just a few more blocks and he would be at the precinct. Then he could search the place and hopefully find one of the bastards who could give him the info he needed. If they weren't there, he decided, he would head straight back to the safe zone, as quickly and quietly as possible.

Suddenly a dark figure streaked by in his peripheral vision. But there was no sound. And whatever it was had moved faster than any human. Weller remembered the encounter with the incredibly pale and incredibly strong man on the night that it all started. How the guy had held him down with one hand like it was nothing. His grip like steel. His eyes somehow strange. Too much or too little of something. But not cloudy like the eyes of a zombie. His eyes were clear and almost luminous in the darkness. He said his name was Derek. But not quite like that. Deer-Reck, or something stupid like that. Some European hipster name.

Weller sensed movement behind him and spun around to see a gruff, small man dressed in a plaid shirt and blue jeans racing toward him. Weller got a shot off before the guy slammed into him, but it went wide. The jarring impact knocked his gun loose and it was a miracle he didn't crack his head on the concrete on impact. He found himself prone, with this ginger psycho on top of him. Drool from the guy's mouth dripped on Weller's face as the little man groaned and made to take a bite out of him.

Weller had both his hands up around the guy's collarbone, trying to hold him off, but it wasn't working. The little man had his hands on Weller's shoulders and he was pulling himself down with them inexorably, like one of those car-crushing machines.

Weller looked into the guy's eyes and noticed that they looked a little cloudy, but somehow bright, too. He saw life in them, and that life looked scared. Weller couldn't figure it out, and he didn't think he would have time to before he was ripped to bits by the mouth that moved slowly toward him, still dripping saliva on his neck and cheeks.

Weller continued to fight the guy off on pure instinct. His conscious brain was scoffing in disbelief. *What a dumb way to die*, he thought. He had half a mind to just let it happen already. *Enough with the suspense. Although, if something miraculous were to happen, now would be the time...* He listened hard, his arms barely able to hold the guy up.

Nothing. No savior.

*Alright. Fine.* Weller let his failing arms go slack, shut his eyes, and turned his head, hoping the zombie would go straight for the jugular— to make it quick. *It'll only hurt for a minute,* he thought.

# CHAPTER SIXTEEN

# AN APOLOGETIC CANNIBAL

A few seconds ticked by and nothing happened. The guy was still groaning and still dripping spit on him. Weller opened his eyes and turned his head to see another face floating in the darkness behind and above the small scruffy guy on top of him. A handsome face. A pale face. A familiar face.

"Derek?" Weller said in an annoyed tone. He had been getting used to the thought of being dead. Now he had to change his whole mindset. *Again*.

"It's pronounced dee-reck," Diirek said. "Is this man bothering you, detective?" Diirek had ahold of the guy by the back of his plaid shirt just below the collar, keeping him off of Weller with one hand. He was, once again, dressed in all black. Combined with his jet black hair, this gave off the illusion that he was just a pale face sitting about six feet off the ground.

"Either get him off me or let him eat me. I hate suspense."

"Very well," Diirek replied and yanked the man off of Weller, sending him flying backward. He landed with a crunching thud on the sidewalk some thirty feet behind Diirek, who kept his eyes on Weller the whole time.

Weller was surprised at this, but he hid it well, getting up off the ground, grabbing his gun, and dusting himself off before standing up straight and looking hard at Diirek.

"Great. Thanks. Be seeing you," Weller said casually and turned around to walk away, gun still in hand. His plan was to double back and follow this guy. This took precedence over his other problem. Anyone who could throw a grown man— a small one, but still grown— that far without the use of a catapult should be kept under watch.

Weller took several steps while straining his ears for any movement, but he heard nothing. Finally, he couldn't take it anymore and he turned around to look. Diirek was directly behind him. This time he couldn't hide his reaction. He let out a girlish scream-sigh and brought his gun up on instinct. Diirek let him.

"What were you going to do, detective? Try to double back and follow me? I don't think your skills are quite there yet."

Weller regained some composure but kept the gun leveled at Diirek in a casual, not unfriendly manner. Diirek had both his hands behind his back. Weller looked him over quickly, and let his eyes come to rest on Diirek's. They *were* kind of luminous. Almost like a cat's eyes in the way they glowed faintly. But it was a red-tinted glow. Weller held his stare and spoke. "What are— what do you want?"

"You're a homicide detective, yes." It wasn't really a question. More of an affirmation, and Diirek continued before Weller had a chance to answer. "I need your help. Some of my friends are being killed. There's a serial killer loose in the safe zone."

Weller looked hard at him. There was something very strange about this pale man. And not just the fact that he seemed to be the strongest person in the world. Which currently wasn't much of a feat, but had the world still been fully populated, he would have been arm-wrestling champion, for sure.

Weller didn't know where to start. He decided to find out more about Diirek's friends. Get a guy talking and he's bound to tell you something about himself. But, before he spoke, another voice piped up.

"Oh, shit. I didn't try to eat you guys, did I?"

Diirek and Weller both frowned at the same time. Weller looked past Diirek, who turned slightly. Standing a little ways behind them stood the small, scruffy, plaid-ed guy who had tried to eat Weller. He was a zombie. And he was talking.

"Uh... yeah. What the hell, man?" Weller said, without much gumption, his surprise too much for him to conjure any sort of believable reaction. But he wanted to keep the guy talking. If this was a new breed of zombie, he needed to know it. Diirek said nothing, staring at the guy.

"Sorry. That happens sometimes. It's pretty messed up. When I get really hungry I kinda... lose myself." He said, walking toward the other two men.

"No worries, man. Seems that a lot of people have been eating other people lately. My name's Kurt. What's yours?"

"Buck," Buck said. "Listen, I'm still pretty hungry, so I should leave. I usually don't come out of it until I've eaten something. Not sure why I'm out of it now, even. Must have hit my head or something." Diirek and Weller looked at Buck as he turned around, a look like remembering on his face.

"Wow. Did one of you guys throw me?" He turned halfway back toward them.

Diirek nodded, still unsure what to make of the little man standing before him.

"Cool... Alright. Later, guys. Sorry again about trying to eat you. Oh, and be careful out here. There's something big and mean around these parts. Watch your backs." With that, Buck started walking away. He slowly picked up speed and was running before too long. And running fast.

"Can you keep up with him?" Weller asked, suddenly.

"Yes, I think so," Diirek said. He wasn't sure. The guy was fast.

"Do it. Come find me after you figure out where he goes. I'll help you with whatever you need. Just find out where he goes." Before Weller finished talking Diirek had taken off, too. He was incredibly fast, and graceful. It was like watching a cheetah.

Weller stood there in the dark, dead bodies and broken glass around him on the sidewalk and in the streets. Things kept getting stranger and stranger here, in the apocalypse. He half expected to wake up, to have it all be a strange dream. But the pain in his back from when Buck jumped on him told him that he was alive, goddamnit.

The worst part was he didn't bring any cocaine. In fact, since he had been unofficially officially deemed an officer of the peace again, he hadn't really thought about the drugs and sex that had occupied his mind for that long and short week during which he had been a civilian again.

Now, standing in the dark after two inhumanly fast men went running off into the night, he felt like he could use some mind-alteration. If this was the new reality, it would take some getting used to, that was for damn sure.

He debated going home, forgetting about finding Pratt and his crew, but he just couldn't do it. If someone was still trying to murder him for something he'd done before the apocalypse, chances are he wasn't safe in the safe zone. They would come for him eventually. Plus, he hated loose ends. It was one of the many traits that made him a good detective. He turned around on the sidewalk and headed further into the outskirts.

A few minutes later he peered around the corner at the station house. There were lights on inside, he could see slivers through the windows on the top two floors. The windows lining the bottom two floors had been boarded up from the inside. There was no glass left. He could see scorch marks on the brick facade. Apparently, the place had been attacked, and not by zombies. Unless they had learned how to assemble Molotov cocktails, which was a scary thought.

He saw no one standing guard on the street, which was smart. He also didn't see anyone on the roof of the building, but that didn't mean there wasn't anyone there. He watched for several minutes, seeing no movement. The building's front doors faced the corner of the block, which meant that they could see anyone approaching from the windows. Surely they had someone up on the top floor, keeping watch. Definitely at the back entrance, too. Weller could remember that the back might be the best way in, if only for the fact that there was an alley there.

The four-story building had white brick along the bottom floors and red brick on the top two. It had windows galore along the front, but he knew that there weren't many in the back. Even before the apocalypse, police station houses had been pretty solid and defensible. Who knows what they had done since.

Weller wondered about the lights. They probably had a generator or two. Gasoline wouldn't be too hard to come by, with most of the population of the city dead. In fact, there was a Chexxon not two blocks down, sandwiched between two apartment buildings. If they didn't have generators, they were using gas lanterns or some other kind of non-flickering lighting. He didn't see any change in the lights while he stood there, peering around the corner.

Finally, he backed away and went a long way around to reach the back of the building. It took him the better part of twenty minutes, but it also didn't bring him anywhere close to those front windows. He saw no one and nothing on the way, just more trash, dirt, and a few dead bodies. He kept expecting one of them to jump up and grab for him, but as he got closer to them he realized that their heads had been smashed in. Apparently, people had figured it out in the outskirts, too.

He approached the alley cautiously, stopping at the corner and kneeling to listen. He didn't hear any movement or breathing, so he slowly crept around the corner, into the darkness of the dank alley backing the station house. There were two back doors, both made out of heavy, reinforced steel, neither one of which was unlocked. That would have been too easy, he thought. The little metal handles didn't move a bit.

He looked up to see the metal fire escapes fixed to the back of the building, but they were too high for him to jump and grab. He eyeballed a dumpster halfway down the alley but figured that moving it would make too much noise. He hadn't come prepared. Not for the first time he thought about Batman, and how awesome it would be to have some of those wonderful toys he always had on his utility belt. *Where does he get those wonderful toys, anyway?* Weller thought, in his mind's best Nicholson impression (it was pretty good, actually).

Weller walked up and down the alley, looking for any way to scale the building and get up on one of the two fire escapes. His efforts were void of any real motivation. Since his little encounter with Diirek and Buck, he just hadn't been able to gather the gumption he'd had when he set out from the safe zone. Normally his gumption served him well. Now, he was distracted, and only half-heartedly trying to get into the station house.

If he had managed to get to the place without running into those walking distractions, he would have found a way. Even if that way was simply knocking on the back door and waiting for someone dumb enough to open it. He'd been successful with worse plans many times in the past. But now his heart just wasn't in it. He muttered something about bullshit under his breath before walking back down the alley, hoping to run into Diirek on the way back to the safe zone. What Weller didn't know was that Diirek had been watching him for several minutes.

What Diirek didn't know was that Merek had been watching *him* since two blocks after he left off following Buck.

# CHAPTER SEVENTEEN

# PAYBACK, BITCHES

D iirek landed softly behind Weller on the alley floor. He always liked scaring humans. It was one of the things that never got old for him. As he landed behind Weller, Diirek deliberately scraped a patent-leather boot on the ground, causing Weller to spin around. The look that met Diirek was lackluster at most. The detective was damn good at hiding his surprise. His mouth did twitch a little bit, which was better than nothing, but Diirek felt a little let down. *American cowboy*, he thought, with an internal eye-roll. Before Diirek could think of something mysterious and dark to say, Weller spoke.

"Did you see where he ended up?"

"Yes. I did. It was a little bar on Franklin Street. But, I'm sorry to say, Detective, that someone tried to murder him on his way home." Diirek paused for effect. "He ate the man."

"He ate the man? The man who tried to murder him?"

Diirek nodded.

"How do you mean? He took a few bites out of the guy?"

Diirek shook his head. "No. He ate the man," he repeated.

"He ate a whole man on his way home? All in—" Weller checked his watch— "half an hour?"

"Yes. He ate very quickly. Oh, and he left the bones behind, on the sidewalk."

"He left the bones behind on the sidewalk," Weller echoed, nodding as if it made perfect sense.

\*\*\*

Neither man noticed Merek, who had moved closer to them in shadow on the rooftops. He solidified and began listening, smelling, and salivating. He was biding his time, preparing for the kill. The vampire would satiate his appetite, at least for a little while. The human would simply have to die.

\*\*\*

Weller began to speak, but his voice was cut off by a scream from inside the station house. A woman's scream.

Both men looked up toward the third floor. Weller thought it came from there, but couldn't be sure. The detective went over against the nearest door, forgetting momentarily about Diirek. Hearing a woman scream always put him into a kind of frenzy. He was like a bloodhound, liable to scratch through brick to find out what was happening and stop it, if he could.

He ran over and checked the other door, no longer worried about being loud. The scream issued again, and Weller thought it was even more pain-filled than the first one. He had to get into the damn building. There was something terrible happening to the woman. He turned around and headed for the dumpster to push it under the nearest fire escape but stopped short when he saw Diirek. The guy was just standing there, watching him, with a somewhat interested look on his face. Weller had forgotten about him, crazily enough. But he was glad he was there, and his perturbation was overcome with relief to not have to move the heavy dumpster.

"A little help?"

"Oh, yes. Of course."

"Can you boost me up to the fire escape here?" Weller asked, gesturing above his head. Without a word Diirek jumped up and grabbed the uplifted stairs, pulling them down to the ground. Only it wasn't a jump. Weller didn't see any sort of spring or tensing of muscles preceding the move. He just sort of propelled through the air. It was a night of firsts for Weller, and he decided he would deal with it later. He walked up the stairs and then turned to see Diirek following him. He stopped and looked back. "I got this. Thanks for your help, but I don't want to put you in danger."

Diirek smiled at him like he was looking at a child. He shook his head slowly at the detective. "There are twelve hostiles in there, from what I can tell, detective. You will die if you go in alone. If you die, I will have to find someone else to help me find the murderer. No, I think I'll go in and make sure you make it out alive. We better hurry. She's alive now, but won't be for much longer."

"How the fuck do— Never mind. Let's go."

The two men walked noisily up the metal steps to the third floor. The window was locked and there was a board nailed inside. Weller was about to put his foot through the window when he felt Diirek's hand on his shoulder, pushing him gently out of the way.

Diirek put both his fists through the glass and the wood at the same time. It was like an explosion; glass flew inward and the board split in two down the middle. Weller closed his eyes in reaction to the sound, and when he opened them, Diirek was gone.

Pulling out his gun, Weller approached the window and looked inside. He was surprised to find that Diirek was already in the dark room, his hand on the light switch. There was a man lying in the middle of the room who looked to be unconscious. Diirek turned back to Weller as the light came on.

They *were* using a generator, Weller decided. He knelt beside the man to feel for a pulse. He still had one.

"Don't kill anyone, will ya? I don't know what or who you are, but if you kill someone, I'll have to attempt to arrest you, which I don't want to do." *Mostly because you'll probably kill me,* he thought. Diirek nodded.

It was a small room with a single desk, probably belonging to a captain. There were papers strewn about the room, a cot behind the desk with a sleeping bag on it, and several guns scattered about the place. The door to the hallway was closed, but Diirek was about to open it. Weller ran up and put his back to the wall next to the door and nodded at Diirek, who opened it like he was walking into his own bedroom. The vampire looked left and right, then stepped out of the office. Weller did the same.

They were in a wide hallway that ran the length of the building. There was a staircase on both the east and west sides. The two men paused for a moment. Growing sounds came to Weller's ears. People were coming.

Weller looked at the stairway to the east. He heard a whimper and another scream from the west. It sounded like there were three or four guys coming up the east stairwell, probably a reaction to the sound of breaking glass and cracking wood.

Weller looked at Diirek, who nodded again. They understood each other. For a second Weller had the feeling that he was working with a partner again. But not just any partner, a partner he'd known for years. *Maybe the guy knows how to read minds*, he thought before turning to head toward the sound of the woman. Diirek went the other way, toward the stairs and the footsteps.

The corridor was full of closed doors, but only one of them had a light shining beneath it. Weller headed straight for it and stopped outside to listen. He immediately heard whimpers and little screams. Holding his gun in his right hand, he tried the knob slowly to see if the door was unlocked. It was.

He opened it.

***

Diirek had no qualms about making noise as he headed down the stairs to meet the approaching men. He slammed the bar on the door to the stairway. A couple of the guys coming up the stairs yelled out a name as a question. He said nothing, but a brief smile lit on his face as he heard the fear in their voices. He wanted them wondering who the hell could be coming down the stairs with such abandon. It would scare them if they were smart. But, since they were most likely cops, he didn't put too much hope on that factor.

The stairway doubled back on itself between floors so Diirek could look down the middle and see hands gripping the railing as the men came to the second-floor landing. Diirek jumped over the railing and landed directly in front of the guy leading the charge.

***

Weller was surprised to find not just a man doing the torturing, but a woman, too. He was even more surprised to find that the person they were torturing wasn't really even a woman, it was a girl. She couldn't have been more than thirteen. She looked at him with tears in her eyes— no hope whatsoever. The couple— both dressed in police uniforms—

went for their guns, which were in their belts on the desk next to where the girl was sprawled.

Weller thought he told them to stop, but revisiting the incident later he wasn't so sure. Maybe he didn't give them a chance to surrender. Maybe he did. Either way, it didn't matter much to him. The scene there was enough to turn his vision blood red.

Both the man and woman reached for their weapons— the woman even got hers in her hand— before Weller shot them. The woman he caught in the throat. She dropped her gun. The man he shot in the face. Blood spattered the teenage girl, her eyes wide and mouth open in a frozen grimace of pain. A pain that, Weller knew, would take years to fade away— if it ever did at all.

The man was dead but the woman was still alive. Weller spared her a disgusted glance and then put her out of her misery. He found the girl's clothes and handed them to her, telling her it was over.

While the girl was dressing, Weller took note of the nametags on the police uniforms. He wanted to know if they had actually been police. Taking care not to step in blood or brains, he dug a wallet out of the guy's pocket. The name on his ID matched the one on his uniform. The glimpse that Weller got of the guy's face before he destroyed it stared back at him with a wry smile from behind the plastic of the driver's license.

Weller found no ID on the woman, but it didn't matter. The world was going insane. No— it had already gone. Ten days ago now.

***

Little, one of the police that had been in on Weller's attempted murder, was at the very back of the line of four men running up the stairs. He was high on four different drugs and didn't really know what was going on, but knew that he'd been conscripted into protecting their little haven. So he had grabbed his gun and come running. But things went sideways when they hit the second floor. Jones, in the lead, was thrown into the light fixture in the ceiling by a black figure. Everything went dark.

Little saw a flash of gunfire ahead of him, the sound echoing violently off the walls. He stepped back instinctively, waiting for his eyes to adjust. He heard what could only be the sound of a bone snapping followed by a scream just ahead of him in the dark. Little remembered the little flashlight in his back pocket. He pulled it out and lit it.

The beam landed on Balzen, who had his hands around their assailant's throat. It was a black-clad, pale, European-looking guy. And he was smiling. Balzen's hands were white from the effort and his face was a sneer of dwindling energy. Little leveled his gun at the European guy but before he could get a shot off, the guy moved.

Balzen was launched backward on the stair landing, his back impacting the tile-covered wall on the other side. Little flicked the flashlight beam over in time to see Balzen fall into a heap from the dented wall. Realizing he'd lost sight of the perp, Little flicked the flashlight back over in time to see what looked like an expensive leather shoe coming fast at his face. Everything went black again as Little's little brain was knocked against his skull impossibly hard.

***

Diirek appeared behind Weller as he helped the girl out of the room. The pale man stepped to the office that they had just vacated and looked inside at the two dead bodies.

"Who's going to arrest you for murder, detective?" he said, half-joking.

"Couldn't be helped." Weller said and turned toward the nearer stairwell as more footsteps approached. "I'm looking for a couple of guys in here. I need to talk to them. You think we can take them all?"

"Yes. It sounds like they're coming up both stairways, though. Four on that side and two on this one. You take the two, yes?"

Weller nodded. He put the dazed and blank-faced girl into an office and told her to hide under a desk. Then he picked a doorway opposite and knelt down to wait, his pistol pointed at the door to the stairwell. He leaned around the door jamb and looked back at the other end of the hall. He didn't see Diirek anywhere at first. Then he looked up and saw that the guy had placed his back to the ceiling above the stairwell door. He had his hands and feet outstretched against the walls, but it didn't look much like he was making much of an effort to stay there, nine feet above the floor, waiting.

Weller was glad Diirek needed his help. Otherwise, he'd probably be a dead man. But it didn't mean he was happy about it. For all Weller knew, Diirek might kill him once he got what he wanted.

He turned back around as the footsteps on his side of the hall stopped. They had reached the door. The metal door cracked open and a hand appeared briefly, throwing something into the middle of the hallway.

A flashbang.

Weller jumped out of his crouch and twisted backward into the office, landing on his stomach. He shut his eyes and placed his palms over his ears. He wasn't about to drop his gun, so with his right hand he only placed the heel of his palm over the right ear.

Even with his eyes closed and a wall between him and the device, he still saw a brilliant flash of light. His right ear started ringing, but his left was doing okay. He spun around, flipping from his stomach to his back, to see a man's legs step into the doorway. He fired at once, the bullet tearing apart the guy's leg just above his kneecap. Weller looked into the man's face as he screamed. It was Pratt. His face was contorted in pain and anger, and he aimed his gun at Weller, shaking. Weller shot his other leg, and Pratt went down hard.

Weller got up and kicked the gun out of Pratt's hand. He heard movement and spun to find himself face-to-face with a man he'd never seen before. They both raised their guns but were too close to even straighten their arms. Weller dropped his gun to free up both hands. He put one to the guy's throat and the other to his gun hand. They struggled into the room, tripping over a gasping and whimpering Pratt and colliding with the linoleum floor. Weller's hand lost grip on the guy's throat so he used it to his advantage, jabbing the guy with two quick, but powerful punches to the nose. The man's eyes screwed shut at the pain. Weller let go of him, scrambled up, and jumped back over Pratt to collect his gun.

"Stay down!" He yelled at the no-name as he stepped back over Pratt.

"Kill 'em, Bill," Pratt groaned, his hands to the wounds in his legs.

"No. Don't, Bill," Weller countered. The guy wasn't listening. He forced his eyes open although they were filled with tears. He brought his gun up from the floor, swinging it toward Weller.

Weller thought of the girl in the other room before he pulled the trigger. Two quick shots to center mass. Bill's gun never made it to Weller, which was a good thing because he fired it in a death spasm. The bullet went into the ceiling.

*I always wanted to kill Bill*, he thought.

***

Diirek was flash-fried by the flashbang. He went completely blind and he felt his skin sizzle anywhere it was exposed, which was really only his face and hands. He'd never experienced a flashbang before, and it terrified him. It was all he could do to not cry out in his spot at the ceiling. He heard muffled sounds of the four men coming through the door beneath him, but he couldn't see them or hear them well enough to do anything. He figured Weller would die, which he didn't want. He had made headway and figured the detective would help him find the killer in the daytime. Plus, he kind of liked the guy. He wasn't like most other humans.

Diirek's vision was slowly coming back when he got shot in the chest. The first man through the door had chanced an upward glance and seen Diirek there. After a moment of confusion, the man fired his weapon.

The burning lead served to piss Diirek off more than anything. He descended on the man quickly, although he could only see blurry shapes. He picked the shooter up by the head and slung him back toward the other three guys, who were still confused and trying to figure out what was going on. They'd seen their buddy fire at the ceiling, and then a dark figure come down, but it just wasn't jiving with their worldview, so they were slow to react. Which sucked really bad for them.

Diirek threw the guy so hard that his head came off in his hands. His body smashed into the three men crowding the end of the hallway, breaking the first man's ribs and knocking him unconscious. He, in turn, slammed into the other two guys, sending one of them bouncing off the wall and the other flying back through the stairwell door. Two down, two to go. One of them dead, for sure, but like Weller said— couldn't be helped.

Diirek grabbed the guy who had bounced off the wall and threw him through that same wall. Then he stepped into the stairwell. The last guy was sprawled on the stairs, trying to get up. Diirek stomped the guy's right femur, which was resting on top of two stairs, and broke it in half. The pointed angles of the stairs served as fulcrum points of sorts, enabling Diirek to kick through the bone easily. If the guy had simply been lying on the ground, it wouldn't have worked out that way. It was a first for Diirek, and he stood there to think about it for a second while the guy passed out. Then he remembered Weller.

He listened for a minute and was happy to hear silence accompanied by Weller's breathing and heartbeat. He smiled. Diirek was thankful that his vision was clearing up, but he needed to heal. He knew his skin was still blistering, and he was bleeding from the bullet hole. He quickly ducked down and fed a bit on the stairwell guy. He felt better immediately. His skin and eyesight started healing quickly.

***

Weller had heard a lot of racket over on Diirek's side of the hallway and hoped the guy fared alright. *But he's not just a guy. He's something else.*

Diirek walked up as Weller was beginning his interrogation.

"Pratt. You get to live. Just tell me why you tried to kill me that day. Why'd you do it, you sorry excuse for a cop?"

"Fuck off, you— Aaaahhhh!" A finger in a bullet hole is a sure way to make a grown man scream like a girl, and Weller wasted no time in employing the tactic. He kept shoving it deeper into the hole in Pratt's leg until the man gave in. Diirek stood back and watched this.

"Okay, okay, fuck. It was Linori. Linori promised $20,000 each to do it. Only we didn't, did we? So we didn't get shit. That fucking stunt you pulled with the gun out the window fucked it all up." Pratt said, his breathing labored and his face growing paler by the minute. He was starting to look like Diirek.

"Linori? Organized crime boss, Linori?" Weller asked. He'd gone after Linori but not for a while. He'd been taken off the case. He never could get anything to stick. *Why would he want me dead?*

"How many fucking Linori's are there in this town, you dumb shit? Yes. That Linori."

"Why? Why did he want me gone?"

"The fuck should I know man. Someone puts a contract out on you, that's your business. We just pull the trigger. Cops like you are harder to do, though. Gotta be careful. Cops don't like it when you kill cops. I never had anything against you though. Just sayin'."

"What about Shellbourne? Or Ray O'Shea?"

"It was Linori. That's all I know. You'll have to find him and shoot him and stick a fucking finger in him to figure it out."

Weller let Pratt go. He had no idea if Linori was still alive or not. He believed Pratt. After years of detective work, Weller knew when people were lying to him. He stood up to go gather the girl and thought about why Linori would want him dead.

Weller stepped into the hallway and looked at Diirek. The pale man's face showed terror.

Before Weller had a chance to figure out what was wrong, a nearby window and wall exploded inward and something massive moved swiftly toward them. Weller froze when he saw the monster racing toward them, fast and huge.

# Chapter Eighteen

# Hand-to-Hand Monster Combat

M erek had been about to make his move when the man and the vampire were in the alley but decided against it when the two sprang into action and got into the building. He didn't want to go into the building— not with all those people in there. So he waited patiently on the roof next door to the station house. He waited for the two to incapacitate the many humans in the place. Then he saw his chance.

He sailed across the alley, smashing into the window. He was so big that he couldn't fit through the window alone, and so took out bricks all around as well. He wasted no time in going for them. The vampire would need to be incapacitated first. He was more capable than most, Merek knew from watching him.

\*\*\*

Diirek knew he was too slow. The monster had taken him off guard. He knew what it was, though. He knew it was the one killing his friends, and he knew now that all the stories he'd heard over the years were true. Maybe not every little fantastic detail, but he couldn't deny that here was something or someone undoubtedly more powerful than him.

The funny thing was that he'd kind of been expecting a visit from the murderer. He would have been dumb not to, with the recent deaths of his vampire comrades. But even expecting it, he was too slow. It made him feel something he hadn't felt in a long time: fear. He hated the taste, and it brought back bad memories of his boyhood and the events that led to his becoming a vampire, all those years ago. He'd have been happier to never have thought about those things again. And to never have felt fear again.

He was used to inspiring the fear, not the one being inspired.

But now, as the bulging monster was almost close enough to touch him, he still hadn't moved. Neither had Weller, but Diirek hadn't expected him to. The detective was much too slow, being human and all. Diirek looked into the monster's eyes and was surprised to see that they weren't that different from his own. They were glowing yellow and had a red circle around the iris. They were vampire's eyes. Diirek's fear intensified. The monster closed.

Just before it reached Diirek and Weller, the monster went tumbling down the hallway to his right, like he'd been struck by a train. Neither Weller nor Diirek had moved and yet remained untouched. Diirek looked to his left to find Lidia strolling toward them. She took her eyes off of the confused monster and winked at Diirek. *Damn, I love that woman*, he thought, full of relief.

They both ran down the hall toward the monster.

"Merek will kill you for that!" His booming voice made both Diirek and Lidia stop and look at each other. "Merek?" they both mouthed at the same time, remembering stories they'd heard from other vampires over the years.

"Wait, so you weren't going to kill us in the first place?" Lidia asked. Merek was getting to his feet at the far end of the hallway. He was slow in getting up, but Diirek knew it was a feint. As was the talking. But he'd take any time he could get to give the two humans a head start. He looked back at Weller and motioned for him to leave.

"Sure thing," Weller said, ducking into the room where he'd stashed the girl, thankful she hadn't seen this— whatever it was. Weller lifted her in a fireman's carry and took her across the hall and down the fire escape via the way he and Diirek had come in.

*** 

Merek rushed them when he saw that they weren't going to fall for his tactics. They were ready for it. Lidia went low and Diirek high. Merek managed to dodge Lidia, who was really just a diversion, while Diirek plucked one of his eyes out. He yelled and swung at the empty air where Diirek had just been.

On the next engagement, he kicked Diirek through a wall, but Lidia managed to break a couple of his ribs from behind with a kick. He spun around impossibly fast and got ahold of Lidia as she tried to back away. Diirek jumped back through the hole in the wall and saw Lidia in Merek's grasp. She was squirming to get away but he had her tight, one hand around the base of her neck and the other gripping her head like it was a small basketball. "Oh, no," Diirek whispered to himself, not believing what he was seeing. He watched Merek's muscles tense as he moved toward the monster.

Just as Merek was about to rip Lidia's head off, shots rang out and Merek stopped what he was doing to look behind him, Lidia still struggling in his hands. It was some bleeding human— the one that Weller

had been torturing— propped up with a gun in his hand. The guy shot
Merek again. Merek yelled and threw Lidia at the guy, slamming the two
into a door jamb. The snapping of the man's spine was loud enough that
Diirek heard it, several yards away. Lidia bounced up quickly, seemingly
unfazed. Merek looked at his empty hands and then at Lidia, seeming to
realize that he had actually thrown her. "Damnation!"

Diirek ran up to Merek and assaulted him with a series of moves that
would have turned a human to sludge. It had little effect on Merek, who
blocked most of the blows. Diirek, for his part, managed to dodge the
monster's powerful strikes, but he was losing steam.

Finally, he saw Lidia running toward him. She passed behind Diirek,
grabbing him as she went. With her other hand she tossed something at
Merek's feet. He looked down at the small black object and then up to
see that the two vampires were nowhere to be seen. Then he looked back
at the cylindrical object, which erupted in searing sunlight, burning his
skin and turning him blind in his one remaining eye. He tried to turn to
shadow but couldn't, so he bowled his way out of the building and away
into the city.

***

Before he'd gone far, he'd already begun healing. But he would need to
rest properly. Let his eye grow back. He'd find them tomorrow night. It
wasn't over. It wouldn't be over until they were all dead.

# CHAPTER NINETEEN
# THE V WORD

S he said her name was Berena after Weller prodded. Berena Frederick. She told Weller, as they hurried away from the building, that her mother had been in there too, but that she had been killed a few days ago. While she was trying to save Berena.

After those few unsure sentences, the words seemed to spill out of Berena. Pretty soon she had told him the whole story. Berena and her mother were from a small community about 80 miles outside the city, and they had been narrowly missed by the missiles or bombs or whatever they were.

They'd heard on a battery-powered radio that there was a safe zone in the city, and they'd been trying to make their way there. They had managed to avoid zombies and gangs until a man in uniform approached them several days earlier. They knew that they were close to the safe zone, and so thought that they were saved when the cop found them. But that didn't turn out to be the case.

As her story unfolded, Weller began to regret not killing everyone in the station house. He was tempted to turn around and head back in, monster or no. But that was when the woman that had saved them in the station house caught up to them.

"I'm Lidia," she said to Weller, who introduced himself and Berena.

"Where's Diirek?" Weller asked.

"Following the monster Merek," she said, a crease in her brow.

"What monster?" Berena asked.

"You couldn't kill it?" Weller said, crestfallen. Lidia simply glared at him. Then she turned her attention to the girl, telling her about the safe zone and how there was still hope. She didn't say anything about the monster.

Weller's mind reeled. Too much had happened in such a short time. His head began to hurt, and the urge to fall back into that deep pit of drugs and meaningless sex found itself on the edge of his consciousness. Only this time he didn't think he'd be able to get back out so easily. A feeling of utter helplessness settled on him like a gang of zombies on an unlucky human.

When they were finally approaching the lights of the safe zone, Weller realized that Lidia was no longer talking. He looked around to see that she had gone. It was just him and Berena, who was looking up at him questioningly.

"It's okay," he said. "We're here."

Weller didn't know what to do with her. He'd damn near forgotten about her on the walk, lost as he was in his own thoughts. There was no one to do intake for her. There wouldn't be until the morning. By the time they got through the safe zone and past Sergeant Antar, who peppered Weller with questions about the girl, he just wanted to slip into oblivion. He thought about JayLynn's place and decided, without much forethought, to take her there for the night. He could come back and get her in the morning to escort her to intake. They could find a home for her.

He felt in a daze as the two of them walked under the city lights toward JayLynn's building. Berena asked him where they were going, but he didn't hear her. Not really. For the second time in as many weeks, he was at a loss for what to do. He felt like he at least had a *chance* of handling things until that monster had literally burst into his life.

What the hell was he supposed to do about an actual, real-life monster? Its strength was like nothing he'd ever seen before. Even what he'd experienced with Diirek and that Buck guy (who was a whole other problem) was no match for the strength of that dark, twisted monster.

Weller was used to dealing with regular, human monsters. He'd grown to find them predictable. And almost always dumber than him. But finding that out was a challenge that he enjoyed. There was an art to detective work that he loved. But what kind of detective work could he do to fight a monster whose very existence was antithetical to everything he'd come to believe of the world. It seemed that his whole worldview would have to shift to accompany the events of the night.

Zombies were one thing. He could deal with legally-dead humans wandering around trying to eat people. There was evidence of similar things happening in nature. Plus about a thousand movies about it. Maybe that was why he'd found it fairly easy to accept the zombies. Because they were familiar in a way. It was almost as if they were inevitable. Like he wasn't all that surprised that there were zombies wandering around. The same went for the missiles that exploded the world: inevitable.

He had only been puzzling over Buck and Diirek when his world had been shattered. But even Buck and Diirek *looked* human. Even if they weren't (and he knew now that they were not) they still looked human. That was a big help in accepting them as reality. But that thing that attacked them in the station house? It didn't look human at all. It was like a demon. Or something out of a nightmare. He didn't know what he could do about it, and it was wearing him down quickly.

Weller noticed a couple of figures hanging out in front of JayLynn's apartment building as they walked closer. Pretty soon he recognized Diirek and Lidia. Despite himself, he felt sort of happy to see them. He wanted an explanation more than anything in that moment. And he figured they were the ones to give it to him.

"Did you find out where it went?"

Diirek shook his head. "He's too fast. I could not keep up."

"What the hell was that?" Weller had meant to approach the subject with more finesse, but his patience and energy were both waning badly. Diirek looked as if he knew this was coming, and he seemed to have all the patience that Weller had lost.

"Detective, do you know what I am? What we are?" Diirek said, gesturing to himself and Lidia. Weller opened his mouth to answer but then remembered the girl at his side.

"Maybe not in front of her? She's been through enough. Let me take her up to my ex. Don't go anywhere, okay?" Diirek and Lidia nodded.

JayLynn was all too happy to look after the girl for the night, even if she was initially upset that Weller pulled her out of bed at such an hour. She made him promise that he would tell her the whole story in the morning.

She had always been good with kids and had wanted three with Weller, but they had never gotten around to agreeing on that one. It was a point of contention. He hadn't been sure he wanted kids when they were married. He sure as hell didn't want them now. Not with the world as it was.

When he had set Berena up with JayLynn, he trudged back down the stairs and into the street. Dawn was still a couple of hours away and the streets were deserted, save the mysterious couple waiting on the sidewalk.

"Okay, what are you?" Weller said as he walked out of the building.

"Well, detective," Diirek said. "We don't like this terminology, but the closest word you have to describe us is 'vampire'. Which is right and wrong at the same time, depending on the lore you believe."

"Does sunlight kill you?"

"Well, yes, but—"

"Do you need human blood to live?"

"Yes, and—"

"I already know you can, like, jump super high and shit. Plus you're really strong. And you're both very good-looking. Sounds like you're vampires to me. You check all the important boxes." Weller was in a huff. He didn't want vampires to exist. He didn't want zombies to exist. He didn't want the apocalypse to be happening at all, but especially not in the way that it was currently happening. *This is such bullshit.*

"Why don't you like the word vampire?" he continued, pushing for a fight.

"It's not that we don't like it. It's just that we don't like humans to use it. It's our word."

Weller stared at them for a long moment.

"I'm sure you know—"

"Not even close to the same thing," Weller said to Diirek. He looked at Lidia. "You should know better than that."

"I was born in France," she said with a shrug.

"Whatever. I'll try to refrain from calling you vampires. No promises though."

Lidia and Diirek looked at each other and then turned back to Weller. "Fair enough," they said at the same time.

"So, now you know. Vampires are real," Lidia said, returning some of Weller's snark. "Congratulations. You're one of only a handful of humans to know this. But we're not all bad. Most of us actually do lots to help humans. Like not killing them when we could— easily."

"Well, it's a brave new fucking world, I guess. So what the hell was that thing back there? Some sort of vampire-hunting monster?"

"Yes and no," Diirek said. "If the stories are true, he is the original vampire. Merek. The one that allowed all of us to come into existence. And he has been feeding on other vampires for hundreds of years. Which should not be possible. Vampires who feed on other vampires die. I have seen it happen. Only this one does not. Which makes us think that he *is* the original vampire. After so many years of killing us and drinking our blood, he has turned into the... thing that he is now. At this point, he probably needs our blood to survive."

"Why, if he's the original, would he want to kill you? Wouldn't you be like his kids or something?"

"The story goes that, after a few hundred years of creating new vampires and killing humans and being an all-around asshole, he found God," Lidia said.

"God? Like, the Christian God?" Weller asked.

"Yes. And he started to feel bad for all the asshole-ish stuff he'd done and set out to make it right. So, in an effort to stop killing humans, he started feeding on vampires. It was like a two-for-one. He could right his wrongs by killing vampires he'd ultimately created while staying alive by drinking their blood. After all, he was still a vampire. He still needed blood to live. Or so some of the stories go, anyway. There are a ton of variations. I'm pulling on the ones that seem to make sense now that I've actually seen him."

"A religious vampire who kills other vampires and drinks their blood. My head hurts," Weller complained. "Wait, but you said he doesn't want to kill humans. But if it's really him who has been committing the murders in the safe zone, he's killed several humans."

"Well, he no longer seems to care about not killing humans," Lidia continued. "That's how he was, back when he was still a normal-ish vampire. Before he mutated into whatever he is now. If there are humans in the way, he doesn't seem to have a problem killing them."

"Personally," Diirek said. "I think he is more insane now than he ever has been. And, for whatever reason, he is only active every hundred fifty years or so. According to vampire legend, he needs to hibernate and rest. Every time he goes deep underground and sleeps, he comes back more mutated and vicious."

"What. The. Fuck."

"We don't know how much of this is true," Lidia said. "We had never actually seen him until tonight. Or met anyone who's seen him. Up until recently, we thought it was just a story that vampires told each other for the hell of it. Like your Boogie Man, or El Cuco. But the nature of vampire communities dictates that we don't really talk much to each other, anyway. We're not sure how many of us are left, especially after recent events. So we don't really have a good way of determining vampire deaths. Or even if someone claiming to be one of us on the internet is really one. We would have no way of knowing if Merek has been making his way around the world and killing off vampires every hundred years. All we can speak to is the number he's killed here, from our little community."

"Okay, okay, I get it," Weller spoke up. "Do you have a plan for killing him? Or making him go back to sleep or whatever? How do we get him the hell out of my city?"

"That's where you come in, detective," Diirek said. "We know he's staying somewhere around here. He has to be. And we're pretty sure he has to sleep during the day, like the rest of us. So we want you to find out where he sleeps. And—"

"Wait. You said you're 'pretty sure' he has to sleep during the day? You're not certain?"

"Well, legend says that he sleeps. And we hit him with a flashbang back there. That seemed to slow him down. So presumably he can't go out in the sunlight. So, yes, we're pretty sure he sleeps during the day."

"Ughhhhhh. I guess I'll have to bring a shit-load of flashbangs. Do I need to bring a stake to put in his heart? Does that shit work?"

"You will want to cut off his head. I don't think a stake will go through all that muscle and bone. Not with a human's strength, anyway."

"Oh, okay. Just cut off his head. Simple as that. Fine. Great. Sounds like a fucking plan."

"Hey, listen, Mister Grumpy," Lidia broke in. "We're not asking you to kill him. Not yet. Just find out where he is staying and whether or not he sleeps during the day. We know he's not active during the day, at the very least. So he doesn't move around—"

"I mean," Diirek interrupted. "If you find him and he is asleep, you might as well kill him, yes? Then you can tell us where he is and we will make sure he is actually, really dead. Unlike us, who are technically undead."

"Oh right. You and the zombies. Undead."

"Yes, the zombies are another problem. But, one thing at a time." Diirek smiled.

"Well, vampires, I must be going now. If I need to be hunting monsters tomorrow, I should get some rest." The sarcasm in Weller's voice was unmistakable. He had to do what they were asking, after all. There was really no doubt about that. That thing could kill the whole city in a month's time if it wanted to. Plus, Diirek had helped him out when he needed it. For vampires, the couple didn't seem so bad. He started to walk away and then remembered something.

"Hey, Derek, where did that weird little guy that tried to eat me end up?"

Diirek didn't correct Weller's pronunciation this time. "He went to a place called Bill's Bar and Billiards."

"Yeah, I know the shithole. Okay, thanks. I've got an idea... How do I reach you?"

"We'll contact you at night. We can't help you during the day, but at night we've got your back," Lidia said, winking at him.

It creeped him out more than a little.

## Chapter Twenty

# DOGS LIKE DRUGS, TOO

I nstead of sleeping, because he knew that would have been impossible, Weller decided to give in to the temptation that had been plaguing him since the encounter with the monster Merek. He did cocaine. And lots of it. He still had quite the stash left over from that night at Bertrand's apartment. The night that the whole world went to shit and Weller killed the mayor's asshole son.

It seemed like a different world, and, to be fair, it was. Everything had changed, and Weller had been doing his best to maintain a sense of normalcy, but that proved harder and harder with every stupid supernatural realization that forced its way into his crowded and increasingly-neurotic head.

To top it all off, the piece of information he'd gotten from Pratt only left him more puzzled about why he'd been targeted for destruction. He hadn't worked a mob case in a while— at least not that he was aware. The FBI had taken over most of the mob-related cases, as there was interstate commerce and other federal-level bullshit going on. So why would they want him out of the way? Sure, he'd made low-level mob guy's lives a living hell when he could, but that was all part of the game. He couldn't remember ever doing anything that would warrant a hit. Even killing a cop was too much heat for the mob. They knew better. It was just one more question for him to answer.

But it was a question he would have to delay until he had attended to the other, more pressing matters. He didn't like the fact that his city had been infiltrated by vampires, but he liked them a damn sight better than zombies. *And I plain hate that monster Merek*, he thought as he cut up his second line of coke in his little one-bedroom apartment in the safe zone. He stared at the line of yellow-white powder, rolled-up dollar bill in hand. Finally, his blank stare gave way to an intense gaze that, had the cocaine been sentient, would have caused the white power to march dutifully up Weller's nose while averting its eyes and crying a little. But, since drugs can't march or cry, Weller snorted the line as if it would give him the knowledge he needed to deal with the myriad of problems arrayed before him.

The drug did little to calm him down. The euphoria he felt was short-lived as his mind started to run a million miles an hour, his consciousness like a hamster on a wheel, just going along to get along. He had never gotten around to unpacking his stuff after the divorce, and boxes crowded his apartment. He thought about unpacking them but decided against it.

Weller had wasted no time in diving into his work after the divorce. But that wasn't really true. He wasted no time in diving *even further* into his work. Instead of working just 12-hour days, he started working 14 or 15 hours. He'd come home with takeout, eat it while watching a game or something on his laptop, and then pass out.

Pretty soon the unpacked boxes began to blend into the space. He had the bare essentials out: coffee maker, a couple of utensils and eating apparatuses, and seven sets of clothes; five of which were suits of different shades of khaki. His toothbrush, electric razor, and deodorant were the only things on his bathroom counter. A bar of soap and a bottle of shampoo the only inhabitants of his shower.

When he'd been taken off the job— suspended for saving his own life— he'd come home to the apartment in the middle of the day, looked around, and left immediately. He knew all the seedy parts of town where one could score various pleasures, and he chose one at random, not really thinking about it. He wanted to explode. What he really wanted was to go see JayLynn, but that was out of the question. His pride was too great; it wasn't an option.

Now, three more lines and several hours later, the sun was shining and Weller was finished planning his day. His apartment still looked like a storage space for sad boxes and even sadder police detectives, but it seemed a small concern at the moment.

He looked at the clock and knew JayLynn would be up— she always was an early riser. Weller could go pick up Berena and take her to intake. Then he could start making some calls and hitting the haunts and finding this monster that was slumbering somewhere in the city. Surely someone out there had seen or heard something. Maybe he could even pick up a trail from the station house, but that didn't seem very likely.

He had to start somewhere. This was what he did. He found people who didn't want to be found. That was half of his job as a detective. Never mind the fact that who he was after was a giant monster that looked like it had been spending its time alternately bodybuilding and getting run over by trains.

After a quick shower and a change into one of his suits, Weller headed out. It was a few short blocks to JayLynn's place, and he contemplated just leaving Berena there and heading straight to start his search for Merek. But he'd gone back on his word to JayLynn more times than he cared to admit. He couldn't do it again. He'd told her that he'd be there in the morning, so he'd be there.

JayLynn answered the door glowing. Behind her, Berena was sitting at the dining table, eating cereal. She looked much better than she had the previous night, but Weller figured it would be a long time before she was back to normal— if she ever was. Weller's ex-wife greeted him with a sly smile. "You're not taking her back," she said. "Not now."

In all honesty, he'd seen this coming. JayLynn was a therapist, after all. If anyone could look after the girl, it was her. "Wow. You look like hell," she said after he stepped inside and she managed a good look at him.

"Thanks, darling," he said, sarcastically. "Well, I've got no problem with you hanging onto her. It's breaking the rules but..." JayLynn gave him a glance that said 'you're one to talk.'

"That's great, coming from you, Mr. I-Make-My-Own-Rules. By the way, what was all that about you losing your mind at a crime scene before the end of the world happened?"

"It's a long story, which I don't have time for just now. I've got other worries to tend to. You need anything?" She shook her head.

Weller said goodbye to the two and headed out. Under normal circumstances, JayLynn would have tried to pry information out of him, but she was preoccupied with the girl, which was fine with him. He was anxious to find the literal monster that was killing both vampires and humans.

He felt himself lagging, and so stopped in the stairwell and pulled out his keys and a little baggie of coke. Just as he put a key bump to his nostril, the stairway door opened ahead of an old lady that Weller knew as Mrs. Millie. He quickly snorted the coke and then brought the key to his eye, as if he had just decided to stop in the stairwell and inspect his keys. The baggy was hidden in his other fist.

"Mornin' Mrs. Millie!"

She stopped and looked at him, a little rat-dog squirming in the crook of her right arm. A long moment passed. "Well," she said, finally. "Are you going to offer me some of your delicious drugs, or is your generation's etiquette that bad?"

Weller, taken aback, slowly scooped some cocaine onto his key again and held it out to Mrs. Millie. But the dog was faster, licking it off the key before she had a chance to snort it. She admonished the dog with a love tap while Weller wiped the key off and then presented her with another snort. This time she held the dog away and got the little mountain of white powder up her nose.

"Not too bad," she said after a moment. "I can get better, though. You just let me know, detective."

"Uh... Okay. Good seeing you Mrs. Millie."

"Happy end of the world!" she cried up at him as she walked down the stairs. Weller couldn't help but laugh. He took another bump and followed her down.

\*\*\*

When he got to the police plaza, it was in full swing. It had become the official headquarters of the whole city operation. The National Guard leaders as well as political leaders came to meet with the police. He was sure it hadn't happened without a fight. In fact, even the firefighters had representatives here, which was almost beyond belief. The fact was that the police station had the infrastructure all set up for this sort of thing, and it was in the heart of the safe zone, not too far from the lake, which was a comfort to most.

"Weller. What you been doing, young buck?" someone said from behind him just after he sat at his desk. Weller twisted in his opposite-of-ergonomic office chair to see his old pal Ralph Hardiman standing near him with a smile on his face. "Hey, Ralph. What are you up to?"

"Not much. Gettin' by. Hey, I keep hearing rumors that the brass are expecting some kind of invasion soon. From whoever bombed us. You heard anything?"

"What?" Weller said, confused. It was the last thing on his mind. "Invasion? No. Unless you're talking about the goddamn deadeyes. If it hasn't happened yet, I don't think it will. I think if there are people left out in the world, they're in the same situation as us." Weller opened his desk and began rummaging for files. Hardiman came over and sat on the edge of the desk, hands in his pockets. "You sure you haven't heard anything? I know you have the chief's ear."

"What?" Weller stopped looking for the file he had on Linori. "Where'd you hear that?"

"People say he's the one that let you out after the thing with the mayor's son. They say you got off easy for some reason."

"Whatever," Weller said, resuming his attempted exhumation of the old paperwork. "What other people say is not high on my list of priorities right now. Besides, when did you start listening to the gossip? C'mon Hardiman. You know me."

"Yeah," The older detective shrugged, glanced away.

"Fuck. Has someone been into my desk?"

Another shrug from Hardiman. Weller switched his attention to the computer now. "It'll be in here, for sure."

"What are you looking for?"

"My file on Linori." Weller had the tip of his tongue out, moving the mouse and clicking on files. He typed slowly, putting his password into the internal City Police database.

"Linori? Is he even alive? Didn't he live in the Palisades?"

"What the shitcicle!" Weller yelled at the computer. "Where is it? How can it just disappear from the goddamn *database*?"

Although it was clearly a rhetorical question, Hardiman shrugged again. "You sure you had more in there?" he said, leaning forward to get a better look at the screen.

"Yeah. I had photographs, recordings, notes. All digitized like five years ago."

"Takes someone pretty talented to hack into the database. Or someone high up the food chain to delete files."

"Yeah..." Weller said, picturing someone with a Guy Fawkes mask on, sitting hunched over a laptop amid a mess of energy drinks and donut boxes. *Hackers.*

He looked at the time in the corner of his computer and cursed under his breath, then leaned back in his chair and looked at Hardiman, who stared back with a raised eyebrow. After a long moment, Weller spoke. "I could use your help. Can you keep a secret? It's a doozy. You probably won't even believe me, but that's why it's a secret. I can't trust anyone around here."

"Sure, Kurt. You know me."

Weller opened his mouth to speak but he couldn't do it. He wanted someone to share the burden with him. Wanted to tell a friend all about what he'd witnessed last night, but he just couldn't. Word would get out, for sure. Impossible for someone to keep a secret like that.

When it did get out, people would most assuredly try to kill the vampires. And Weller wasn't sure that was a fight they could win. He wasn't sure that he wanted them dead, either. They did seem alright, so far. He needed more info, like how many there were in the city. Yeah, he needed a vampire census. *List the number of people in your lair/cave/castle/coffin/household who need to drink human blood regularly to stay alive.*

*Enough screwing around,* he thought. *First I need to deal with Merek.*

"Never mind. I'll tell you later. Right now it's just conjecture, anyway."

"It's about Linori? He's still alive?"

"I'll tell you later, Hardiman," Weller said and stood up. "Be safe."

He headed downstairs recalling the name of his destination: Bill's Bar and Billiards.

He signed out more from the supply room than he was supposed to, but the clerk owed him one or three from way back when. By the time he finally left to go find Buck, he had a duffel bag full of supplies in the trunk; he hoped they would help if he ran across Merek today.

# Chapter Twenty-One

# A Big, Bright, Shining Star

Weller pulled up in front of Bill's Bar and Billiards in the early afternoon. It looked like the place was open, as signified by the guys stumbling through the door. Weller sat and watched for a little while, hoping the little guy would show up. He didn't. Finally, he got out of the car and stepped across the road and into the dingy little bar.

The windows were blacked out from the inside, blocking any sunlight that tried to find its way in. Red neon lighting lined the bar. There was a badly tilted pool table in the back under a dim light. A few tables were occupied by skeletal creatures with deep-set eyes and bad skin. The guy behind the carved-up bar was huge, but the bulge in his pants looked about average to Weller. *Above average for a guy as white as this*, he thought, guessing it was a fake.

"Beer, please," Weller said to the guy, thinking back to a scene near the end of a little movie called Boogie Nights. The bartender had a little smirk on his sledgehammer face as he moved toward the taps. Weller couldn't help himself. "Are you a star?" he asked the bartender. "A big, bright, shining star?"

The smirk on the big man's face died. "What?"

"Nothing. Could you help me out with something, buddy?"

"You want to drink or ask questions all day?"

"Both," Weller said, simply. "You seen Buck lately?"

At this, a man a few seats down the bar looked at Weller.

"Who's asking?" he said. It came out 'Ooose assinn?' The guy was sloshed.

"Detective Kurt Weller. Who are you?"

The guy looked at the bartender questioningly, then down at the bar, then back at Weller, his head swiveling slightly the whole time.

"Name's Charlie." Namess Shaarrlie.

The bartender came back over and set a pint of beer in front of Weller.

"That'll be fifty dollars, cop." He spat the last word.

"Fifty dollars? Are you fucking crazy?" Weller had heard about this. Money was in a precarious position just now. Some people still believed in it, while others didn't. For the time being, anyone could head to one of three locations and get essentials like food, soap, toothpaste, and shampoo for free. Provided they could prove their identity. But the idea was to get a small economy up and running soon. Weller was glad he wasn't in charge of that. As a result of the ambivalence toward money, some businesses that were actually opening had started charging exorbitant prices, because no one was stopping them. Clearly, people had been happy to pay the prices in this place. Weller pulled out a $10 bill and slapped it on the deformed wooden bar.

"Keep the change."

"I said, 50 dollars, cop."

Weller pulled out his pistol and set it on the counter. "And I said keep the change."

"You're a dead man," the bartender said, matter-of-factly, as he stepped over to his cash register— without grabbing the money— and reached for something next to it.

"It's a brave new fucking world," Weller said, standing up with his pistol in hand. "No one's going to miss a crotch-stuffing bartender. The way I see it we're all walking dead, anyway—" Weller stopped for a quick second, thinking. "Actually now that I say it, that doesn't make much sense. Anyway, you reach for that gun, I have no qualms about shooting you. I already killed the mayor's son and got away with it."

The bartender stopped, looking up at Weller with disappointment and confusion all over his face. Word had gotten out about the mayor's son's death, and then the mayor's after that. It garnered respect in certain company. He stepped back and took Weller's ten dollars off the bar, grumbling.

"Good bartender. Now, Charlie," Weller said, turning his attention to the dead-beat-dad looking guy at the bar. "You know where Buck is?"

Charlie nodded. His eyes lost and regained focus as he looked at Weller.

"He's upstairs. But, he hasn't been himself lately. He's been really weird."

Weller had to focus to make out the slurred words.

"Yeah, I'll bet he has. I need his help. Can you take me to him?"

"What's in it for me?" 'Whaas inut fer mee?'

"I'll buy you a drink, how about that? What'll you have?"

"Just one drink? I dunno..."

"Or we can forego the drink and I can drag you out into the street and beat the shit out of you," Weller whispered in Charlie's ear. He was quickly losing daylight— and patience. "Take your pick."

"Hmmm. Okay. Bill? I'll take a whiskey."

"A reasonably priced whiskey, *Bill*," Weller corrected.

The big-fake-dicked bartender glared at Weller, but served up the whiskey and took the twenty that Weller laid out on the bar. Weller noted the names and words etched into the bar but paid them no mind, save one that said 'Fuck You' in big letters, just next to where Charlie sat.

"Yeah, fuck you, too," Weller said a little too loudly. Charlie and Bill both looked at him, surprised. "To the bar," Weller explained. "It says fuck you, so... Never mind." Bill rolled his eyes and turned back to the till. *I'm fucking losing it,* Weller thought. "So, you've had your whiskey, now show me where Buck is."

Charlie got unsteadily up from the bar and led Weller out the front door, turning around to tell Bill that he'd be back soon, and not to throw away his beer. "No promises," Bill said. As an afterthought, Weller stopped to flip Bill the finger. The bartender returned the favor.

Next to the bar was a door to a stairwell. It took them about five minutes to reach the third floor, what with Charlie almost falling backward every three steps. If Weller hadn't been there, the guy would've been dead at the bottom of the stairs with a broken neck.

Finally, Charlie came to a door with the number 314 on it. He pulled out his keys and started the process of trying to get the key into the lock. After two tries, Weller took the key from him and slipped it inside, unlocking the door and heading inside. Charlie followed, stumbling.

"He's tired during the day. Can't hardly get him up to drink with me."

Weller found the guy on a twin mattress on the floor of a sparse bedroom. He kicked the mattress. "Get up, Buck, I want to talk to you." Buck didn't move.

"I told you," Charlie said, leaning against the doorway behind Weller.

"Charlie, go back downstairs. Remember to use the handrail. I'll bring you your keys."

"Okay. Good luck." Charlie stumbled away, chuckling.

Weller yelled and kicked and flipped Buck over without so much as the twitch of an eyelid. Finally, he found some water and poured it on Buck. That did it.

"What the hell?!" Buck sat up on the mattress and looked around.

"Remember me? You tried to eat me last night?"

"Oh, shit. Yeah. I said I was sorry, dude. What do you want?"

"You go to the outskirts every night?"

"No way. That's crazy, man. No way."

"Alright," Weller said, reaching behind him for his handcuffs. "If you're going to lie to me, I'll just have to take you in."

"For what?"

"Assaulting a police officer, that's what. Unless you answer some very basic, very fucking important questions. Now."

"Fine, fine, fine. Yes, I go out there almost every night."

"Good. Now, have you ever seen anything weirder than you out there? Like, say, a big, strange-looking... thing?"

Buck nodded, rubbing his eyes. "Do you know what it is? It tried to kill me once, you know. It was crazy. Too bad I'm already— " Buck stopped suddenly.

"Already what?" Weller asked.

"No, nothing. Yeah, I've seen it. Up close."

"Do you know where it stays during the day?"

"Umm. Maybe? I have an idea of an area where no one goes anymore. Supposedly because of that thing. Even the crazy gangs don't go there."

"Where? Is it in the city?"

"Oh yeah. Off of Reagan and 24th."

"I know the area. There're a lot of buildings there. Do you have any idea where he stays there?"

"It's a he? How do you know that?"

"Just answer the question, Buck."

"Yeah. I think. I mean, I guess I could show you. Tonight."

"Nope. Now. We'll go now."

"No way man, it's too bright out there. Plus, I'm so tired. I couldn't make it."

"Well, that's too damn bad. Wear sunglasses. I'm not going to look for the thing at night. No way. So get your shit together. We're going now."

Buck whined and groaned and tried to go back to sleep as soon as Weller left the room to find a bathroom. But another dose of water got him back up again. When Buck was ready, he had almost every inch of his skin covered with clothing. He wore gloves, a long-sleeve plaid shirt, pants, and a beanie. On top of the beanie, he had a baseball cap. And sunglasses.

Even all that barely helped him when they got out in the sun. Buck groaned and whined until they got in the car. Weller remembered that he had Charlie's keys, so he ran them back into the bar. When he got to the car again, Buck was asleep.

"What the fuck? A goddamn narcoleptic zombie-person-thing? Great." He started the engine and drove to the only official exit out of the safe zone.

The day shift was working, and they knew Weller, so they let his car through quickly. Soon enough they were cruising slowly down the streets in the outskirts, weaving between parked cars, garbage, and bodies littering the roadway.

Buck snored, slumped in the passenger seat. Weller saw people scramble for cover as they heard the car approaching. He knew it was risky coming out here in a car. The sound of the engine might attract deadeyes, which was the last thing he wanted. But, he also didn't want to walk around the outskirts looking for a monster, asking to get murdered and eaten by roving gangs in the meantime.

When they pulled up near the area Buck had named, the streets were empty. No shadowy figures darting away. No birds chirping. No squirrels frolicking. Of course, there wasn't really any place for them to frolic aside from the metal, concrete, and glass making up the city.

"Wake up, buddy," Weller said, shaking Buck. He took off the smaller man's sunglasses, thinking it would do the trick.

"Whaaa?' Buck said, looking around in a daze. When his eyes finally landed on Weller, he seemed to remember what was happening.

"It's so bright. Aghhhh."

Weller gave him the sunglasses back. "Lead the way, little bud."

Buck sighed and adjusted his hat and put the sunglasses on. He stepped out of the car and looked around. Weller followed suit and then proceeded to the trunk to get some supplies. Buck came back to see what he was doing as Weller was filling his pockets.

"Whoa! Those are sweet guns. Is that an AR-15?" Buck said, pointing at one of the guns in the bag. "Is that an AK47?" he said, pointing at another.

"No. And, no. Are you just repeating gun names you heard on tv? This one's an M4 Carbine and this one's a shotgun."

"Oh, right, right, right. Which one can I have?"

"You can have none. You're strong and you eat people. Those together are enough of a weapon. Hell, you might be unkillable for all I know."

"No," Buck said, looking away. "I don't think so."

Weller swung the shotgun over his shoulder and handed Buck a hacksaw he'd grabbed from his apartment when he left. "Here, you can carry this," he said.

"Sweet. Is this a chainsaw?"

Weller rolled his eyes. "Which way are we going?"

"I dunno, man. I told you that I'm not sure where he is. It's just a guess."

Weller looked around. The streets were still empty of any movement. He looked at the buildings, trying to see anything that would give him some sort of clue. Finally, he just decided to start walking. Buck followed along behind him.

# CHAPTER TWENTY-TWO

# THE BUCK STOPS HERE

Almost four hours later, Weller and Buck had cleared a couple of buildings with no luck. There were a few bodies in them, but none that had their heads ripped off. Most of the buildings were empty, and there was nothing indicating the presence of a monster. But there were still several more buildings in the area. Several times Buck had sat down and fallen asleep while Weller cleared a building. It was beginning to irk the detective, and his dejection only grew as the day wore on.

"If you fall asleep again, I'm going to see if you can survive being shot. I'm sick of dragging your ass around all day."

"I'm sorry man. I've been super tired during the day ever since I had an accident in the outskirts one night. It sucks for me, too. I've got stuff to do during the day."

"Like what? Drink?"

"No!" Buck scoffed at this, even though it was true. "Like work and find food and help people."

It was Weller's turn to scoff.

"Alright, we've spent enough time out here. Let's head back to the car."

"Fine," Buck said. "I'm sorry it didn't work out. I tried man."

"Wait," Weller said, stopping on the sidewalk, the mid-afternoon sun casting shadows from the buildings. "Let's circle this block and take a look, then we'll go back. I just remembered that the Paredo Building is here."

"The Paredo Building?"

"Yeah. The one with the weird dome on top. Looks like a mausoleum, but it's really an office building?"

"Whatever you say, boss," Buck said, shrugging and dragging his feet.

They rounded the corner and the building came into view on their left, in the middle of the block. Weller squinted, seeing something strange. As they walked closer, he decided that he was right, there was something strange; a broken doorway. Like something big had barreled its way through it. They paused outside and looked up at the facade.

"This place screams 'vampire'," Weller said to Buck, who just nodded, suddenly nervous. Weller slung the shotgun off his shoulder and up into his hands and started inside.

"I think I'll stay out here," Buck said, holding his ground on the sidewalk. Weller turned around and looked at the small man.

"Fine," Buck said and started inside.

Weller led the way, up the stairs, stopping at each floor to listen for movement and then clear the many rooms. He saw no more damage like that at the front doors, but that didn't mean anything. He pictured Merek, upset from the damage Diirek had done with the flashbang, busting through the doors and then slowing down necessarily to take the stairs. His gut told him that the monster was here. It was just a matter of finding him.

The Paredo building had fourteen floors, and it took the two men almost two hours to search the building thoroughly. But they found nothing. No deadeyes, no humans, and no monster vampires. The last place to check was the roof, which didn't seem likely for a monster who could die in sunlight, but Weller headed there anyway, remembering the domed structure on top. Buck followed reluctantly.

The access door opened onto the roof at the back of the building, and the sun was weakening as it made its descent toward the western horizon. A little under an hour before sunset, Weller figured. They had some time.

He thought that the dome on top of the building was for show, but that didn't turn out to be the case. It had a blank metal door at the back. The material looked like stone from afar but was really some sort of concrete treated to make it look like the graystone of the rest of the building. It was about the size of a small house and would easily fit a monster.

Weller fingered one of the flashbangs in his pocket, unsure of whether to pull it out yet. He stopped at the door and listened for about a minute, but he heard no movement. The heavy door and concrete walls could have been the reason for that. He turned around and gestured a three to Buck with his fingers, then he dropped it to two, one, and then he pulled open the door and rushed into the darkness.

To his credit, Buck followed Weller into the dark, windowless dome. Weller cleared the area inside the door by the light falling through the entrance. Before going further, he pulled out his phone and shook it, turning the flashlight function on. There was a line of large electrical boxes in the middle of the room and old office supplies piled against the walls.

Weller looked down and saw large footprints in the dust on the concrete floor. He stopped and listened, hearing only his own breathing. He looked back at Buck, who was wide-eyed behind him, his sunglasses now resting on the bill of his cap. Weller couldn't hear the little man breathing, which startled him almost as much as what was surely behind the electrical boxes, where the footprints seemed to lead.

He gave Buck the flashlight and secured the pump-action shotgun against his shoulder, making sure it was ready to fire. Buck stayed behind

Weller as the two made their way around the pale blue electrical boxes, shining the light ahead so Weller could see. As they rounded the corner, following the footprints, the light picked out the hulking shape of Merek standing just behind the electrical boxes. Weller flinched back and went to pull the trigger, but a powerful hand stopped him. His insides knotted up before he realized it was Buck's hand on his arm.

"He's asleep," Buck whispered, shining the light up to the monster's face. Though his eyelids were closed, they could still see his staring eyeballs behind the faintly cloudy skin. Weller could see massive black muscles sitting cramped under translucent skin, and dark blue veins traversing those muscles like the map of a highway system in a population-dense area.

"How the hell did you know that?" Weller asked in a harsh whisper.

Buck shrugged. "I could kind of... sense him when we came in here."

"And you didn't think that was information to share with me? I'm human, remember? I can't sense things like you apparently can."

"Sure you can. You brought us up here, didn't you?"

Weller thought about that and decided not to argue about it further. The guy was right, in a way. Weller's gut *had* told him they were in the right spot. Instead, he asked, "Why is he sleeping standing up?"

Buck shrugged again. Weller looked back at the statuesque monster and thought for a minute. He looked at the ground and noticed the footprints they'd made in the dust. If he left now to tell Diirek and Lidia about the hiding place, Merek would surely be gone when they came back. It would be hard to miss the footprints that he and Buck had made in the dust.

He looked at Buck, who had the hacksaw looped over his left shoulder. He remembered Diirek and Lidia saying that guns wouldn't do the trick and that the best bet was to cut off his head. But he felt sure that Merek would wake up the minute the blade touched his neck. Weller had handcuffs, but they wouldn't fit around the monster's massive wrists.

He had zip-ties, too, but those looked too flimsy to hold the limbs of a monster who could smash through doorways.

"What are we doing, man? Sun's going down!"

For the first time in his adult life, Weller was at a loss in the middle of a dangerous situation. His finely honed instincts and experience were failing him when faced with a supernatural monster. He froze and, ridiculously, began thinking about how the Incredible Hulk was tamed. That's pretty much what he was up against, the fucking Hulk. He didn't have a pretty woman nearby with an emotional connection to the monster, so that was out. He thought about dressing Buck up to look like a woman, but the guy's beard scruff would give him away. It was out of the question for Weller himself. He simply exuded masculinity.

*How else was the Hulk put down in the comic books?* He thought, standing there, within grabbing distance of Merek. Buck had begun to dance around like he had to pee, causing the light from the phone to move around the room.

Suddenly, it dawned on Weller what he needed. Another superhero to battle the Hulk. The rest of the Avengers had to fight the Hulk at one time or another, right? Yeah... Weller looked at Buck, who was the closest thing to a superhero he had on hand.

"Whaa?" Buck said, not liking the look in Weller's eyes.

"Listen," Weller said, bending down to address the smaller man. "Do you think you can swing that saw hard enough to cut off his head? Maybe even a couple of chops? Right? You're strong. You would've killed me last night if it hadn't been for Diirek—"

"Whoa, what? He'll wake up! Bigass monsters don't like having their heads chopped off any more than you or I. He'll tear me to pieces!"

"Yeah, maybe. But you're already dead, right? You don't breathe and you eat humans. You're like a weird zombie, anyway. So who says you'll actually die. Besides, if he wakes up, I'll just shoot him a bunch until you can get away."

Buck had been shaking his head the whole time Weller was talking, but he stopped suddenly, looking over Weller's shoulder. "Uh, where'd he go?" he whispered, his voice tinged with dread.

Weller spun around to find that Merek had disappeared. "Oh, fuck." He raised his gun and began looking wildly about the space.

"The fucking sun's still up!" Buck declared, incensed.

"Maybe he's on east coast time. Goddamn tourist vampire-monsters." To Weller's surprise, his voice was calm, even if nothing else about him was. "Stop swinging the fucking light around. Here." Weller put the barrel of his gun on Buck's right shoulder. "Point the light where I move the gun." By applying pressure through the gun, he told Buck where to move the light as they inched their way toward the door. The flashlight flung shadows around the space like confetti at a goth party, but they didn't see Merek.

"Stop," Weller said when they were still several feet from the door. "What's that?" The light had landed on a shadow, but it didn't look like the other ones. It was darker— denser somehow. Then it moved toward them.

In the span of a second, the shadow morphed and solidified into Merek, moving on the two men quicker than either of them could react. But while Weller was still in the process of figuring out what was happening, Buck was pulling the hacksaw off his shoulder, getting ready to swing it. He wasn't fast enough.

Merek snarled as he reached Buck. The phone was knocked out of the little man's hand as the monster grabbed him. It fell face down, so the flashlight was still shining straight up, allowing Weller to see what was happening— kind of.

Buck made a noise akin to a cry of pain as the sound of cracking bones and rending flesh filled the concrete dome. Just out of the illumination, Merek's back muscles were boiling as he bent over Buck, making violent motions that told Weller that Buck was surely dead. Reacting, Weller snatched up his phone and pulled two flashbangs out of his jacket pocket. As he reached the door he pulled the pins on both and turned around to throw them inside the dome. Merek's glowing yellow eyes turn toward him in a fury. Buck's blood was all over Merek's face. Weller felt sick.

He threw the flashbangs inside and shut the door, hearing them go off a second later. He pulled the other two out of his pockets, primed them, and threw them in, too. He heard shrieking and banging from inside. Something large and heavy hit the door, but it didn't open. It sounded like the monster was running around inside crashing into stuff.

With no saw and no more flashbangs, Weller debated what to do. Nausea took hold in his stomach as he ran off the roof and into the building. He hoped he could find Diirek and Lidia before the monster recovered. They could come back and finish him off.

"Fuck!" Weller yelled as he ran. He'd just got Buck killed, and the tearing sounds he heard were still echoing in his head as he reached his car. It was full dark when he reached the safe zone fifteen minutes later.

"Hello, my friend," Sergeant Antar said when he saw it was Weller trying to get back into the safe zone. "You must have been out there for a while. Official business?"

"Listen, Antar, I'll tell you all about it later, but right now I've got to find some friends." Weller sped past the now-empty intake area and turned the corner. Immediately he started honking his horn. He didn't know what else to do, so he pulled over and kept honking, looking around. It didn't take long for them to show up.

"Okay, Detective," Lidia said, appearing out of the dark next to his window. "That's enough." Weller looked over her shoulder to see Diirek's ghostly face floating out of the darkness. "Well, you guys don't have fucking cell phones. 'We'll find you,' you said. I thought it was stupid then, and I still think it is. Might as well have a goddamn bat signal. Hey— can you guys turn into bats?"

Diirek and Lidia looked at each other, and back at the rambling detective. "Did you find him?" Both the vampires said at once. Weller slouched in his seat and nodded his head.

"Where?"

"Reagan between 24th and 25th. The old Paredo building. At the top, in the dome thingy. I think I injured him, but I'm not sure how bad. I threw 4 flashbangs in with him. But he got Buck."

"He stole a dollar from you?" Diirek asked, perplexed.

"No, no. That guy who tried to eat me. The one you followed to the bar last night?"

"Oh, yes. Interesting fellow. I told you about him," Diirek looked at Lidia. "The one who wasn't quite a zombie, but wasn't a human, either."

"Well, it sounds like our next problem has been solved, thanks to you, Detective," Lidia said.

"Your next problem?" Weller slung his door open and stepped up to Lidia. "What the fuck does that mean? I didn't do it on purpose. He was a good kid…"

Diirek raised an eyebrow. "Was he? You are very quick to forgive someone that tried to eat you. Good to know. What would you have done with him if he hadn't been killed? Surely he would have spread his disease like the zombies do. You couldn't let him roam free, could you? Surely not. This way is better. He died for something good."

"Yeah," Weller said, his anger fading back into sorrow, but a sorrow not as deep as it had been minutes earlier. "Anyway, you're wasting time. I'd go see if you can take him now. Hopefully, he hasn't recovered yet."

"You're right, Detective. We'll be back."

"Wait," Weller said while heading to the trunk. He opened it and handed each of the vampires a flashbang. His last two. "Just in case." Diirek and Lidia looked at each other and then back at Weller. They both nodded at the same time before turning to leave.

The creepy couple disappeared into the newly-formed night.

Weller sat on the hood of his car and looked up at the clear night. He could see more stars shining through than he ever had before. It made sense because more than half of the city's lights were off. And would probably stay off for a long while.

Weller took a deep breath and tried to settle his mind for the wait. It was something he was used to doing. Hurry up and wait. The night was beautiful, the breeze coming off the lake smelling of summer.

The sounds of Buck's body being torn apart played on repeat in Weller's head.

# Chapter Twenty-Three

# ONCE YOU POP...

A fter several long minutes of finding sitting a chore he was unequal to, Weller left the car parked where it was and started walking slowly, heading nowhere in particular. He had walked all around parts of the city today that no longer felt like they were a part of the whole. They felt strange to him, like some city on another continent. A city he'd only seen pictures of but never visited. He looked around and took solace in the fact that the safe zone still felt like home.

*Home.* The thought brought to mind JayLynn, and he decided on a whim to go see her. It was still early, just past 8 o'clock. He headed that way.

Her building was in sight when Weller felt a presence behind him. He spun around to see Diirek walking stiltedly toward him. "Did you find him?"

Diirek nodded. It was then that Weller noticed the vampire was holding his left arm tight against his body with his right.

"Oh, shit," Weller said, seeing that the arm was hanging on at the shoulder by what looked like a flap of skin that was about to break. Blood was soaking the vampire's dark clothes around the wound. Diirek's face held a barely pained expression.

"Come with me," the vampire said. "We must do something crazy, I think. It is as I suspected. He's too powerful." He began walking away from Weller, still holding his left arm with his right. Weller followed, realizing that Lidia wasn't with him. "Where's Lidia? Did she..."

"No, she's still alive," Diirek was walking quickly now, Weller almost running to keep up with him. "She's keeping him occupied, but we must hurry."

They said no more in the few minutes it took them to get to the nearest subway station. They ducked under the police tape and scared a bunch of teenagers who had decided to party in the subway. Weller flashed his badge and waved his gun and the kids scattered. He was sure none of them got a good look at Diirek's arm, which was for the best.

Diirek led Weller through a series of access tunnels and service doors until he wasn't sure where he was under the city. Along the way, as they rushed through the almost total darkness, Weller got a cryptic warning about a vampire named Elena. Just as he was about to ask Diirek to elaborate, the vampire spoke.

"We're here." Diirek stood in front of the door and closed his eyes. Waiting for something to happen, Weller looked around at the old brick walls and the gaslight fixtures that sat dark in the walls. He figured the station to be over a hundred years old and disused for almost as long. When he looked back at the door, Diirek was gone.

"What the—?'

"Up here, detective."

Diirek had thrown his bad arm back over his neck and had propped himself between a support beam and the wall, about seven feet off the ground. With his good hand, he found the holes in the brick that served as a doorknob. Weller felt a little queasy, looking at the arm slug non-chalantly around the vampire's neck, but he kept his eyes up as Diirek pulled the hidden door of bricks open. The bleeding vampire disappeared onto the other side. Weller jumped up and grabbed the bottom of the makeshift doorway and scrambled his way up. On the other side, he dropped down onto plush carpet, gasping for breath.

Diirek stood on a platform next to the movable wall of bricks. When he saw Weller was through, he pushed the door shut and jumped down.

"You don't look so good. Do you need me to—" Before Weller finished his sentence, Diirek stumbled and fell face-first onto the carpet. The separated arm bounced up on impact, seemed to wave at Weller, and then came to rest against the wall of the narrow hallway.

"Oh, man. What do you need? Blood?" Weller shook the vampire, but to no avail. Weller figured if he was human, he'd be dead. He'd lost a ton of blood.

He looked around and decided to venture on. Diirek had brought him here for a reason. He stopped at the end of the hallway and slowly opened the door there. He looked through with one eye and saw an old subway station dressed up like a midtown loft for twenty-somethings. There were couches and televisions around. Game systems, books, laptops, headphones, comic books. It was a big place. He saw no one moving around, and so opened the door wider, his hand on the pistol still in his shoulder holster. He stepped inside the room, and the door slammed shut behind him.

Weller spun around to see a teenage girl staring at him, fangs poking out between her lips. He felt hands on both his shoulders. He tried to move but the hands held fast. He looked right and left, seeing a middle-aged man and an older woman standing at either side, staring at him, fangs protruding.

"Oh shit."

"Are you him?" the teenage girl asked.

"He's human, dummy. Maybe he works for him. How did you find the place?" This from the older woman on his left.

"Doesn't matter," the man said. "He found the place, so he has to die. It's the rule."

"Let's share him," the girl said, in a cheery voice. "It's only fair."

"Fine," the woman said, licking her lips. "I'm starving." The three vampires moved in on him.

"Wait! Derek! Dear-rack! Dare-reek! Deer-wreck! Whatever his name is, he's in the hall. He brought me here. That thing— Merek— ripped off his arm. I was looking for blood. He needs blood. I think." The words came pouring out as sweat beaded his body. The three vampires stopped, looking at him, skeptical. The teenage girl, whose fangs were suddenly gone, went to inspect the hall. A few seconds later she came in, Diirek draped over her shoulder, his left arm carried in her hand like it belonged to an oversized doll.

The man and woman released their grip on Weller when they realized he was telling the truth. The girl walked over to a couch and laid Diirek down, then she turned to Weller, fear and anger on her face.

"Why didn't you give him your blood? You were right there!"

"Hey, little girl," he said, his confidence returning now that he wasn't under immediate threat of exsanguination. "I don't know how this shit works. I was afraid he'd drain me dry. I don't know if it's a Pringles situation, or what. I'm willing to help out, but not at the expense of my life, okay?"

"Pringles? What the hell is he talking about?" asked the old woman.

"The Pringles were an addictive chip that no one could stop once they popped, apparently," the man said. Then he turned to Weller, "Food references are lost on most vampires. We don't eat."

"Whatever. Bite me," Weller said, unthinking. "But not really," he quickly added.

The teenage girl was unmoved by this exchange. "Come here," she commanded the detective.

"Don't you have like, a supply of blood down here or something?" Weller asked, standing his ground.

"Sure we do, but Elena will never give Diirek any. She'd rather see him dead."

"Oh yeah, Diirek said something about her— wait, how many of you are there?"

"Where is Lidia?" the girl asked, still glowering at Weller.

"He said that she was keeping Merek busy."

"Oh my god, they found him. We have to hurry—" the girl stopped suddenly, looking around. "Damnit, Gretchen already went to tell Elena. Ricardo, please bring the man here."

Weller looked around to notice that the old woman had disappeared, just as Ricardo propelled him toward the couch with one hand.

"Your blood," Ricardo said.

"Alright, fine fine. I said I would. Damn." Weller rolled up his sleeve and pulled out a small pocket knife that he always carried. He cut the skin on his wrist and held it over Diirek's open mouth as the blood welled up. A small but steady crimson stream poured onto the unconscious vampire's pink tongue and then flowed from view as it made its way into the dark depths beyond. The girl held Diirek's severed arm to his shoulder and Weller watched in amazed horror as the skin began to heal itself.

After what Weller thought was about a pint of blood, Diirek's eyes flew open and he sat rapidly up on the couch, all at once. Weller jumped back. "Jesus! That's some Pulp Fiction shit right there," he said, holding a hand over the wound on his wrist.

"Wow, detective," Diirek said, licking his lips. "You taste good."

"Ugh. Don't ever say that again."

"Thank you, Isabelle, I'm feeling better now."

Isabelle hugged Diirek just as a whole colony of vampires stalked into the room from further in the abandoned tunnel, a very young girl leading the way.

Weller was caught completely off guard by the pudgy little vampire at the head of the pack. Her face was a child's, but there was something very old in it. Like a combination of a spoiled kid and a privileged yet cynical adult. He assumed this was Elena, and he immediately disliked her. When she opened her mouth and spoke, he felt justified in his brash judgment.

"What the hell are you doing here?" she said in a high whine, crossing her little arms in front of her flat, adolescent chest.

"Elena, listen," Diirek said, sitting on the couch, patience radiating from him. Weller couldn't imagine what he was feeling. His woman was out with that monster, keeping it busy, whatever that meant. *The guy must be dying to get back to her, yet he needs to deal with this bullshit first,* Weller thought.

"No you listen," Elena pronounced, stomping one little foot. "You're not allowed here anymore. And who the hell is this? You brought a human down here? Now we'll have to kill him and move."

"The fuck you say?" Weller wasn't having it. This little vampire was pressing all his buttons and he'd only just laid eyes on her.

"We found him!" Diirek said, interjecting. "Lidia's out there right now, keeping an eye on him. Provided she's not dead."

"So? Why are you here and not out there helping?" This from one of Elena's sycophants.

"He's too powerful. I wasn't fast enough. Lidia barely is. Barely. We need to use the blood. And we need your help. Everyone's."

Elena looked at the ground, and so did her lackeys. *Seriously?* Weller thought. He didn't know what it was like to back down from a fight. He couldn't remember a time he ever had. It would get him killed one day, but it wasn't something he could help.

Diirek continued. "We've got a plan. It'll work, but we need everyone. And we need that blood."

"What if... what if the stories are true and we all die? If he's the one that started us all... Killing him might kill us," a timid-looking man said, from the back of the group.

Weller counted 24 total vampires. He wondered if that was all. He slowly pulled out his Sig and held it by his leg. He didn't know how this argument would go, but he didn't like his odds.

"We might die, yes. But if we do nothing, we will die by his hand. Besides, Lidia doesn't think there's any truth to that. She thinks it was something he made up centuries ago to protect himself. She's done the research."

"But there's no way to know."

Diirek shook his head. "Not until he dies, no."

"What about my blood?" Elena asked.

"We'll get you more. There's plenty of humans still inside the safe zone. We can keep half-feeding. This is more important. We're losing time."

The old little girl looked up at her lackeys and then back down at her shoes, thinking, taking her sweet time.

"No," she said, finally.

Weller had seen this coming and was ready for it. He shot Elena three times in the face in quick succession, collapsing her skull inward, and blowing the back of her head apart. Before anyone could make a move, Isabelle was on Elena, tearing her head off with her bare hands. There wasn't much left to tear.

Two vampires— a man and a woman who had been standing directly behind Elena— came after Weller. He slowed them down by emptying his clip into their chests, but it didn't work for long. Just as they were about to close in on him, Diirek body-checked the man into the brick wall, sending dust and broken chunks everywhere. The woman grappled him and the two of them started crashing around the room like a scene from the Matrix.

Weller ran up to the man who was just pulling himself out of the wall. He pulled a flashbang out of his pocket, primed it, and waited until the vampire saw him. The guy, who looked to be related to Elena— maybe her father— came full force at Weller. The detective noticed that his placement was as good as ever. The tight grouping of his shots had made a fist-sized hole in the vamp's chest. Weller faced the oncoming assailant head-on. When the vampire was upon him, he shoved the flashbang into the ragged and gory chest-hole and let himself fall backward. Using the guy's momentum, he rolled toward his head and used his limbs to propel the vampire toward the tunnel. He landed awkwardly on his stomach, hearing a muted pop and a sound like gravel raining down.

When Weller scrambled up and turned around to look, the vampire was gone, and ashes were floating to the ground. He looked around to see Isabelle had finished with Elena and was heading to help Diirek, who was standing on the woman's shoulders he'd been fighting, yanking on her upper jaw. He yelled and pulled and the woman's head came apart at the jaw.

None of the other vampires were making a move. Seeing that Diirek was victorious, Isabelle turned toward Gretchen and made a "come-on and fight me" gesture. Gretchen shook her head emphatically. Only one or two other vampires looked to be upset. The rest, Weller saw, had smiles forming on their faces. He figured it would be the case. But he noticed that a couple of the vamps had disappeared.

"Where's the blood?" he asked Isabelle.

"She'll show us," she said, gesturing at Gretchen again. This time the woman nodded her head and turned around to lead the way. But before she could get very far, the vampires who had disappeared during the fight came running up the tunnel with two duffel bags. One of them was Ricardo.

"Here it is. Where are we going?" Ricardo said.

"We've got to find the horde," Diirek said, moving quickly toward the exit, dropping the woman's jawless head as he went. The rest followed.

# CHAPTER TWENTY-FOUR

# ALONE IN A CROWD (OF ZOMBIES)

On their way out of the underground, Diirek recounted the story that gave him the idea they were moving swiftly to enact. It had happened the three nights after the world ended. He had gone out to explore the outskirts. Okay, so he was looking for prey, but he didn't have to tell everyone that. He was still getting his head around the self-imposed limitation of half-feeding, and he wanted one last indulgence. So he went looking for a douchebag to drink.

What he found, though, was an asshole. Two assholes, in fact. But that wasn't apparent right away. At first sight, it looked like one asshole and one victim.

The people in question were on top of a small building in the warehouse district. Assumed-asshole number one had another man up there with him, but they clearly weren't friends. In fact, the other man's legs were missing. Well, maybe not missing, because they were there on the roof. They just weren't attached. Apparently, the two men knew each other because, as Diirek stopped at the edge of the roof to figure out what was going on, the legless guy was pleading for death.

"Please, Mark," the man said. "Just let me die. Let me die. Please. Oh god, please." The guy with his legs gone looked to be in his 60s. His hair had receded long ago and his skin was faintly wrinkled. But he still looked tough enough— after all, his legs had been removed and he was still talking. Diirek had to tip his hat to the guy— if only he'd been wearing one.

Mark, who had a bloody saw lying next to him, was just finishing tying a tourniquet on the older guy. "Shut up, *Jim*," Mark said in a sneer. "I'm not done with you yet."

The smell of blood made Diirek's mouth water and his fangs hurt. In his mind, the mere act of cutting off some guy's legs was enough of a reason to choose this Mark as a meal. But before he was about to make his move, the plot thickened.

He listened intently as Mark explained to Jim why he was doing what he was doing. That Jim, who had apparently married Mark's mom, had been less than civil in raising him. There were beatings, verbal abuses, and even the hint of sexual abuse, which Jim denied vehemently.

In the end, Diirek decided to take care of them both. After all, Jim had clearly lost a lot of blood, so he wouldn't be too filling. Plus, he would welcome death. He'd said as much many times since Diirek had been listening.

As for Mark, well that was a no-brainer. Abuse or not, any person who was not a psychopath would opt for a less brutal form of punishment. Cutting the legs off a person is pretty messed up. At least it was in Diirek's mind. So, he made his way toward the two men who were still in passionate conversation.

"Hello, gentlemen," he said when he'd come close.

"What the fuck?" Mark said, diving for a shotgun lying several feet away. Diirek moved with a speed unmatched by any human and hit Mark on the head, knocking him out. On looking back, it was a stupid thing to do. He should have taken care of Mark first, but he didn't. At the time, he wanted to put Jim out of his misery first, as the man was clearly suffering. Plus, he was losing blood by the minute, which Diirek saw as a terrible waste. So, he approached Jim, who was now pleading with Diirek to kill him.

"That is the plan, James," he said, picking the incomplete older man up easily. He unhinged his jaw and got a few swallows in when he heard movement from where Mark had been laying. Diirek spun around, still holding Jim in front of him, just in time to watch Mark pull the trigger on the shotgun. The shot hit Jim directly in the back, spraying blood, bone, and bits of muscle all over Diirek. The vampire took a few pieces of bone or bullet in his chest, but nothing too serious. Nothing a quick feeding on Mark wouldn't cure.

Before he could get another shot off, Diirek threw the remains of Jim at Mark. Instinctively, Mark raised the gun to fend off the tattered body of his stepfather. Diirek was on him in an instant, breaking both his arms to get him to drop the gun.

The feeding was quick. Diirek was pissed at himself for letting it happen, but he was also pissed at Mark, whose body crumpled at his feet when he was done.

Looking at himself, Diirek decided to cut his night short and get home to take a shower. As much as he liked drinking blood, he didn't like to have it all over him. After all, you don't like having spaghetti sauce or ice cream all over you, do you? So he floated down to the street and began his walk home. Only he ran into the horde on the way.

Not thinking anything of it, he headed straight for them, knowing from experience that they had no interest in vampires. He shouldered his way into the horde, his eyes fixed ahead to where the buildings were closer together. He preferred traveling by rooftop, but just now it wasn't an option. He made his way deep into the horde before he realized something was wrong.

Hands were grabbing at him and the zombies were actually *looking* at him. They had never done that before. One snapped at him with big, rotten teeth, but Diirek moved back. Pretty soon there were hands all over him and everywhere he looked there were gape-mouthed zombies. He was surrounded.

Diirek turned toward the nearest building while fending off the zombies as they came at him. He wasn't sure what a bite would do and didn't want to find out. The building was a good hundred yards away. It had a fire escape zig-zagging up the side of it, thank goodness.

He pushed forward against the zombies in front of him, toppling them into the uncoordinated figures behind them. Then he used his legs to propel himself backward, arms spread. The result was much like that of a boxer getting knocked back into the ropes, only instead of ropes, there was a mass of zombies. They fell back, giving him a brief respite from the grabbing hands and snapping mouths.

Having cleared himself some small amount of running room, he ran forward, using the zombie-ramp he'd formed ahead of him to get on top of the horde. He wasn't sure his desperate plan would work. It wasn't like he could float on command or anything. He knew how to make himself weightless— sort of. He could jump high and run fast with minimal effort. He was incredibly strong. And he knew he had a tendency to float a few inches off the ground when he was about to feed. It was all pretty automatic, and he hoped this would be, too. He'd never tried running on top of a seething crowd of people, dead or otherwise.

The first few strides atop the horde were slippery and somewhat tentative, but then he got the hang of it. Diirek began to smile. He ran toward the building while hands reached up and tried to yank him back down into the depths of rotting flesh rippling beneath him.

He felt overripe skulls, shoulders, and spines give way under his feet as he ran joyously atop the horde. But he was moving too fast for them to affect his momentum much. He kicked at hands that came up before him, knocking purple and green fingers out of sockets or off altogether. A couple of hands came off at the wrist and sailed through the air to slap or punch an unsuspecting zombie in the distance. One hand, he could swear, flipped him the bird before it disappeared into the horde some 20 yards away.

He saw a particularly tall zombie off a little way into the billowing crowd. It had a machete blade stuck halfway into its neck. He thought of Lidia. It was too good to pass up. He veered off toward the irregularity, traveling fast on heads and shoulders. When he came to the zombie he made like he was kicking a football. The head came off and sailed far into the crowd, striking another zombie in the head with a satisfying crunch.

Diirek was laughing by the time he reached the fire escape. He jumped up onto the second-floor balcony and took off his soiled jacket, hanging it over the upturned rotting faces below him. He watched, fascinated, as the zombies began climbing on top of each other in an effort to reach the jacket.

Pretty soon they were in grabbing distance, but Diirek walked up another flight of metal stairs and hung the jacket over again. Still, they climbed each other. It wasn't exactly teamwork. The ones on the bottom who fell were simply trodden on by their brethren. They were mindless, but still, they kept making the pile higher as Diirek kept moving up away from them. Some of the zombies reached out to brace against the lower levels of the fire escape, but none of them stepped onto it from the pile. Not that they could step anywhere, really. Only the few who made it to the top had any real freedom of movement. The rest all had zombies resting or climbing on top of them.

Soon enough the pile reached critical mass and the whole thing toppled down sideways. Diirek looked at his coat and decided it was pretty well ruined anyway. He let the soiled and expensive black velour coat fall down into the horde.

When the zombies got ahold of it, the coat was gone in only a few seconds, ripped to shreds by hungry mouths. He didn't imagine it was too satiating, but that wasn't really the point. He noted the experience and headed home, via rooftops this time.

When Lidia got home later that night, he told her about it.

"Good to know. Don't get caught in the horde covered in blood," she said.

"It's strange, though. They don't seem to bother us, even if we've just fed. We technically have blood running through us. If you cut me, I bleed. Not as much as a human, but still. So what's the difference?"

Lidia didn't seem too interested in the conversation. "You know how we always talk about our abilities like they're magic?" she asked. Diirek nodded his head.

"Well, we call it magic because we don't have any other explanation for it. Would you agree?" Again, Diirek nodded.

"I've already ruled the zombies under the magic heading. Nothing about them makes sense. Just like nothing about us makes sense. We both defy current scientific knowledge. So, I guess that's why we don't see it as such a big deal. We're used to defying the laws of physics. We only really care about the zombies because they'll negatively affect our food source."

Diirek gave her a look.

"Well, for the most part. I do like humans— some humans— and so do you. But I think that's more because we used to be human than anything else."

"Yes, I suppose that is true," Diirek said.

"So," Lidia continued. "It's good that you figured out that the zombies can smell or sense human blood. But leave it at that. Trying to figure out why is an exercise in futility, no? How many years did we spend trying to figure out what made us possible?"

"Too many."

"Exactly. So that's how I look at it. When I kicked a zombie's head off the other day, that was an addition to our knowledge. We use it to survive, not to understand. We damn near got ourselves killed many times in our search for answers about our existence. I don't want the same happening again. I want to stay with you for at least another five hundred years." Lidia sidled up beside Diirek with this last sentence, and he welcomed her.

"I know how you get," she said, softly. "But I don't want to lose you to an obsession again, okay?" Diirek kissed her in answer, which was about the best she was hoping for.

They spent the few hours until dawn devouring each other passionately, as they'd been doing for decades.

# Chapter Twenty-Five

# PUNY HUMAN

"Well, I could've done without that last part about you guys devouring each other, but, I see what you're getting at," Weller said as they approached a barricade. This one was on a small side street and it wasn't guarded. There would be a patrol around every 15 minutes or so, but Diirek had memorized their schedules.

Most of the twenty-odd vampires climbed deftly over the wall made out of flattened cars stacked four high and four across. A few— including Diirek— sailed up and over the barrier with the speed and grace of a jungle cat climbing a tree. Their hands and feet touched here and there, so it wasn't quite flying or floating, but it was close.

Weller watched as a vampire that may have been an African Queen in her past life made it to the top easily. When she disappeared over the side, and he lost sight of her wonderful backside, he snapped out of it and realized that he was alone on the wrong side of the barrier. He climbed over with considerably more difficulty, panting as he dropped to the other side. He wasn't sure if the vampires didn't want him there or if they just weren't used to a slow human tagging along. One thing was sure: he wasn't staying behind. He needed to see the monster go down. He needed to be sure.

The vampires were up ahead in the gloom, grouped around Diirek. He was too far away to hear what their new leader was saying and he jogged toward them, trying his best not to let his anger flare. Just before he made it to the group, Diirek and two others darted off into the dark, away from the safe zone.

"Where are they going?" Weller asked the African Queen whose ass he'd been admiring at the barrier.

"Why are you here, human?" she asked, looking at him like he was crazy. "You'll die quickly out here. Go back." Weller wasn't surprised to hear an accent as she spoke. Maybe she really had been a Queen. She certainly had the looks for it. The other vampires glanced at him but paid him no further mind. They started walking briskly in the direction the three others had taken. Weller walked with them.

"So where are they going?" he repeated.

"Diirek," African Queen said with a sigh, "is going to find Lidia and Merek. The other two find the horde. They come back and tell us where to wait. But you should go back. It's dangerous out here for a human."

"I'll show you dangerous, you sexy fiend," Weller said, under his breath. She looked at him then and smiled. "Thank you."

Weller blushed. *This is bullshit. Stupid sexy vampire hearing.*

Two figures darted out of the cross street ahead. Diirek reached for his gun before he realized that it was the two vampires assigned to find the horde. One of them was Isabelle, he noticed.

"Follow us," she said to the crowd. The two took off the way they'd come. The rest of the vampires started running. Fast. Even the ones carrying the duffel bags full of packaged blood were regular track stars, the weight not slowing them down a bit.

The distance between the crowd and Weller grew exponentially. He ran after them until his heart pounded behind his eyeballs and every breath felt like he was inhaling coarse cotton. They ran straight for five blocks and then turned right before Weller lost sight of them. He ran until he developed a sharp pain in his side, at which point he slowed to a fast walk. He turned the corner, hoping to see them ahead. They were gone. Nowhere to be seen.

He kept walking for three blocks, glancing down side streets only to see prone rotting bodies, abandoned cars, trash, and the occasional far-off zombie limping along. Holding his side and still recovering his breath, he walked to a short brick building bordering an alley entrance and leaned against the rough stone.

"Shit!"

Although he hissed it, the word still echoed quietly off the buildings around. His heart was just slowing down when a hand shot out of the dark alley and grabbed his arm, yanking him off his feet. Weller sucked in breath and choked for a brief moment before he saw that it was Isabelle. "Come," she said.

"Christ on a Christmas tree," Weller said, his heart thudding in his throat.

Isabelle let go of his arm and he followed her into the alley. They walked through and stopped at the other end. Isabelle peeked left out of the alley. Weller joined her. The horde was there, half a block down, but it seemed to be moving away. All Weller could see were the backs of zombies at the edge of the crowd.

Weller had heard reports and seen a few pictures of the mass of zombies. A few stragglers on the outer edges were always wandering off in search of food, but for the most part, the horde had become one giant organism. Weller had figured it was a couple hundred strong, but it looked to be much larger than that.

"Let's go. Quietly," Isabelle said. They ran across the street and into the next alley. The waiting vampires were arrayed all around in the dark. Moonlight fell about their shoulders and heads like it was attracted to them by some invisible force. Seeing the vampires there felt a bit like seeing a fish in water or an asshole drinking Sud Light. It was *natural*.

One of the vampires said he heard something and left to inspect. The rest of them stayed in the alley. They were waiting on a signal from Diirek, Isabelle said. If Merek saw them all, he would surely disappear. Maybe for another hundred years or so. Weller nodded at Isabelle and then walked up to African Queen.

"What's your name?" he asked her.

"Binta," she said. "You are Detective Weller."

He nodded, although it wasn't a question. "None of you have ever seen Merek in person?"

"No," Binta said. "There are only stories. Lore. I didn't believe he existed until all this started."

"So, let me ask you, do you think that a zombie bite will turn Merek into a half-zombie half-crazy vampire hybrid?" All the other vampires turned to him then, their eyes wide.

"What?" she asked, appalled. "No. I don't think so... I don't know."

"You guys haven't thought about this?"

"No. It's Diirek's plan," another vamp spoke up. "I just assumed he would have thought of it. He knows what he's doing."

"I mean— are there any other options to get rid of this guy?" Weller asked. The vampires were silent.

"All the lore says is that he can only be killed by having his head removed," Binta said.

"Damn. Have you seen where his head is? He doesn't even have a neck. There's like, a shell of muscle around that thing."

"You've seen him in person?"

"Yes. I'm the one who found him. Not even two hours ago now."

"And you are alive? A human?"

"I got the feeling he was interested in the guy I was with more than me. He hunts vampires, after all. I think Buck was a vampire. Or, half vampire, anyway." The vampires all looked at each other, questioningly.

"We haven't turned anyone. How would he be a vampire?" Binta said.

"I don't know. I was hoping you could tell me. He tried to eat me last night. Diirek stopped him."

A vamp who hadn't spoken yet stepped forward. She was about as pale as Diirek and looked like the stereotypical version of an eastern European vampire: dark hair and eyes with pale skin and a thin, toned body. "Was he small man? Red-ish hair?" She asked in a heavily-accented voice.

"Yeah. Dressed like a 90s grunge guy. Stupid plaid shirt, old holy jeans, and black and white sneakers. At least every time I've seen him."

"Hey!" hissed one of the vampires in a hurt voice. Weller looked at the guy, who was wearing pretty much the same outfit he'd just mentioned. Weller shrugged and turned back to the European vamp. "So?"

"Yes. I think it was me who did this. I am feeding on him and he stab me with knife several times. I drop him and he gets my blood in his mouth. Then he gets bit by zombie. It was... how you say?" she paused momentarily to ponder. "Ah, yes. Freak accident."

"Goddamnit Val. Why didn't you say anything?" This came from Ricardo.

"I didn't think it was issue. I thought he get eaten by zombies. I don't know he a vampire-zombie until now," Val said, defensively.

"So, chances are that if this thing goes sideways, Merek will become a hybrid? That can't be good." Weller asked.

"So, we make sure it no go sideways. We kill him tonight," Val replied, performing a very Russian-looking stomping gesture.

"We fucking better," Weller said.

# CHAPTER TWENTY-SIX

# BLOOD AND FURY

L idia was getting tired.

Even hurt, Merek was fast in the open. Almost as fast as her. She jumped from a rooftop, soared over the dark avenue below, and crashed through a window of a building across the street. As she rolled onto her feet in a room filled with cubicles, she felt the floor shake as Merek landed just behind her. She didn't turn around. She ran as fast as she could toward the window on the opposite side. She felt Merek gaining on her. If he had been strong enough to turn to shadow, he would have, she knew.

She'd managed to hide from him a few times. Once he even gave up and started to move deeper into the outskirts, but she followed him, afraid to lose this chance. When he sensed her it was as if he got *faster*. She was barely able to stay ahead of him.

She wondered where Diirek was as she ran toward the large floor-to-ceiling window. She hoped he wouldn't be much longer. If he was, she'd be dead. Instead of jumping through the window, she turned sharply to the right and rounded the corner. Then, while Merek couldn't see her, she ducked into a cubicle. She listened as Merek cut the air and kept going. But he stopped not far away. She heard him growl and start stalking around.

She needed to feed. Resting wouldn't do much good. It was a matter of blood; she didn't have enough in her. She realized that she couldn't hear the monster anymore and her eyes went wide. She listened hard, sending her hearing out. Nothing. *Oh no*, she thought, and began to move quickly out of the cubicle. A giant hand came down and knocked her back. Before she knew it, he was on her, his terrible eyes fixed on hers, his lips slipping back over his razor teeth, getting ready for the kill. She squirmed, trying to get free, but Merek put his hand on her chest, and the other held her legs down. But her arms were free, the left of which she used to pull a black cylinder out of her pocket. It was her last chance.

She knew the flashbang would probably hurt her more than it would Merek, but it would distract him long enough for her to get away. Maybe. If she was too damaged, it would only prolong the inevitable. *Where are you, Diirek?* she thought again, pulling the pin with her arms above her head as Merek's mouth moved to close over her face. She released the catch, which caught the monster's attention. He stopped and looked at her hand, eyes wide. She thought about trying to throw it around Merek's bulk, so his body would block her from the blast, but it would also mean that only his back would be burned. She wanted his eyes and face burned. So she went to shove the device in his mouth, but he was too fast. He caught it, burying both her hand and the flashbang in his own giant fist.

The explosion tore both of their hands apart. She saw the light flash out before she went blind, and she knew by the pain that her hand was gone and her face and torso badly damaged. But then, even that knowledge was gone. All went black.

\*\*\*

Diirek spotted the flash from outside the building. It wasn't all that bright, but he didn't like it. Lidia promised him that she'd only use it as a last resort. He suddenly felt sick, but he jumped across from the roof and in through the broken window. He ran fast and made the corner, heading to where the faint flash had come from. Amid the maze of cubicles, Diirek saw Merek standing up, raising his arm. His hand was gone at the wrist, and the skin of his face and chest was charred and pocked. Blue-black blood oozed out of gouges, and only one of his eyes was open. He hadn't spotted Diirek yet, who was waiting for Lidia to show up from wherever she had hidden.

She didn't.

Instead, Merek reached down with his good hand and grabbed something from the floor. The monster lifted a ragdoll form, limp and bleeding, to his mouth. Diirek moved then, horrified, realizing that the limp doll was Lidia. She looked worse than Merek, the flesh of her face blackened and burned. Merek lifted her up and let her head tilt limply into his mouth, just as his over-large jaw unhinged. Diirek screamed.

Merek looked up and smiled briefly before clamping down on Lidia's neck with his teeth. He yanked her body away and pulled his head back. The pop-crunch sound that issued as the monster's teeth severed Lidia's head at the spine made Diirek explode in a white-hot mixture of pain, anger, and despair. Before Diirek could reach him, Merek jumped away, still holding Lidia's body in his left hand.

Seeing his century-long lover and best friend headless and limp opened something in Diirek.

Suddenly he felt himself move faster than he ever had before. His legs pumped and arms pistoned and a humorless grin of determination came over his face. He followed as Merek shouldered straight through the disused cubicles in his way, sending computers, cheap wooden desks, headsets, and partitions flying out of the way. Exploding through the nearest window, Merek dropped to the street below, Lidia's body still clutched in his good hand.

When Diirek got to the window, Merek was nowhere in sight. He glanced around the street below. He tried to listen for movement but there was a cacophonous rage blaring in his head. He knew that Merek was somewhere draining the last of Lidia's blood into his mouth. He would heal quickly, and the odds of his defeat would skew steeply in the wrong direction.

Diirek dropped down to the street, his rage causing him to overlook the obvious.

Merek came at him from behind— he'd doubled back into the ground floor of the building they'd just been in. The glass windows had been smashed during the looting, like so many others had in this area. It was stupid of Diirek not to realize it, and he knew this as Merek's hand wrapped around his head, the fingers like concrete tentacles.

Diirek had only a second, but he used it to open his mouth wide. One of Merek's fingers slipped inside and Diirek clamped down as hard as he could, his teeth severing the oversized digit at the first knuckle. Merek cried out but didn't let go. Diirek felt the giant hand tighten around his seemingly fragile skull. The pressure began to overwhelm him as the taste of Merek's blood exploded in his mouth.

A corona spread through his mind and poured like lava into his body, turning the fire already there into an inferno. The taste was like gasoline, battery acid, and animal blood all mixed together. The effect was like nothing Diirek had ever experienced. His muscles thrummed and swelled, his senses sharpened and focused as an immense calm settled over him like a lunar eclipse.

Vampires couldn't feed off of other vampires. When they did, they died quickly. Diirek knew it, but he didn't care. He was ready to die— as long as he took Merek with him.

He reveled in the feeling. Was this what Merek felt like when he fed? Did he feel this, or something like it, all the time? Diirek started sucking on the still-bleeding stub of Merek's finger, savoring the sickening taste and the effects accompanying it. Merek tried to move the single finger away from Diirek's mouth, but he couldn't do so without losing his crushing grasp.

Perhaps conscious of what would happen if the vampire kept feeding on him, Merek grabbed Diirek around the neck with his other, half-formed hand, and let go. But his other hand was not finished regenerating. The fingers were still forming.

Diirek spun around and slipped easily out of his grasp. He ran to the street and snapped off a metal post with a crosswalk sign on top. Without looking he knew that Merek was moving toward him. His senses were on overdrive, and he felt like he was almost an even match for the monster— for now. He jumped into the street and turned around, flinging the broken metal post at Merek all in one fluid motion. It penetrated the monster just above the collarbone in the middle of his almost non-existent neck. A little less than half of the post stuck out high on Merek's overly-muscular back. The rest, including the thin metal sign, was in front.

This development surprised both parties. Diirek was acting on instinct— with the help of the monster's blood— and it was paying off.

Then Diirek glanced Lidia's headless body behind Merek, discarded on a glass-laden floor. "I am going to rip your fucking head off," he growled at Merek, who was still looking in surprise at the metal post sticking out of him.

The monster went to pull the post out. Diirek jumped at him and kicked it back in. For the moment Merek forgot about the post and came after Diirek, who took off down the street. As he ran, the vampire saw movement on a nearby rooftop and looked up. Boris was there, signaling him the way to go, and then disappearing into the darkness.

Diirek kept running. The trap was set, and they had a chance. Already he felt the effects of Merek's blood wearing off, and he spat out the tip of the monster's finger, knowing he'd gotten all he could out of it.

Again, he sensed Merek stopping and he turned around. The monster was trying to pull the post out again. Diirek stepped toward a nearby building and punched a hole in the brick facade. His hand came out with a mostly-intact brick and threw it, hitting the top of the post, negating the progress Merek had made. *Maybe it's not wearing off, after all*, Diirek thought when he realized he'd punched a hole in a brick wall. He was strong, but not that strong.

The monster made a frustrated sound and reached forward to grip the metal sign on either side. He yanked down, snapping it in half (his nubby fingers on his bad hand were now formed enough to do that, at least). He came at Diirek again, this time with a thin, sharp piece of metal in each hand. It wouldn't be hard to take a head off with one of those, Diirek knew, as he ran again.

He got another signal from Boris to turn left at the next block, which he did. The horde was now straight ahead. He didn't see any of the other vampires. But he knew they were there somewhere, waiting.

## Chapter Twenty-Seven

# Sexy Zombies and Ugly Monsters

E ach of the vampires now had a bag of blood in a hand. A few gulped some down to put the edge on their strength. Weller looked around the alley at the silent vampires. They seemed nervous. He sure as hell was. He shuffled a little bit, then started pacing up and down the alley, noticing a couple of corpses on the alley floor for the first time.

It was disturbing that he'd gotten so used to seeing dead bodies in the outskirts. Both those that walked upright and those that didn't move at all. He saw a figure come into view at the mouth of the alley and froze in place. It was a zombie, dragging a dangling foot along like a hit-and-run victim that was too drunk to realize it. It paused and looked down the alley. Weller swore that the thing was looking right at him. It moved its head then, and Weller thought that it was sniffing the air. *No fucking way.*

Finally, after what seemed like several minutes, the zombie limped on down the road, apparently seeing nothing of value in the alley. Weller breathed a sigh of relief. The last thing they needed now was to draw the attention of a bunch of zombies. It would surely alert Merek, whom the other vampires seemed to think was on the way.

Weller looked at Binta, his eyes wide and a small, relieved smile on his lips. She raised her eyebrows in an approximation of sympathy, but he didn't think she was too concerned about it. After all, from what they said, the zombies weren't interested in them. Only Weller, the sole human in the group, was in danger.

"They're getting closer," a woman vampire said from her perch on the fire escape half-way up the back of the building. Weller stood still for a moment, but then he started pacing again. He was beginning to lose it. His heart was beating so hard it was giving him a headache, and his breath was sour with fear. He held his pistol in his right hand, just because it made him comfortable. It wouldn't do much good against what was coming, and he knew it. He had no idea what he was going to do when the monster got here. *Die, maybe,* he thought. *What the hell was I thinking? I'm up against a fucking mons—*

A sticky, bony hand clamped against Weller's ankle. He made a yip sound and pulled instinctively away from the hand. It held fast. He looked down to see one of the corpses that had been decorating the alley floor was grabbing him. Somehow this old dead man had lost his legs, and Weller was dragging his top half along the alley floor, his panic mounting inexorably.

Dead eyes stared up at him from a ragged and torn face, while viscera trailed out of the bottom of the zombie's torso. The stench that floated up from the spilling guts made Weller want to puke. He kept trying to shake him off, knowing he couldn't use his weapon, lest he alert Merek to their presence. The dead man stayed latched to Weller's leg by a surprisingly powerful hand. In an effort to kick the zombie in the head while simultaneously stepping backward with his other leg, Weller brought his foot too close, and the rotting mouth closed around his ankle.

He watched it happen in slow motion. He knew the panicked kick was a bad idea as soon as he did it, but the momentum was unstoppable. He expected pain as the zombie bit his ankle, but there was none. For this he was thankful, but he felt it was a small mercy.

He would have to kill himself now. A bullet to the brain to prevent him from turning into one of them.

One of the vampires kicked the zombie's arm, splitting it in half at the elbow. Then a second kick sent the corpse flying against the alley wall with a wet thud. The hand still clung to Weller, but the rest of the zombie was writhing against the wall on its back, trying to flip over like an overturned turtle. Weller yanked the hand off and threw it away. He walked over and stomped on the old dead man's head. It gave way under his heel like an unripened melon.

"Fuck!" Weller said, a little too loud.

"Sshhh," several of the vampires said in unison.

"Some fucking help you guys are. I'm dead now. He fucking bit me. Not that any of you give a shit," he said, bending down to inspect the strange, painless bite that surely meant his death.

"Sshhh," came the same reply again.

Weller was expecting a hole gouged in his ankle, but he didn't see one. He lifted up his pant leg and inspected his calf. Nothing.

Then he saw it. On his black sock, there was some kind of slime right where the guy had bitten him. *What the fuck?* He stepped over to the now-still zombie and carefully thumbed open the mouth. Mercifully, Weller had missed the bottom half of the dead man's face with his single stomp. Black and red gums bordering a swollen and discolored tongue stared back at him. The guy had no teeth.

"Ha!" he said, and then gagged at the smell emanating from the mouth. He stepped away and was about to tell Binta, who was the closest and also, Weller thought, the prettiest vampire there, but he saw the look on her face. She knew already.

"How?" he said.

She pointed to where the zombie had been propped against the wall earlier, playing dead. Lying next to the wall on the ground was a pair of dentures. "Holy shit!" Weller said, a profound joy filling his mind in the dank and smelly alley. He smiled a pearly smile and Binta smiled one back.

Then, Weller watched as her smile faded and she moved swiftly up to the top of the fire escape, getting ready. All the others did the same, settling on the rails and stairs near the top of the 5-story building.

Merek was coming. With Diirek and Lidia, presumably. Weller looked up at the vampires perched on top of the fire escape like carrion birds waiting for their supper to die. He heard movement from a door right behind him leading to the alley. He knew immediately what was happening. He saw earlier that the door had been propped open with a broom handle, but hadn't given it much thought. He should have— but he hadn't.

He turned to see what must have been the best-looking and most well-dressed zombies in the whole city. There were three of them, two women and a man. Weller had no way of knowing it, but in their past life, these zombie's names were Kirri, Serena, and Robbie.

The women looked like they could've been wearing zombie Halloween costumes designed to look more sexy than scary— aside from their gruesome injuries, of course. The dark-haired woman was missing half of her arm, which would've been a feat of epic proportions for any special effects artist without a green screen. Even the guy, with his high cheekbones, piercing dead eyes, and large hole in the neck, looked like he could merely be wearing some gory makeup.

They reached for Weller, their dead eyes staring forlornly through him. He scrambled away from them, tripping on the old guy's severed hand and falling against a dumpster with a booming thud. *Oh shit.* He scrambled up again and took a few lunging steps away from the sexy zombies. He glanced up and saw that all of the vampires were gone. Merek must have been close.

Weller knew that hitting the dumpster may have alerted the monster, but at the moment he had bigger concerns. It wasn't so much the three zombies in front of him that were the issue. It was the group of twenty or so that had started streaming into the alley behind him, no doubt drawn by all the noise he'd been making. But, no big deal, really. He could take on three zombies and then escape... *Oh, double shit.* The other end of the alley, behind the model-zombies, was now filling up with deadeyes.

No way out. No vampires to help.

*This is such bullshit.*

\*\*\*

Diirek was getting close when Merek threw one of the metal sign pieces at him. He was traveling fast, but Merek was faster. Diirek heard a small grunt and a second later felt the metal slice into his leg, just above and behind his right knee. He cried out and began to tumble forward, knowing he was as good as dead.

He twisted as he fell so he could face his attacker and he came to rest about 200 yards from the edge of the horde. He could hear them shuffling, their mass of rotting flesh rubbing together as they moved. Merek loomed over him, the other half of the metal sign in his monstrous hand. He pulled the thin sharp metal back in his good hand and took aim at Diirek's neck. No way he could miss from this range.

A rock pinged off of Merek's head. Diirek looked over and saw Gretchen standing there, not far off. "No!" Diirek yelled. "Run Gretchen!" but before he even finished moving his mouth Merek had thrown the piece of a metal sign at her. It was a clean cut right under her chin. The metal, once it had cut off Gretchen's head, stuck into the stone building behind the quickly-dying vampire. Gretchen's head cracked as it hit the sidewalk before her body fell on top of it, spurting blood from the neck.

Diirek made a move to get up but Merek was still right there. The monster, finding himself sans a head-chopping implement, reached down to grab him, but the signpost was still sticking out of his upper chest, and his arms weren't quite long enough to reach past it. Instead, he just poked Diirek in the stomach with the metal, which hurt a bit, but not nearly as much as getting his head ripped off. Of that, he was sure.

Merek's eyes went wide as his hands swiped at the air between him and Diirek. So close but so far away. Diirek got ready to spring up when Merek lifted the post off of him, hoping that, in his rage, the monster wouldn't realize the alternative.

Diirek watched Merek's eyes, set in the craggy and dark face. For a second it looked like Merek would stand back up, freeing Diirek, but he didn't. His eyes narrowed and he began pushing himself forward, pressing harder into Diirek's stomach with the post, using the leverage to push it further out the back of his neck.

Diirek did the only thing he could, he put his feet up against Merek and pushed with all his might.

Merek stumbled back three steps, the push only enough for a few feet of separation. Diirek scrambled up and ran toward the horde. His right leg wasn't working well and he ran in limping strides.

The edge of the zombie horde wasn't far in front of him, but Merek was still gaining. He could hear him. Diirek burst into the horde, sending zombies sprawling. Merek burst in after him like a two-ton truck plowing into a Halloween parade. Putrefied bodies were torn asunder, sending rotting guts all over, limbs spinning through the air, and severed heads rolling their eyes wildly as they spun sloppily through the dark city air.

Several more figures began powering through the zombies on a beeline for Merek. The monster roared close behind Diirek as two blood bags hit him simultaneously, thrown from different directions. The bags exploded on impact, the sight almost comical, like a morbid water balloon fight. Merek stopped chasing Diirek then, turning to look for the assailants. Two more vampires ran past him through the crowd and threw two more blood bags at him. The blood coated his entire upper body and the zombies were starting to take notice. The post still sticking out of Merek's upper body dripped the viscous red liquid slowly.

Diirek saw a zombie bite Merek on one blood-coated arm. A swat from the monster sent the zombie flying away in an untidy collection of separating bones, organs, and juices. More bites. Merek roared and started swinging and swatting the horde closing in on him. Chunks were taken out of his flesh everywhere that the zombies could reach.

Isabelle managed to hit a bullseye on the end of the post in his chest, splattering him with more blood. Binta jumped high over his head and dropped a bag on him like a pilot expertly dropping ordnance on a military target.

Diirek backed away, dodging flying zombie parts that flew like bullets away from the frenzied Merek. The horde kept coming. And so did the blood. Vampires jumped out of windows, off of roofs, and up from the horde to splatter fresh blood on Merek. Diirek watched in sheer amazement and vengeful glee when he was out of the horde. He jump-climbed onto the roof of a three-story building adjacent to the action. Boris threw him a bag of blood. He guzzled it hungrily and felt his leg and his other wounds healing.

Below him, Merek's legs gave out and the monster fell to his knees. Now the zombies could reach his head and shoulders with their snapping mouths and unyielding hands. Merek grew slow as more bites were taken out of him, only managing to push or pummel the occasional zombie away.

As Merek slowed, so did the vampires, which was just as well. There weren't many blood bags left. Many of the vampires gathered on the roof around Diirek to watch the once-great monster die. Of course, there was still a chance that they would all die, too. If Merek was, in fact, the original vampire. They had no way of knowing, and so they waited, many of them thinking that if this was their last deed on earth, it was a good one.

Diirek was ready and willing to die. He almost hoped for it. Life without Lidia seemed so dull and pointless. He'd seen plenty of people come and go in his time, humans and vampires both. With so much experience in death, he hoped it would hurt less. It didn't. Watching Merek die slowly was some help, but the satisfaction he felt was already fading away.

Merek groaned weakly as the zombies ate away the flesh of his neck and face and chest. They were eating around the metal signpost still impaling the monster, but they didn't seem to mind. Finally, the bulk of the monster faded into the crowd, only a badly-eaten arm sticking briefly up above their heads, as if hoping for a dark savior. None came.

Diirek looked around, remembering. "Where is the detective?" he asked.

***

Weller found himself in an unenviable position in the alley. Deadeyes closing in on him from all sides and not an escape route to be found. He looked around for another open door, or a reachable fire escape, or anything to help him get out alive. He found nothing.

Looking at his Sig Sauer, he thought about using it on the zombies, but that would only delay the inevitable. Not enough ammo left. Then he thought about using it on himself. He decided that he would if he got bitten. Until then, though, he still had a fart's chance in a room full of fans.

The three model-zombies were closing in on him, making them the most immediate threat. He looked past them at the door they'd come out of. It was still propped open an inch or so. He dodged around the three zombies and opened the door— to see a crowd of zombies inside. They hadn't spotted him yet, maybe he could— two cold hands grabbed him from behind. Weller turned around and stepped back just as teeth closed on the air where he had just been. *Shit*, he thought, trotting away from the male model-zombie that had tried to bite him. Both ends of the alley were now thick with zombies, heading slowly his way.

He dodged around the three model-zombies and opened the door again. This time he was greeted with a green and bloody face. Behind that face were several others, heading toward the alley. He kicked away the broomstick and slammed the door. It meant that he couldn't escape that way, but it also meant that they couldn't come out— unless they learned how to open doors.

He looked at the nearby dumpster while holstering his Sig. Maybe he could flip it on its top and hide in it until they all went away. But it was heavy with old trash and he didn't think he could flip it by himself.

*Damn vampires, leaving me to die*, he thought. He looked at the corpse of the old guy who had gummed his ankle. A slow smile spread across his face as he looked down at the zombified old-timer.

He ran up to the first model-zombie, the blond, and grabbed her by the back of the neck, propelling her away from her friends. She snapped half-heartedly at him and tried to turn around, but he had her by the shoulder and the neck. She was probably a dime over a hundred pounds, which made her easy to move.

He took aim at the edge of the dumpster and slammed the dead woman teeth-first into it. Then he did it again. And again. He tripped her and she sprawled out on the ground to one side of the dumpster.

Weller looked around. The zombies were closing in fast. Well, as fast as they could, anyway. He had to make this quick. He ran up to the other two sexy zombies, the brunette woman and the chiseled man, ducked their arms (one and a half arms, in the woman's case), and got behind them. He grabbed each one by the back of the neck and propelled them forward like he'd done to the first. Again, teeth-first into the side of the dumpster. The man was a little heavier than the woman, but not by much. The crunching sound their teeth made against the metal was sickening.

By the time he was done with them, the blond was getting up off the alley floor a crowd of zombies closing in from either side. Weller grabbed her by the dress and tanked her toward him. He pulled the other two, as well, hoping to god he'd gotten all of their teeth out. He surrounded himself by the three, and briefly closed his eyes as they opened their mouths to bite him.

Weller was only slightly taller than the women, and about a head taller than the man. He felt a mouth on the back of his shoulder through his clothes. It was soft. So far so good.

Another mouth closed around his ear, like a lover in ecstasy. He shuddered and waited for the pain of a lone surviving tooth piercing his skin and spelling his death. It didn't come.

Another mouth grabbed ineffectually at his neck. He giggled a little and shivered at the slimy touch. *Whoo.*

Now the other zombies were upon him, but the models stuck to him like suckerfish to a whale as he moved slowly toward another door in the alley. The edental and bloody mouths kept trying to find purchase somewhere on Weller's body while other hands reached and grabbed at him. He kept his hands loose at his sides to shove away any toothy zombies that came close.

He reached the first door in line and tried it. Locked. He felt something touch his leg. He yanked it away. Teeth bit through his slacks but missed his flesh. He pulled the other three members of his gruesome foursome as close as he could. They were still gumming and grabbing at him. Other hands reached past his makeshift protectors and yanked at him. Weller's heart was pounding and sweat was dripping into his eyes.

He put his back to the alley wall and moved the brunette from his back to his front, making a zombie barrier. He inched along to the next door. As he reached his hand out to try the door, a tall zombie pushed through the models and grabbed Weller by the shoulders. It took both hands to keep the zombie from biting him. As he struggled, others were pushing at his walking-dead protectors. They did their best to keep their prize, but they were just too light. He saw his protection begin to break up.

Weller pushed the tall zombie away as far as he could and then swung his head forward while yanking the dead man toward him. The vicious headbutt caved the zombie's skull in and it fell back against the sea of bodies behind it. Weller reached for the door and tried it. It opened.

He shoved all the zombies away from him and scrambled into the door. He was halfway in when hands grabbed his legs and jerked him back. He kicked frantically, feeling bones break and teeth shatter as his blows connected. Suddenly he was lying inside. He jumped up and pulled the door shut. Hands reached into the crack of the doorway, pulling it back open.

Weller adjusted his grip on the push bar across the door with sweaty hands. He yanked as hard as he could. The door bounced once and he yanked it again, feeling it close after a little resistance. A pile of 20 or so fingers came clattering down to the floor like the contents of a split package of moldy hotdogs. He felt like he was hyperventilating, but he didn't have time to breathe. He heard something behind him.

Weller spun around to see a zombie clad in a tattered blue police uniform staggering toward him. He didn't recognize the guy, thank goodness. Weller pulled his Sig out and took aim. But, behind the cop-zombie, the stationary store he found himself in was still full of tottering zombies. Not all of them had noticed him yet, but they definitely would if he fired a shot. To Weller's left, there was a stairwell. To his right, a supply closet.

He bolted up the stairs and came to a small office filled with cardboard boxes and stale paperwork.

Another door from the office led to a hallway. He went to the front of the hallway and looked out the window. The horde was a seething mass of decrepit flesh one story below him. The moonlight gave them all an even ghostlier look, if that was at all possible. They seemed to have been attracted by something out in the street and to his left, but he couldn't see what it was. There were too many zombies on top of it, reaching and grabbing down. He hoped it was Merek. That the plan had worked. That his city was safe from a super-vampire with an affinity for removing heads.

There was nowhere else to go, so Weller ran up the stairs and found roof access above the third floor. As soon as he burst out into the calm night air, someone said, "There he is, Diirek." Weller looked around at the group of vampires on the roof. Diirek was over on the edge of the roof, looking back over his shoulder at Weller.

"Detective. I was just asking where you were," the vampire said, solemnly.

Weller's eyes were wild, his fists clenched, his heart beating profoundly. "I'm lucky my whereabouts aren't in a hundred zombies right now, you assholes." Diirek looked around questioningly. Most of the gathered vampires ignored Weller. Others shrugged at Diirek.

"Leaving me in an alley full of zombies. Christ in a souped-up sedan," Weller said, walking toward the edge of the roof. "So, it worked, I take it? That's what they're feeding on?"

"Yes. It worked quite well, Detective."

"So why the fuck are you so— " Weller said, then stopped, looking around. "Wait. Where's Lidia?"

Diirek's answering look said it all.

"Oh, no, Diirek. Damn, that—" A commotion below cut him off. It was as if the zombies were bulging up off of the street suddenly. What happened next happened fast.

Merek appeared from below the exploding bulge of zombies with a fearful scream of pain and revenge. He propelled himself toward Diirek, who had begun to move already.

Weller watched in abject horror as the bloody monster flew toward him through the air. His bulk had been eaten, and Weller could see red bone in some places where the flesh was missing. His whole body was a mess of bite marks, blood, and whatever blue-black substance had been running through his veins. The metal post still stuck out of his neck just above the collarbone in front and out of his still-substantial back and shoulder muscles that came up to meet the back of his skull.

Weller's human reflexes were not up to the task of saving him then. The vampires were scattering, leaving him staring dumbly at the crazed monster coming at him from the mass of zombies below. But it wasn't him that Merek wanted. It was Diirek he was after.

As Merek reached the roof he swatted Weller out of the way with a powerful hit from a skeletal hand. Weller felt his right arm and a couple of his ribs break with the hit. He cartwheeled like a ragdoll across the hard surface, coming to rest at the back of the roof, his torso hanging over the alley he'd escaped just minutes before. His eyes shot open and he tried to cry out, the pain dizzying and unbearable, but he could make not a sound. He tried to move— to pull himself back up— but nothing seemed to work. He felt himself slipping, the weight of his upper body pulling him slowly over the edge, the zombies below looking up at him with their dead eyes.

*This is such bullsh*— he never finished his thought. Pain flared and the light of his consciousness switched off.

\*\*\*

Merek paid the human no more mind. He was focused on Diirek, who was standing near the side of the roof, looking scared and unsure.

Two vampires jumped at him then; one from the back and the other in front. Diirek knew them as Boris and Lewis. Merek didn't know their names and surely didn't care; he was running on fumes, pain, and a hatred so deep and embedded that only death would wrench it from his gnarled heart.

The attacker behind him kicked the back of his leg and Merek went down to one knee. At that moment the one in front was coming in for an attack. Merek's involuntary kneel made the vampire change the direction of his approach; a moment that the monster took advantage of. He smacked the onrushing vampire with such force that it whipped his head around 180-degrees on cracking vertebrae. The vamp collapsed in front of him.

Sensing movement from the vampire behind him, Merek gripped the metal post impaling him and jerked it back through his body several inches. His hand still on it, he felt it connect with his attacker. A choking sound told Merek that he had indeed impaled the vampire through the throat, or close to it.

Meanwhile, the one with the broken neck was squirming in front of him. Merek picked him up by the feet and swung him at several oncoming vampires, knocking them down. The violent movement caused the impaled vampire behind him to slide off the post and soar into the horde below.

Merek, still holding the vampire by the feet, swung him savagely down into the hard surface of the roof, right in front of Diirek, who had been among the attacking vampires he'd knocked down. The vampire's head splattered, sending pieces of it all over Diirek and the other vampires who were getting up from the roof.

Merek dropped the limp body of the forever-dead vampire he'd been holding, and looked around, smiling. The remaining vampires were arrayed around the roof, stone-still like boring gargoyles, staring at him. He was pleased to see that some of them had already fled. The look on Diirek's face made him forget briefly about the immense pain he was feeling. He was going to win. This time and every other time. Until they were all dead.

Merek stepped casually forward to pick up the smashed vampire body ahead of him and drink its remaining blood, but he felt a tug on the metal post. Someone was holding onto the back of it.

"Hey," said a dreary and pained voice from behind him. "You're bull-shit, you know that? Why don't you just fucking die already?"

***

Weller let go of the post as the monster turned slowly around, seemingly unable to believe what was happening. His right arm hung limply at his side, the angle at the elbow all wrong. It was severely swollen and there was a rattling sensation deep inside any time he made the slightest move. It took almost all his energy to hold his pistol in that hand. With his left, he pulled his right hand up at the wrist and shot the monster once in the chest. He tried to shoot again but his finger wouldn't work. The pain made him want to throw up.

Merek looked at the hole in his chest, which might have been a paint-ball shot for all it affected him, and then looked at Weller. He started for-ward toward the detective but there were suddenly vampires all around him, holding onto his legs and keeping him from moving any further.

Weller laughed, took a step back, and then collapsed onto the roof. He watched what came next with the detached interest of a man slowly dying from internal injuries.

***

Weller's gambit had given the vampires time to move into position. There were eight gathered around his legs, holding him down. Three more attached themselves to each of his arms, taking him by surprise. He struggled and threw a few of them off, but those vampires he thought had run away were merely trying to come upon him from different angles, and they joined in now.

Diirek got around to Merek's front and grabbed that end of the post. Isabelle grabbed the other end. They yanked it one way, pulling it through the tough tendon, muscle, and bone. Merek made a strange noise that wasn't quite yelling and wasn't quite screaming. Isabelle and Diirek reversed direction, widening the hole in the monster's neck. Merek made no more noise, but his eyes remained wide and staring, the pain evident there. They reversed direction again. And again, using the metal to tear through the monster's flesh. Diirek's face showed that effort and sick joy he felt as he did it.

The pole yanked loose of the mess of bone, muscle, and sinew, leaving Merek's head attached only by an inch or two of flesh on the other side. Diirek took the pole into his hands like an oversized baseball bat. Merek was still alive, and he could do nothing but watch as Diirek swung the post savagely at the remaining flesh holding his head on. The gnarled head came off with the impact, bounced to the edge of the roof, and came to rest looking at the night sky.

Diirek walked up to it and stared.

He began to stomp on it, much like Weller had done to the dead geezer's head in the alley. Merek's head took some doing before it turned into slush.

The vampires that had been holding the monster stepped away and let his body crumple. They all stared at their work for a moment, sure that it was over.

All the vampires watched in silence as Diirek continued to stomp Merek's head, which was no longer recognizable as such. It *was* finally over.

Diirek stopped and looked up at the moon sitting blithely over the city. He cleared the tears out of his eyes and headed over towards Weller, whose eyes were now closed.

"Damn. He messed up," Val said, looking down at the delicious blood soaking Weller's khaki suit. "Maybe it too late for him? Shame for him go to waste, eh?"

"No. Not him," Diirek said. "I like the detective. He helped us. We need to get him back to the safe zone. They can take care of him."

"I don't think he'll survive the trip back," Isabelle said. "I can hear his heart struggling in there."

Diirek thought for a moment. "Maybe it would be better if he joined us? It might be his only chance to live. I can turn him here. Do we have any blood bags left?"

"Yes, a few," Binta said.

"Okay," Diirek said. "We shall turn him into one of us. To save his life." The rest of the vampires nodded solemnly. "It's the only way," a few said. Diirek leaned down to begin the process. He opened his mouth, unsheathing his fangs, and—

"No fucking way!" Weller croaked, his eyes shooting open. "Take me to the safe zone. The hospital there. You crazy bastards." He managed to prop himself painfully on his left elbow. "I've got a few broken bones and I lost consciousness for a minute. So what? Happens all the time. Is this how you solve all your problems? 'Just turn him into a vampire. It's the only way.' You guys are as bad as Catholics. I'm surprised there's not more of you. Christ."

The gathered vampires couldn't meet his accusatory gaze. A few of them turned around, pretending like they weren't a part of it. One of them even started whistling.

"We did it," the battered detective said. "We killed the asshole. Great. That's fuckin' teamwork, everyone. Now, please get me to the hospital. It's about time for some really, really strong drugs."

# CHAPTER TWENTY-EIGHT

# THE END...

Things settled down for the safe zone once Merek was dead. At least, as settled as things could be. The world outside the zone was still an apocalyptic hellscape filled with crazed gangs and roving zombies. Plus, it wasn't like anyone inside the safe zone ever knew about Merek, anyway. Aside from those poor humans that happened to be around when Merek decided to go hunting. But, they didn't live to tell about it. As for the vampires, well they sure as hell weren't going to tell anyone. Having Weller know of their presence was unnerving enough.

The second night of Weller's week-long stay at St. Christopher's hospital, Diirek came to visit him. Weller was half asleep in his bed, doped to the gills, when suddenly a figure was standing by his bed.

"Jeezly crow!" Weller said. "Derek, you scared the morphine out of me."

"It's Diirek."

"Right, Diirek. What's up?"

"I wanted to thank you for your help, detective. And I wanted your word that you will treat the rest of my people fairly."

"That depends. If I start finding dead bodies in the safe zone again— bodies with no blood in them— I'll be visiting you. You can guarantee that."

"What if they do their hunting in the outskirts? People who... deserve it, shall we say?"

"Who determines that? And why do you keep saying 'they'? You leaving, or something?"

Diirek nodded, his movie-star good looks covered in a dark shadow.

"Where are you going?"

"To see what has become of the rest of the world. To make sense of my loss and the existence of Merek. I've got questions I want answered."

"Ah. Wandering in the desert for 40 years and shit. Gotcha. That's actually not a bad idea. If you can find a way to get me messages as to the state of the world, I would greatly appreciate it. You do that, and I'll take care of your people. I'll even try to get them blood bags on a regular basis."

Weller knew that there wasn't really anything he could do to control the vampires anyway. Anything short of killing them all. Telling anyone about them would either raise more panic or get him kicked off the job for good. But he desperately wanted info on the rest of the world. If the higher-ups knew anything, they weren't telling.

"You have a deal, detective."

"I'm sorry about Lidia," Weller said, simply. Diirek nodded and then disappeared into the shadows in the corner of the room. *Now I know how Commissioner Gordon feels*, Weller thought.

A week later, Weller, JayLynn, and Berena were in Weller's apartment. JayLynn had all but legally adopted the girl, and from what Weller could tell, it was the best thing for her. For both of them, actually. Berena seemed to be doing well, despite the atrocities done to her. JayLynn seemed happier, too. And, in fact, it seemed to be good for Weller, in a roundabout way. Not only did he like the girl, but JayLynn seemed to be opening up to the possibility of spending more time with Weller. He supposed it could be the injured card he was playing— after all, his right

arm was in a cast and he could barely move without his ribs hurting—
but he didn't think that was totally it.

Of course, he made up a lie about a gang in the outskirts to explain
his injuries. He wasn't ready to tell anyone about what happened out
there. Not yet. JayLynn and Berena had come over to help Weller finally
unpack. He felt it was an excuse to see him. He and JayLynn had been
making progress.

Weller finished a box of random living room paraphernalia and moved
the empty aside to start on the box below. JayLynn was unpacking a box
of books onto a shelf on the other side of the room. Their eyes met and
held for a long moment, the look on her face one that Weller remembered
from their dating days. An ember of hope flared in his heart.

His days in the hospital provided him with a sense of clarity about
what he needed to be in this changed world. JayLynn visited him every
day. Some days Berena was with her and some days she wasn't. Berena
had made a friend of a teenage neighbor girl whose parents were all too
happy to watch the two young girls. On those days, they talked for hours.

Weller knew that those talks were the basis for their tentative rela-
tionship that was forming anew. They had heart-to-heart talks that they
should have had while they were going through the divorce. Weller was
never around to talk back then. He was never around for much. He was
consumed by his need to fix everything that fell outside the parameters
of his marriage. A drive to clean up the city kept him out at all hours.
JayLynn had recognized this drive even before they were married, but she
thought that together they could funnel that energy into their relation-
ship. Her energy was there, waiting to be complemented by his, which
never came.

Weller recognized it. He knew she was right. And he told her that this
post-apocalyptic world needed a different kind of drive from him— and
from everyone. The old ways wouldn't work. The old ways would simply

lead them back to the old world. He saw this tragedy that had befallen them as a chance to start again.

Now. Now was the time to make a change. But not if he went around chasing revenge again, spending his energy on fixing the little things that did nothing to fix the bigger problems that plagued communities like the one he grew up in.

No, he needed to look forward. He needed to focus on the community and his family and steering the ship toward a better future.

He told all this to JayLynn, in so many words, at the hospital. When he was finished JayLynn was crying. She hugged him. Their embrace lasted a long time.

Presently, Weller smiled at the memory and felt pretty good about everything. Determination pulsed in his chest side-by-side with the love he felt for JayLynn. He opened up the next box in the stack he was working on and started digging stuff out with his good arm. There was a box of pens, a plastic container of paperclips, random odds and ends.

And a stack of manilla folders, each filled with papers.

He pulled them out, a slight frown creasing the dark skin of his smooth face. They were old case files. That much he knew. Unable to help himself, he started flipping through them, a distant memory rushing up out of the fog to seat itself in his frontal lobe.

He came to a folder labeled "Linori Crime Family" in his small, neat handwriting. He opened it up and flipped through the loose papers, looking for a stack of photos he knew were here somewhere. The pile of 8"x10" surveillance pictures was at the bottom. The top picture was a close-up of Linori sitting at a breakfast table by a window. Weller had taken the picture from the top of an adjacent building on a cold and windy winter morning. The dark clouds were reflected in the window, the other side of which sat Linori, his mouth open in frozen laughter, eyes crinkled, small teeth framed by thin lips. But through the passage of time, through the clouds reflected in the window, and through the window itself, Weller spied a hand. It was resting on the table, the body attached to it obscured by blue velvet curtains.

On one finger of that hand rested a striking ring. A deep blue stone set in a decorated black band on the man's plump digit. It was a ring he'd seen on Chief of Police William Roan's hand what seemed like a lifetime ago but was really just over two weeks.

The strange conversation he'd had with Roan suddenly clicked into place. He'd been telling Weller to stop looking for *him*. It was a quid-pro-quo. Let Weller off for the whole thing with the mayor and his son, provided he stop looking into the botched murder attempt. It explained everything. Shellbourne and O'Shea pressing him to get in with the dirty cops, the assassination attempt, the decision to put him in with gen pop the day he was arrested, the files missing from the computer. It all could have come from Roan. The chief knew Weller was onto him before Weller even did.

A feeling took hold in Weller's stomach that was much like the morphine he'd had at the hospital. It was a warm feeling, radiating out through his limbs and vibrating his soul with impassioned energy. He suddenly realized that this feeling was warring with the other in his chest— and in his head.

Weller looked up from the photograph to JayLynn, who felt his eyes and turned toward him, smiling. Weller looked back at the photograph for a long moment and then at his ex-wife once more.

Her smile was gone.

"Damn," Weller said, under his breath. "This is bullshit."

# EPILOGUE

On the roof of the Paredo building, a pigeon landed and began its idiotic waddling, pecking occasionally at scraps. The sun was going down, a crest of boiling blood on the horizon. The door to the electrical-room-turned-storage closet sat slightly open. The darkness inside was total, but the pigeon paid it no mind. Pigeons can't pay anything much mind but food.

The dirty gray bird bobbed its head purposefully as it passed by the door, searching for more scraps. Gray-blue feathers littered the ground around the bird, evidence of some terrible happenings that had befallen its brothers and sisters. It paid no mind to these sundered feathers.

The hand that came out of the darkness to grab the bird was fast. It was a hand crusted with dry blood. It was a hand attached to an arm inside a tattered plaid shirt. The bird never had a chance.

No one was around to hear the sucking and crunching sounds that came out of that room. There was something in there, and it had eaten a dozen pigeons. It was slowly regaining its strength, getting ready to venture back into the world. Getting ready to find a certain detective and make him pay. The time was near.

# Undead Assimilation Teaser

The story's not over yet. Keep reading for the first three chapters of the second book in the Undead Trilogy!

# PROLOGUE

Joseph burst out onto the roof, sweat glistening on his balding pate, breath hissing between his brown teeth. He surveyed the rooftop of the building quickly, noting without interest the concrete dome in the middle. A demented smile cracked his only-a-mother-could-love face as he placed grimy hands on the strap across his chest. He ducked his head, pulling the strap off and the Remington 700 rifle to which it was attached.***

He walked toward the edge of the building, glancing down at the errant bird feathers that scattered the roof. He frowned slightly, his eyebrows momentarily joining to make one long, angry, black caterpillar. *They're for the birds*, he thought of the feathers, and laughed at his own awesome wit. The strange smattering of feathers quickly left his mind as he approached the three-foot rim of the roof, crouching as he neared it.

The sun was touching the horizon to his left, but it wouldn't be a problem. He knelt down and pulled the 700 to his shoulder, angling it right, away from the sun. He peered through his scope, made a few adjustments, and silently thanked his former employer, the city police department, for providing him with his toy.

It had been nearly a month since the apocalypse began, and Joseph had been having himself a good old time. He'd killed a few blacks and Hispanics during his short tenure as a police, but the end of the world provided him with so many excellent opportunities to have his fun. And without all the paperwork and investigations and bullshit that came with shooting someone as a cop.

He had never—not even for a second—regretted his decision to strike out on his own, here in the outskirts. The way he saw it, there was really no choice. Stay in the safe zone and risk getting caught for killing people, or put up with the dangers of the outskirts and kill as many people as he wanted?

There had never been an easier decision.

Now, as he knelt in the fading daylight on top of the Paredo building, he thought back to his first kill as a free man. Or, rather, his first several kills. He'd gotten the first few with his trusty 700, from a roof not unlike the one he was on now. A couple of big, tattooed guys with guns walking down the sidewalk like they owned the city. He got one in the neck and the other in the head. *Bam, bam.* Then a third guy, too. There were two women with them, which he had hoped to get alive, but that hadn't worked out. Too bad. They had been lookers.

Then, his favorite part happened. His partner, whose name he couldn't remember now, got all bent out of shape about it. Like the world hadn't already gone to shit. Like there were still rules. Like fucking zombies weren't roaming the goddamn streets. But he had taken care of that little bitch with a nice shove off the roof.

Joseph got a little excited as he thought about the noise the guy made as he hit the concrete. *Best day of my life*, he thought. *But maybe today will take its place.*

He had one eye to his scope as he relived that day, Z-Day, as it was now known. The first day of the new world, where zombies roamed the streets and chaos reigned supreme.

The zombies were easy to handle. It was the gangs that you had to worry about.

And the do-gooders.

Presently, Joseph's breath caught as he saw movement through the scope. *Here they come. Too far to shoot, though.* He would have to wait for them to get close. It was a rather large group of people, clearly not familiar with the city, because they were going the wrong way. Of course, it helped that Joseph had moved the signs that the do-gooders had put up to lead people to the safe zone. He liked corralling people into his little traps.

Watching through the scope, he debated which one he would get first. It looked like two families traveling together. Five adults and six kids. He debated killing the smallest of the kids first. They were harder to hit; small, quick bodies that could easily hide once they realized what was happening.

He finally decided on who to shoot first when he heard something like the creaking of a rusty hinge. He looked up from his rifle, toward the domed structure. From his angle near the corner of the roof, he could see that the door was open. *Was that door open when I came up here?* He couldn't remember. He'd been so excited about this current batch of victims . . .

*It must have been open*, he decided, looking back through his scope. They were almost in range. Joseph started slowing his breathing in preparation, getting his mind into shooting mode. No need to load a bullet; he always had one in the chamber.

He set his crosshairs on the gray-haired man in the middle of the group. The bullet would drop a little and move slightly to the left, catching the kid holding the old man's hand as they walked. That kid looked fast. Best to get him first. The adults would be so concerned that they would all bunch up around the dead kid. Maybe he could even get two-for-one today. He'd always wanted to do that.

Joseph moved his finger inside the trigger guard, his breath slowing, his mind zeroed in.

A scrape sounded close by on the roof, causing Joseph to jerk his head away from the scope and look. A badly deformed man in a plaid shirt, jeans, and sneakers stood an arm's length from him, staring with wide, bloodshot eyes. One of his arms was canted at a bad angle in the middle, and the fingers of that hand pointed in all directions.

The man opened his mouth, his eyes going wider, and reached toward Joseph with his good hand. Blackness seemed to pour out of the guy's mouth. Joseph stood up and swung his rifle toward his attacker. The man yanked the rifle out of his hand, turned it around, and jammed it through Joseph's right foot. Joseph screamed in agony as the blunt barrel smashed through skin, muscle, tendon, and bone. It passed through his foot, through his boot sole, and into the hard scrim of the roof, pinning him in place. The deformed man let go of the rifle, which stayed upright, swaying slightly.

"Oh god, oh god, oh please, what do you want?" Joseph said as the man reached for him. Joseph put his right hand out, an unconscious gesture of pleading.

"Duuuude," the man said, just before chomping down on Joseph's trembling, pleading hand. Joseph screamed as the man's teeth snapped and separated three of his fingers from his hand.

By the time Joseph finally lost consciousness, he'd decided that this was the worst day of his life.

Of course, who can blame him? It's hard to stay optimistic when you're being eaten alive by an unlikely monster.

Or, for that matter, any kind of monster.

Avoid it if you can.

\*\*\*

When the monster, whose name was Buck, finished picking Joseph's bones clean, he spoke. "Much better than pigeons," he said to himself as his broken arm began to heal. "Now, where the fuck is that asshole detective who brought me up here? We're going to have words."

A voice answered that only Buck could hear, and he nodded in response as he walked toward the door that led to the staircase. The sun was a thin slit on the horizon, and Buck felt better than he had in days. He felt alive. But, most of all, he felt a righteous fury expanding in him like an oxygen-starved fire swooping through a newly opened door.

That fury had one person and one person only in its sights.

# CHAPTER 1

## A New Breed

D etective Kurt Atticus Weller pulled his left hand out of the hole in the wall. His teeth were clenched in pain and anger. The dark skin of his hand was spotted with blood and powdered with drywall dust. The sight of blood on his hand made him even angrier, and he headbutted the wall, denting it inward and sending a wave of pain through his skull. He stumbled backward and sat on his bed, jarring his slowly healing cracked ribs.

*If you're not careful you'll break your other hand*, he thought to himself, looking down at the cast on his right arm. Technically, his right hand wasn't broken. It was both the bones of his forearm that had been snapped three weeks earlier. Still, it hurt to use his right hand for anything, much less punching a wall, which was a habit of his lately, as evidenced by the dozen or so holes in his bedroom walls.

He wiped his forehead off with his left hand and got up, dressed only in his boxer briefs. He walked out past the kitchen and into the living room, glancing at the clock on his wall, not surprised to find out that it was the middle of the damn night. Sleep was ever elusive for the detective, no matter how he tried, which was one of the many reasons he felt obliged to put holes in his walls.

He resigned himself to another sleepless night and picked up a small silver analog recording device with his left hand, ignoring the drying blood and white dust still stuck to his skin. He pressed the appropriate buttons and brought it to his mouth, clearing his throat as he did so.

"Okay, where was I?" he asked the recorder. He wasn't about to rewind it and listen to his own voice from the previous night. Not because he didn't like his voice, but because he barely knew how to operate the damn recorder. "For my ex-wife JayLynn Whittaker, formerly JayLynn Weller, in case I die, blah, blah, blah. Apocalypse, bombs falling, zombies roaming the streets, we're all infected, yadda, yadda, yadda. Oh yeah. I was getting to the vampires. Yes, they exist. So far as I know, I'm the only living human who has been trusted with that most unholy knowledge. And these fuckers are old. Unlike the zombies, they aren't a product of the apocalypse.

"Plus, there was this crazy big guy named Merek who used to be a vampire, but he turned into something else. Like a vampire who fed off vampires. And he was on a mission to kill all the vampires here. Again, nothing to do with the apocalypse. Just bad timing. He's the one that broke my damn arm and ribs." Weller paused, his eyes focusing on the memory that wasn't even three weeks old yet.

"It could have been worse, I guess. And before that, there was this guy named Buck. A real grunge-type loser, but he wasn't all that bad. Anyway, I accidentally got him killed. Which was kind of all for the better, because he was some sort of weird zombie-vampire hybrid. He tried to eat me the first time we met. Like he was in some sort of fugue state."

Weller paused again, looking at his ceiling while the spindles in the recording device spun. "Oh shit, I forgot to tell you about Diirek. He's the first vampire I met. His wife or girlfriend or whatever got killed by Merek, so he's out wandering the wasteland like some sort of depressed messiah . . . I guess that's redundant. All messiahs are pretty depressed.

"He told me he's trying to figure out what caused the apocalypse because no one knows, but I think he's just writing emo songs about his dead girl and crying blood tears. You know, because he's a vampire.

"Anyway, I said I'd watch over his little group of twenty or so vampires here in the safe zone in exchange for information. I don't know how he'll get that information to me, though, seeing as how we don't have working cell phones or internet. Or even damn landlines. Maybe he can turn into a bat. He told me he couldn't, but maybe he was lying."

Something occurred to the detective, and his dark face narrowed. "I can't remember the name to this song I have stuck in my head. That's neither here nor there, but maybe you can help me figure it out. Well, actually you'll only listen to this if I'm dead, I suppose. By then I won't have a head for a song to be stuck in. At least I don't think so." He paused.

"If I die without knowing the name of this song, I'm gonna be pissed. The chorus goes like this—"

A sound like a bucket full of rabid cats being tossed on an angry hippo assaulted him from the street. (It was a better sound than would have emanated from Weller's mouth, so we'll just call that good timing.)

"What the hell?" Weller jumped up, tweaking his ribs in the process. He arrived at the window in time to see a blue-gray figure tear down the street in a frantic blur, four floors below. "Dammit," he yelled to his empty apartment. "What the shit is it now?" Then something caught his eye in the other direction. It was a goddamn vampire, sitting in the street.

Weller couldn't see his face, but he thought he recognized the vamp. He stepped back from the window and walked backward to the couch. He sat down when his calves touched imitation leather. He still held the recorder, spindles turning the seconds away. "I'm so sick of this shit," he said to the silver device. His eyes were wide, staring at nothing. "Why can't I just get one night of decent rest? It's always something. Things were bad enough when it was just humans fucking up the world. But now . . ." Weller trailed off. He forced his eyes to focus and looked at the night outside his window.

He clicked off the recorder and threw it at his couch as he stood up. "Goddammit," he said, stepping behind the couch and grabbing his Sig Sauer P229 9mm pistol from his shoulder holster on the back of a chair. He was out the door before he realized he was only wearing boxer shorts and a cast. By then it was too late to turn around. He knew that if he went back into the apartment, he wouldn't be able to force himself out again.

The late-spring night was pleasant, and the breeze felt good on his skin and through the thin material of his purple-and-white striped boxers. Half of the streetlights were out to help conserve power for the safe zone. There wasn't another soul on the street. Including the vampire, if the lore was correct. For his part, Weller didn't know if he believed in souls or not, but he sure as hell believed in vampires. Seeing is believing, after all.

The night was quiet now. The strange sound had apparently been an anomaly.

He approached the vampire, his bare feet padding along the sidewalk. As he got closer, he knew something was wrong. He *did* recognize the vampire. His name was Ricardo, and his eyes were wide open, as if in surprise, staring the way the blue-gray blur had gone. He sat in the middle of the street, his feet splayed in front of him, his pale skin glowing in the light of the moon.

"Yo, Ricardo," Weller said.

"Ahhh!" The vampire twitched violently and looked accusingly at Weller. "What the hell, man? You know how dark you are? You're like a cast, a pair of boxers, and a gun floating through the night. Scared the hell out of me."

"Oh, a joke about a black guy at night. Real original, jackass. Plus, you're a goddamn vampire. How is anyone going to sneak up on you?

When—" Weller stopped, noticing something. "What the fuck is that?" he said, pointing to the right side of the vamp's chest. Just under his pectoral muscle was a dent about the size and shape of a fist. The vampire's black T-shirt was stuck in the dent, making it visible to Weller.

Ricardo looked down. "Oh, that's what hurts. Damn, that thing was fast." The vampire got up off the ground. As he did so, Weller could hear his smashed rib bones grinding together like a rock polisher.

"Ah, man," he said, wincing. "And I thought *my* ribs hurt. Wait—what 'thing' was fast?"

"I don't know. Whatever it was that punched me and took off down the street. If I knew what it was, I wouldn't say 'thing' now would I? I'd say, 'that kangaroo was fast.' or, 'that heavyweight boxing champion was fast.'" Ricardo clutched his damaged ribs as he straightened and then pulled his plain black t-shirt out of the dent.

"Don't tell me we have another vampire-hunting monster in the city. We just finished with that bullshit."

"No, I don't think so. This thing was fast, but not as fast as Merek was—or as powerful. I thought it was a zombie at first. I was on my way over here when I saw the thing. It kind of looked like a zombie, but it wasn't moving like one. And it seemed . . . almost intelligent. Anyway, it was just strolling along. So I followed it for a little while, then I guess it noticed me because it started running, so I chased it. Then it stopped, turned, and came at me. And punched me."

"I heard some kind of crazy noise. Was that you?"

Ricardo looked defensive. "I was scared and hurt. That thing was crazy. You'd be scared too. Just get off my back already," he said, rapid-fire.

"Oh, Christ," Weller said, throwing his hands up, one of which still held his pistol. "Can't we just have a nice quiet apocalypse for a change? I've got other shit to deal with."

"Whatever. You love it, you sick bastard. Oh, hey, you think I can get some blood? I gotta heal this thing. Hurts like a bitch." Ricardo gestured at his now-hidden wound.

"What? No. Go find some asshole in the outskirts and do the world a favor."

"C'mon, Detective, why do you think I was coming here in the first place? It's a quiet night everywhere. Unless you'd like me to break into one of these brownstones and drink some innocent blood . . ."

"What do I care? You guys are half-feeding anyway, right? If you're not, I'll know. I start finding dried-up bodies, I know where to look."

"Alright, if you say so, Detective." Ricardo started walking away, backward, smiling at Weller. "Where does your ex-wife live again?"

Weller glared at the vampire. "Alright dammit, come on," he said, turning back toward his apartment building. "I have some blood in the fridge. But this is not a regular thing. And my ex is off-limits. And after this you go find whatever the hell that thing was that punched you and, I don't know . . . Figure out what it is. And let me know."

"Oh, Detective, you love us, don't you?" Ricardo said in a high, dramatic voice. "You keep blood in the fridge for vampires, don't you? I knew there was a reason we all liked you. You're a celebrity in the Underground, you know that?"

"Whatever. The blood is for emergencies only. This will not become a habit."

Weller scowled. Ricardo smiled. They headed into the apartment.

# CHAPTER 2

## WAKE UP, GOD. IT'S ME, DIPSHIT

"What is it?" Dipshit asked, trying to sound calm.

"I don't know," Sicko said, out of the darkness beside him. "Probably nothing, but the alarm was tripped. Maybe it's just a walker."

Dipshit peered out through a crack between the boards covering the window of the old farmhouse. "I don't see a walker. I don't see anything out there," he said. "Where was the alarm tripped?"

"Damnation, Dipshit, just think for a minute, will you? It was the front alarm. Why else do you think I would be here looking out the *front* of the house?"

"Sorry," Dipshit said, casting his eyes down. His real name was Fred, but no one called him that at the farmhouse. He had turned seventeen two days before the apocalypse, and although he'd done a lot of growing up in the month since, he still felt like a little kid. Especially around the tough grown men at the farm. He admonished himself silently for asking such a stupid question and affirmed that he deserved the name bestowed upon him by Sicko and the others.

He looked out the crack again, tracking along the coiled barbed wire that sat on this side of the farm's short wooden fence. Sometimes a walker would manage to get over the fence and caught in the wire, triggering the alarm, ringing one of six bells inside the house. He'd never known a walker to get back out of the barbed wire, though. The fact that he didn't see anything out there made him uneasy. He gripped his .22 hunting rifle tighter.

The shrill insistent ringing of another bell blasted Dipshit's ears. He and Sicko turned around, the latter clicking a flashlight on and shining it at the six bells fastened near the ceiling of the living room. The one that was ringing had a label under it that read "backyard."

"Wake the others," Sicko said, heading to the viewport at the back of the house.

Dipshit set his rifle against the wall and then hustled down the hall while digging his own small flashlight out of his pajama bottoms. He burst into the master bedroom and started shaking the man lying on the bed there.

"God? Wake up, God. Sicko said to get everyone up. Two alarms have gone off," he said in a high, hurried voice.

God, who didn't look anything like the God Dipshit had grown up learning about, opened his lids, revealing striking and cruel green eyes. The man tossed the sheets off with one hand and swung his unusually hairy body up to sit on the edge of the bed. He stood, the elastic of his stained white underwear struggling to stay put under his giant, ripe beer belly and over his nonexistent ass. Dipshit stood there, a full head taller than God, his mind a blank like it nearly always was lately.

"What the fuck are you still doing here?" God said in his reedy, ungodlike voice. "Go get the brothers up, Dipshit."

Dipshit's mind snapped back to attention like an old rubber band, and he headed out of the room and across the hall. He opened the door to the other bedroom and started yelling as politely as he could at the two men sleeping in the wooden bunk beds.

"Dementor, Scorpion, wake up! The alarm's going off. Someone's trying to get in."

The two brothers shook the sleep off and got up while Dipshit headed out of the room. As he stepped into the hallway, he heard glass breaking and wood snapping. He ran down, snagged his rifle from where he'd propped it, and headed to the back. The alarm bell had stopped ringing, but Dipshit couldn't recall exactly when.

He ran through the living room and around the corner to the den, to where the viewport was. He stopped short when he saw the state of the boards that had been covering the window. Most of them had been broken. There was a hole large enough for a man to fit through.

"Sicko?" he said, quietly. His heart jangled like an alarm bell in his chest and his vision started to narrow as he crept to the window, his rifle at his shoulder, the flashlight held against the barrel with his left hand.

The only illumination was from his skinny flashlight and the half-moon that floated crooked over the earth. The back lawn had been cleared of all the paint-chipped metal barrels, rusting farm equipment, and overgrown bathroom fixtures that had littered it when God and his crew had arrived. It was Dipshit's job to keep the lawn trimmed, which he had only done once since he'd been conscripted into God's service just under two weeks earlier. The fence was backed with rolls of barbed wire here, too. As was the case all around the farmhouse. Beyond the fence was a small copse of trees, lush with greenery. The deep shadows under the foliage made it impossible to see what may or may not have been lurking there.

Dipshit leaned out the window and pointed his flashlight down to see if Sicko was there. He wasn't, but there was a small amount of blood marring the short grass. Dipshit gulped. A branch snapped off in the distance, causing the boy to jerk his gun up and shine the flashlight futilely at the trees.

Nothing.

"What is it?" God said from Dipshit's elbow, causing the teenager to jump and swing his gun at the small man. God, now dressed in grimy shorts and a matching t-shirt, grabbed the barrel and shoved it away. "You do that again I'll kill you myself, you fucking Dipshit."

Not for the first time, Dipshit thought that this God *did* share some traits with the one he'd learned about—the one from the Old Testament, anyway. This small, hairy God wasn't one to forgive and forget, that was for sure.

"I—I—I heard a branch snap," Dipshit said, visibly shaking, as God looked out the smashed window from behind the barrel of his AR15.

"I don't see—" God's voice was interrupted as Sicko came swinging down from the roof above the window, face-first, his hands fastened behind his back. Sicko's forehead and nose smacked the still-intact bottom board nailed across the window. The momentum carried the rest of Sicko's upper body through the hole there. God and Dipshit watched as the man's neck folded nearly in half backward, hearing vertebra and something else—the rain gutter maybe—crack and snap. It was clear that Sicko's feet were fastened to the roof somehow. His body swung back out, allowing his neck to straighten, then it came back, and his neck folded again, this time with less force.

Dipshit realized with horror that the other snapping sound was that of Sicko's knee joints folding the wrong way as they met the framing above the window. The boy looked away as God cursed and started gibbering.

Dementor and Scorpion came running into the den, all eyes and automatic weapons.

"What in the Sam Hell?" the brothers said together.

"Battle stations," God yelled, looking smaller than ever.

Dementor and Scorpion looked at each other, then they looked back at God, their brows furrowed. "'Battle stations'? What the hell are you talking about?" Scorpion asked. Dipshit didn't have any idea, either.

"Just find a window and protect it. Dipshit, you stay here and guard this window."

The teenager's eyes went wide. "What? N—No way!"

Sicko's body started twitching at the window. The three men and the boy froze, looking over in shock. Their compatriot's body was jerked out into the night by some unseen force. It tumbled through the air and landed on a roll of barbed wire against the fence, ringing the backyard bell once before the weight snapped the line.

God stepped up to the window and started firing wildly. "Fuck you!" he screamed into the night.

Dipshit backed away from the window.

A sound of smashing glass issued behind him, barely audible over the firing AR15. He spun around to see a pale face floating in the darkness of the living room. Scorpion and Dementor had been shoved headfirst into the previous owner's china cabinet. Scorpion in the plates, Dementor in the bowls and teacups. They both lay there, bleeding, limp, and unconscious—possibly dead.

Scorpion groaned and the pale man turned from Dipshit and kicked the noisy brother, launching him into the nearby wall. Scorpion came to rest covered in pieces of broken drywall, his face a mess of blood and china shards.

The pale face came toward Dipshit, who was praying to God (no, the other one) for a swift and painless death. The terror expanded in him, and he felt a blubbering hysteria gather in his throat. But he wouldn't cry. He refused.

God stopped firing the AR15 as the pale figure approached the teenager, who closed his eyes and waited.

And waited . . .

"Gahh! What the hell?" God said from behind Dipshit. The boy opened his eyes and turned around to see the pale man lifting God off the ground. With the moonlight shining through the window, Dipshit noted with something resembling relief that the man wasn't just a pale floating face. He had a body; it was just dressed in the blackest of black clothes.

"Hello, God," the pale man said. "My name is Diirek. And I will be the one judging *your* sins tonight."

***

To continue reading, grab your copy of <u>Undead Assimilation</u>. It's available for purchase on Amazon and free on Kindle Unlimited.

# ALSO BY MATTHEW DOGGETT

## The Undead Trilogy

**Things get even crazier — and bloodier — in the second and third installments of the trilogy.**

- *Undead Assimilation* - Available on Amazon and Free on Kindle Unlimited

- *Undead Extermination* - Available on Amazon and Free on Kindle Unlimited

## The Rise of the Vampire Merek

Witness the vampire Merek's journey from man to monster in this Undead prequel. From Viking warrior, to warlord, to deformed and bloodthirsty monster, this novella takes you inside the mind of the Big Bad from Undead Annihilation.

Exclusively available for free to those who sign up for Matthew's mailing list at **MatthewDoggettAuthor.com**

## The Devil's Playground: Tales of Terror to Keep You Up At Night

These collections of short stories will have you checking under your bed before you go to sleep. From serial killers and paranormal creatures to insanity-inducing experiences and monsters from parallel dimensions, these stories are perfect for horror fans everywhere. 20 chilling stories per volume!

Available on Amazon

## The Trouble Thrillers

"Absolutely thrilling." -Amazon Customer.

Check out these adventure thrillers featuring Terrence "Trouble" Rubble fighting for justice in the streets of America. Read these standalone books in any order or start with the first and work your way through.

*Dead Man's Hatch* - Available on Amazon and Free on Kindle Unlimited

*The Deadly Divine* - Available on Amazon and Free on Kindle Unlimited

*The Death Dealers* - Available on Amazon and Free on Kindle Unlimited

*Too Much Trouble* - Available on Amazon and Free on Kindle Unlimited
*Trouble* - Available for free at MatthewDoggettAuthor.com/Trouble

Printed in Great Britain
by Amazon

30202535R00169